Just between Friends

CINDI GAINES

Copyright © 2020 Cindi Gaines
All rights reserved
First Edition

PAGE PUBLISHING, INC.
Conneaut Lake, PA

First originally published by Page Publishing 2020

ISBN 978-1-64701-529-9 (pbk)
ISBN 978-1-64701-528-2 (digital)

Printed in the United States of America

It seems like the six of us have been friends forever. Carmen and I met first and became instant friends. She introduced me to Gloria Farris and Elizabeth Ross, along with Virginia Carpenter and Nikki Johnson joining the group by chance. Carmen and I have lived in the same subdivision for over ten years. We've seen each other through the death of parents, the birth of children, and girls' night out. I know you've heard the phrase "living for the weekend." Well, our weekend was Thursday nights. It was the time that we got to just be girls again. No husbands, no kids, and no worries, just girls being girls made for a great night out.

I guess I really need to start at the beginning. Carmen and I moved into the Westley Estates about a month apart. My husband, Marcus, and I had just moved to Burnsville, Minnesota, from Florida. Marcus is a corporate attorney for Blasdell, Jacobs, and Tranor. I forced him to transfer when I learned he had an affair with a paralegal at his firm. We had gone to counseling for about a year, and I still didn't feel comfortable with him working around Pam every day. Marcus was on track to make partner before he turned thirty, and I was happy that the transfer would not affect his chances.

Marcus wanted desperately to save our marriage, so he really didn't object when I suggested that we move. We have been married for five years and have a beautiful daughter named Dylen. I always thought we had a pretty solid marriage, but don't most women who discover their husbands have been cheating? We were college sweethearts—how corny is that? All our friends thought we were the perfect couple. Most of them are separated or divorced now, but we're still hanging in there. I was devastated when I found out about the affair. I never believed that crap about the wife being the last to know.

I always figured that if you know your man, then you know when something's not right. Marcus had become distant, not his usual self. He was staying late at the office and making excuses not to make love to me. This had been going on for about a month now. I wanted to ask him several times, but I just didn't know how to bring it up.

I got my answer two days later. Marcus normally had his American Express card bill sent to the office, but the Lord works in mysterious ways, and it was accidentally sent to the house. I opened it, not knowing it wasn't our joint account, and there it was—$450 for a suite at the Four Seasons Hotel. My heart stopped, I couldn't breathe, and I started to have a panic attack. I picked up the phone and called the hotel and asked for reservations. "I would like to book a suite for Marcus Covington," I said. The reservation clerk politely asked if Mrs. Covington would be joining him again. I dropped the phone. I couldn't breathe, and I thought I would pass out. I thought about our daughter and how much she loved her father and how much a divorce would hurt her.

I quickly gathered myself and dialed Marcus's office.

"Yes, Mrs. Covington, I understand, but Mr. Covington is in a very important meeting."

"Please, Miriam, this is important. I urgently need to speak with my husband." While I was on hold, I tried desperately to stay calm and rational.

Marcus picked up the phone all frantic.

The only thing I could say was "If you want to say goodbye to your daughter before we leave for the airport, you'd better get your ass home right now," and I slammed down the receiver. As I rushed around the house packing and talking to myself, I couldn't cry. I was so shocked I couldn't cry. Marcus had given up so much to be with me, and now he was cheating on me; it just didn't make sense.

I remember going to meet Marcus's parents at Christmas break. His father was a judge, and his mother was a Florida socialite. The moment I walked into the house, I could see the shock and horror on his mother's face. I had spoken to David and Shelia Covington several times, and I had just assumed Marcus had told them I was black, but I guess not. The moment Shelia saw me, she ordered Marcus into the study. I could hear her screaming at the top of her lungs.

"If you marry that black bitch, you won't get a dime of my money," she said.

"I don't want your money, Mother," said Marcus. "I love her, and nothing you say is going to stop me from making her my wife." Marcus stormed out of the study and ordered me to get my coat. We made a quick exit and spent the rest of the holiday in a cabin in Aspen, Colorado. A couple of weeks later, we received a letter from Shelia stating Marcus had been taken out of her will.

We did marry the following year, and two years later, our daughter, Dylen, was born. We sent pictures of the baby, but she sent them back. Marcus tried several times to reach out to his mother, but she always resisted. We sent cards on her birthday and, of course, holidays, but still nothing. After a while, Marcus just kind of let it go, and we went on with our lives as though his parents didn't exist.

Lost in thought, I realized I was still rushing around the house like a madwoman.

Damn him for hurting me and with that woman. Pam was a bleached-blond tramp who wore too much self-tanner and makeup. She tried to screw every attorney at the firm. I couldn't believe that Marcus would be attracted to a sleazy, opportunistic social climber like her. As a matter of fact, I never even knew Marcus to be attracted to white women, but why wouldn't he be? He was white after all. When I first met him, he was dating a Hispanic girl, and the guys on campus always teased him about having jungle fever.

By the time I put the last suitcase in the car, I heard Marcus drive up. Dylen ran to him.

"Daddy, Daddy, we're going on a trip."

Marcus grabbed Dylen and took her upstairs. Fifteen minutes later, he came downstairs and told me he was taking her next door to Amy's. Marcus rushed back in the house and shouted, "For God's sake, Jennifer, tell me, what's wrong? What's happened? Why are you leaving me?"

I took the credit card bill and threw it in his face.

He picked it up, looked at it, and I could see his heart sink. He looked at me and fell down to his knees crying.

All I could say was "Do you love her?" I had gone over in my head what I would say when I saw him, but none of it came out.

He looked at me lovingly and said, "Sweetheart, it meant nothing, I swear."

"I'm sure it meant something when you were fucking her!"

"Jennifer, it only happened once. Please, baby, you must believe me. Don't break up our family," he said.

"Is that supposed to make me feel better that it only happened once? And you should have thought more about our family." I sat there and started to cry as he grabbed me and held on for dear life.

"Please, Jen, don't leave me, just give me a chance to make this right."

Marcus went to the car and started to take the luggage out. He called Amy and told her I wasn't feeling well and asked if Dylen could spend the night. Marcus gathered up some clothes and took them over. After he came back, he went into the kitchen and opened a bottle of wine. We sat and talked and cried for hours. He had this scared look on his face, but he told me I could ask him anything I wanted to know.

"Is it Pam?"

"Yes."

My eyes welled up with water again as I tried to hold back the tears. Marcus took a deep breath. "You remember last month when we had that meeting at the Four Seasons? Well, that's when it happened," he said. "Pam and I decided to stay after the meeting and have a few drinks. It was totally innocent at first, then one thing led to another, and the next thing I know, we had checked in. Once it was over, I realized I had made the biggest mistake of my life. I had risked everything that was important in my life. I swear to God, it meant nothing and it will never happen again."

"Marcus, I don't know what's worse: the fact that you cheated on me or that you would risk everything for a cheap thrill that meant nothing to you. I mean, what kind of rational sense does that make?

And now you want to promise me that it will never happen again. You don't have that right to ask anything of me."

The next couple of months were really rough. We went to therapy to try to get our life back together, but nothing seemed to work. When I couldn't take it anymore, I told Marcus to ask for a transfer. I knew he couldn't fire Pam, and I couldn't stand the thought of him being around her and interacting with her every day. Marcus respected my wishes and put in for the transfer. Marcus transferred all his open cases to another attorney, and we were off to Minnesota.

After a month of living in Minnesota, my life with Marcus started to take on a resemblance of normality again. He had even started to talk about having another baby. He wanted a son so badly. He prided himself on being a much better father than his own. His father wasn't abusive or anything; he was just a workaholic and was very distant.

I, on the other hand, was not ready for another child. I was secretly contemplating returning to work. I had a family law degree but had not practiced in a while. When Dylen was born, I wanted to stay at home with her until she was ready for the first grade. With everything going on in the world, the rapes, murders, and child molestations, all I wanted to do was to protect my child from all the monsters in the world.

We moved into the Westley Estates in August of 1995. It was a new area in Burnsville, and I was excited about buying our first home. Once again, we were a happy family. Marcus started on his career, and I set up housekeeping as usual. Play dates at the park for Dylen, dinner on the table by the time Marcus got home from the office—life was good, except I was extremely lonely. I hadn't made any friends since we arrived, but it had only been a couple of months. Marcus kept telling me I just needed to give it some time.

Then I had a lucky break. Dylen and I were outside putting up Halloween decorations when a moving van pulled up next door. The cutest little boy jumped out of the car that pulled into the driveway. Dylen was so excited to see someone her own age that she ran to the little boy. I tried to stop her, but they were already laughing and playing before I reached her. So I walked up and introduced myself to a petite woman whom I assumed was the little boy's mother. Carmen and I became instant friends. Even Marcus and Carmen's husband, Jeff, hit it off. We started to hang out together and even spent the holidays together. We even planned a trip to Jamaica together for the spring, and my life started to feel more and more complete.

Six months into our friendship, I started seeing bruises on Carmen's arms and legs. She always had some excuse about rough-housing with River or moving furniture. I mentioned it to Marcus, but he said I should mind my own business, so I let it go. After a month or so of noticing bruises, Carmen mysteriously fell down the stairs and broke her arm. I didn't see her for weeks. Every time I tried to call her or go by, Jeff would make up an excuse about her sleeping.

One day, Dylen saw River playing in the backyard, and we decided to walk over. I asked him where his mother was, and he said, "In the kitchen washing dishes."

I knocked once and walked in. "Hello, stranger," I said, startling Carmen. She jumped so suddenly that she dropped the bowl she was drying. When she looked up, I could tell she had old bruises on her face. She still had some black around her eyes, and a cut was healing on her lip. "My god, girl, what happened to you?" I asked. "Why did you stop calling me? Did I do something wrong?"

"No, I just didn't want you to see me like this," she said.

"Girl, is Jeff doing this to you?"

Carmen started to cry, and I pulled her close and held her tightly as she cried.

"Look, girl, forget this bullshit, pack your stuff, and move in with us. Carmen, you don't have to put up with this shit from him," I said.

"Jennifer, Jeff is just having a rough time at the office right now. He lost a big account recently, and the other partners are pretty upset. I can't kick him when he's down. We just bought this house, we're overextended on our credit cards, and Jeff is just really stressed out right now and gets a little upset with me. I asked him if I could return to work to help out, but he insisted my help was not needed."

"So what are you going to do? Carmen, that son of a bitch has no right to put his hands on you. I don't care what he is going through."

"Jen, the only thing I can do is to try to be a better wife."

"Do you need any money or anything?"

"Heavens, no...Jeff would die if he knew I told you about our financial situation, let alone take a hand out from you."

"Listen, Carmen, I understand being supportive, but don't be a punching bag for this man. Has anything like this ever happened before?"

"Once, but not to this degree."

"Carmen, I have a great idea. Why don't you and River come to lunch? We miss you guys so much. I will make something really nice. We can sit and talk, and the kids can play. What do you say?"

"Thanks, Jen, but not this week, but we'll take a rain check, okay? Jeff doesn't want anyone to see me like this, so I better stay at home," Carmen said.

"Okay, girl, but if you need me, don't hesitate to call."

"I know you'll be there for me, and I appreciate that so much. Jennifer, I would like to ask one favor of you, though."

"Whatever you need, hun."

"Will you let Dylen spend the night? River misses her so much."

"Carmen, if you're sure Jeff won't mind, then it's okay with me. She will enjoy that. Once her dad gets home and she sees him, then I'll bring her over."

The next couple of weeks were lonely without Carmen. River came over occasionally, but I missed my friend. Finally, Carmen came around, and we started to go out for lunch again and take the kids on play dates. It was really great having my friend back. Carmen started to return to her old self, and she invited me to a girls' night out. Marcus invited Jeff over to watch the game so he would have no excuse for not letting Carmen hang out.

The club of choice was called the Gay 90s. It had a great drag review on Thursday nights, and Carmen had arranged to meet some of her old friends whom she used to hang out with prior to moving to Burnsville. This is where I was first introduced to Gloria Farris and

Elizabeth Ross, who goes by Beth. The club was packed. They didn't have clubs like this in the South. It was unbelievable. There were half-naked men dancing on the bars, guys kissing guys, girls kissing girls. This was some wild shit. It didn't bother me, though; I was a regular fag hag in college. I had tons of gay friends. Marcus didn't like my gay friends, but he didn't disrespect them either. He always thought they were too over the top.

I clicked right away with Beth and Gloria. They were wonderful, and we just hit it off. We watched the show and had some drinks and danced until 2:00 a.m. I knew Marcus wouldn't mind me staying out late, but I did want to call and check on Dylen and River. I was worried about Carmen, though. I knew what a temper Jeff had, but Carmen assured me everything would be fine.

After closing down the club, we said goodbye to Gloria and Beth and promised to see one another next week at the same time. Next week, Ms. Kitty was making her debut, and Gloria raved about how awesome Ms. Kitty is, especially her Celine Dion impression.

On the way home, Carmen filled me in on Gloria and Beth. "Gloria is a teacher, and her husband, Donald, is a commodities broker, and she's having an affair with a teller at her bank," said Carmen, smiling. "Beth just got married six months ago, and she and her husband, Richard, are having problems already. It seems that Beth only likes sex in the missionary position and refuses to give Richard head. According to Beth"—laughed Carmen—"the only way she will even have sex with Richard is when she has been drinking. Richard has suggested counseling, but Beth refuses to go. She doesn't think she has a problem."

"What kind of work does Beth do?" I asked.

"Nothing, girl. That bitch got it made. The only thing she does is spend Richard's money. That's her job," said Carmen. "Whatever she wants is okay with him. He just wants her to be happy."

"So, Carmen, what is the girl's problem? Was she not giving up the booty before they got married?"

"Jennifer, from what I understand, he thought it would change once they got married. I guess he thought she was just holding on to the booty, trying to trap him, and once he married her, he would be in booty heaven," said Carmen.

"Girl, we need to rent the movie *The Brothers* and show that sista how ol girl almost lost her man in the movie because she was not giving up the head. Honey, like the comedian Monique, says, 'What you won't do, another bitch will.'"

"Jennifer, you are a nutcase." Carmen laughed.

"So, Carmen, let me ask you a question. Do you think Jeff has ever cheated on you?"

"I'm not sure, Jen. That's not something I think about. I don't really think so. He's much too busy at work to have time for an affair. Shit, he rarely has time for me. To be totally honest, the majority of the time, I am the one who initiates sex. He's never been really aggressive in the bedroom. I think that is one of the things that made me fall for him. I was molested by an uncle as a child and didn't like sex all that much. When I met Jeff, it was refreshing to meet someone who was interested in my mind and not just my booty. You know what I mean? Why do you ask, Jennifer?" said Carmen.

"I was just thinking about Marcus. He had an affair right before we moved to Minnesota. Well, actually, that's the reason we really moved here. I miss Florida so much, and sometimes I question whether or not it was the right decision demanding that we move. I am just starting to really trust him again. The betrayal was so hard on me. Marcus and I have been through a lot with his family, mainly his mother not wanting him to marry me because I'm black. I made his ass get an AIDS test and every STD test known to man. I told him we're getting one every six months until I am satisfied that everything's okay. Carmen, I know I love him, and I know I want to spend the rest of my life with him, but if I ever think he would cheat again, I would have to let him go. I know how corny this is going to sound, but Marcus is the only man I've ever been with sexually."

"Get out of here," said Carmen.

"No, girl, I'm serious. You know, I kissed and messed around with a few guys in high school, but nothing serious enough to make me want to have sex with them. My grandmother was very strict and overprotective. Besides, my high school was predominately white, and the guys wouldn't date black girls, and I always thought the only reason black guys wanted to go out with me was because I was light skinned with long curly hair."

"Well, that's what you get for being a half-breed."

"Carmen, that's not funny. I'm really sensitive about my biracial heritage. Plus, Miss Thang, you can't talk your light bright and damn near white your-damn-self. I know I got Indian in my family."

We both laughed so hard we nearly peed our pants.

"Girl, we got too many black folks now who use that excuse when they're vanilla yellow with a decent grade of hair. So you need to get some new material, honey."

"Carmen, I know you love Jeff, but I just think it would be more difficult to live with a man who beat me."

"For the record, Jen, I told you Jeff doesn't beat me. He can get a little rough when he's angry, but he is not a violent person."

"Shit, he sounds like the Incredible Hulk to me."

"Jennifer, let's just listen to Luther and enjoy the ride. I don't want to talk about Jeffrey anymore."

"Fine with me. But, Carmen, you know you my girl and I got your back, okay? I would just like to thank you for inviting me out tonight. I had a wonderful time."

"Anytime, Jennifer. You know I got you, girl."

Once I got home, I snuggled next to Marcus and told him how much I loved him.

"Did you have a good time, honey?" he asked.

"Yes, baby, I had a great time. Marcus, baby, I was just thinking the other day that maybe we should seriously consider having another baby."

"Jen, are you serious?"

"Yeah, I am, and if you're not sleepy, maybe we can get started tonight."

Marcus pulled me close to him and began kissing me deeply. I could feel the heat between my legs as he kissed my neck and then my stomach. I could feel his tongue enter my wetness as I began to squirm. I loved it when he went down on me. The sex was incredible, and afterward, I laid my head on Marcus's shoulder and tried to fall asleep. I thought about Gloria and Beth, but most of all, I worried about Carmen. I finally drifted off to sleep thinking how wonderful my life is. I am so happy right now, and I thought life could only get better for my family.

* * *

The next morning, Carmen called me and invited me to a new gym that had just opened. They had an area where the kids could play while we worked out, so this was going to be great. I needed something to motivate me to get back in shape, and this might be what the doctor ordered.

Nikki was a Pilates instructor at Mind and Body. Carmen had met her at the grocery store, and she had given her a business card and invited her to the grand opening. We got there about ten o'clock, and it was jam-packed. We stood in line for about twenty minutes, waiting to register and sign up for memberships.

While standing in line, we met Virginia Carpenter. She and her husband, Brian, had just recently moved back to Saint Paul. Her husband was an army officer, and he had just returned home from Iraq. He had been injured and decided to retire early. Virginia had had a baby four years ago and never lost the weight. She had been living in Fort Hood, Texas, the last eight years and was happy to be back in Minnesota. They had been high school sweethearts and had gotten married right after high school.

As luck would have it, Virginia knew Nikki. They had grown up together in Saint Paul, and she was more than happy to help Carmen and me get a break on the membership fee. I had a good feeling about Nikki and Virginia, and after the killer workout, we decided to go for smoothies. Nikki told us her husband was an investment banker, and he had helped her and several other partners get money to open up Mind and Body Day Spa.

We sat and talked for hours. Dylen and River were getting restless, so we said our goodbyes and ended the afternoon, but not before inviting Nikki and Virginia to girls' night out. We told them about Beth and Gloria and what a great time we had at the Gay 90s. They were very excited about going out with us Thursday night, because this was the week Ms. Kitty would be performing.

I decided to have a dinner party. I wanted all our husbands to meet. I felt like Marcus needed a few more guys to hang out with other than his partners at the office and Jeff. Marcus seemed to really enjoy Jeff's company in spite of what I had told him about how he treated Carmen. They hung out together at football games and played golf, but I always felt like Jeff treated Marcus like the naive little white boy whom he resented for being married to a black woman.

The party was going very well, and we discovered during the meet and greet that Beth and Virginia were already acquainted. They attended college together. We all ate too much and drank way too much, but we all clicked and had a great time. At the end of the night, we all promised to get together at least once a month at somebody's house for dinner or drinks. Marcus was really excited because Beth's husband, Richard, had season tickets to all the Minnesota sporting events.

The next morning, after getting Marcus off to work, Dylen and I lay back down. We lounged around until about eleven o'clock, and then I called Carmen to see if she and River wanted to come for lunch.

"Of course, girl, we can do lunch, but why don't you and Dylen come over here? We need to contact the girls to make sure we're still on for tonight. Everyone raved about what a good time they had the night before and how great the food was."

"Carmen, do you mind watching Dylen while I run to the store? I don't have a thing to wear tonight. Of course, I will. But, Jennifer, with all the clothes in your closet, girl, you don't need to buy another thing."

"Anyway, you know we're always searching for the perfect little black dress, so I'm going to run to Dayton's to see what I can find."

I walked around Dayton's for hours looking for a dress, but no luck. Afterward, I decided to go downstairs to the food court to grab a latte. I was standing in line at Starbucks when I noticed Jeff having lunch with a handsome young man who appeared to be around twenty-five or so. As I watched them, it became obvious they were having an argument. Jeff was getting up from the table when the man grabbed his arm. I was about to walk over when the man said, "Jeffrey, I love you. Why are you doing this?" It stopped me dead in my tracks.

Jeff turned and looked at him and said, "I knew you were going to do this. That's why I didn't want to meet you in public. I'm doing everything I can possibly do right now, but like I told you before, I am not leaving my family." Jeff turned to see if anyone was looking and kissed the young man on the lips. He looked at him lovingly and said, "I love you too, but as I explained when we met, I have a family I love very much. This was supposed to be a fling. I never meant for it to get this involved or for it to get this out of hand. I told you I'm not gay." And Jeff turned and walked away.

I was so engrossed in what Jeff was saying I didn't hear the lady saying "May I help you?"

"Lady, are you going to order or what?" said the frustrated young lady behind the counter. I'm not sure how long I had been standing in that one spot, but a line had formed behind me. I ordered and paid for my coffee and sat quietly in the food court for over an hour. I didn't remember driving home. When I arrived, Marcus had been waiting.

"Honey, where have you been? I have been trying to reach you for over an hour. Sweetie, are you okay?" he asked.

"Yeah, I'm sorry, I had some errands to run, and I was trying to find a new dress, and I guess I just lost track of time."

"I just wanted to let you know I invited the guys over tonight to watch the game. We'll order pizza or something, so don't worry about trying to cook anything. We'll even watch the kids while you girls go out and get your groove on."

"As if you had a choice." I smiled. "And, Marcus, don't say 'groove on,' baby. That is so 1980s."

"Honey, are you okay? You seem so distracted."

"No, I'm fine, Marcus. I'm still a little shaken from this guy on the freeway cutting me off," I said, lying to my husband.

"Well, why don't you go upstairs and take a long, hot bath and I will bring you up a nice, cold glass of wine?"

"Baby, that would be great. Plus, I was hoping we could fool around a little before it was time to meet the girls."

I went upstairs to bathe, and I noticed Marcus had rose petals on the bed, candles, champagne, and a cute little red teddy all laid out for me. Tears started to roll down my face. How could I be so happy with what I had discovered? I turned on the water but decided to take a shower instead of a bath. I let the warm water run down my face. I contemplated on what I should do. Confide in Marcus? Tell Carmen? God, she is going to be devastated. How could I hurt my best friend that way? All the books I have read about brothers on the down-low did not prepare me for this secret. All my gay friends were open about their sexuality. I have met men at the Gay 90s who have asked me out, and I have often wondered, *If you're so straight, what in the hell are you doing at an openly gay club by yourself?* No matter what I did, this was going to end badly. Most of all for Carmen and River, so I decided to put it out of my mind for now and make love to my handsome husband.

Just as I was rinsing the soap from my body, I felt Marcus kiss the back of my neck. He turned me around and kissed me, his tongue going straight into my mouth, and I pressed my breast against him. He took my hand and led me from the shower. I lay on the bed with my arms open, begging him to take me. I loved feeling his wet, naked body pressed against mine. I felt him enter me as I thrust my pelvis forward. I couldn't remember a time during our lovemaking that I was ever this wet and horny. Marcus lunged forward, thrusting and thrusting until my body exploded in ecstasy.

I lay next to Marcus for a few moments then got up to shower again. I dressed for the evening in a little black dress and the new tennis bracelet Marcus had surprised me with. The guys had started to arrive when I went next door to pick up Carmen. Jeff answered the door, and it was difficult to be cordial. He invited me in for a drink while Carmen finished dressing.

"Jennifer, is everything okay?"

"Yes, Jeff, things are great."

"That's good, but you seem kind of distant this evening."

"No, Jeff, like I said, everything is fine, I assure you."

"The reason I'm asking is because things are starting to pick up at work and I was thinking about taking Carmen away for a romantic weekend, and I was just wondering if you and Marcus could take care of River."

"Of course, we would be delighted to," I said as we made polite conversation. "Jeff, I'm going to hurry my girl up, if you don't mind."

"Sure, go right ahead."

I ran up the stairs. "Knock, knock," I said, opening the door. "What's up, Ms. Thang? Let's get this party started." I looked at Carmen and fought hard to hold back the tears. I loved my friend, and I wanted so much to protect her, but I didn't think she could handle the truth about Jeff. I decided to put it out of my mind for right now and just enjoy girls' night out.

Gloria was the cutup of the group. She flirted with every man in sight, but she loved Donald. They had their issues like most married couples, but Gloria's problem was, she liked to party, and she loved the kids. She was a bigger fag hag than I was. The kids loved Gloria because she was always the life of the party.

Everyone had arrived except Nikki. She was late as usual, so we ordered the first round of drinks. We tried calling her on her cell phone, but still no Nikki. Two hours later, and still no Nikki. Around ten o'clock, Nikki came waltzing through the door with a big grin on her face. Virginia was the first one to speak up. "Bitch, where the hell have you been?"

"What are you guys staring at? I would have been here sooner, but I had a class that ran late."

"Yeah, tramp, I just bet you did," said Virginia. "So spill the beans, bitch. Where have you really been?"

"Well, I had this fine white man in my Pilates class. Girl, he got me so turned on I had to go home and get some dick before I came and hung out with a bunch of fags."

"Okay, bitch, details, details."

"Virginia, don't be so crass," I said.

"I left my class thinking I was going to run into the house, change clothes, and be out, but when I arrived, Bruce was in the bedroom watching a porno. He does that quite often, and I don't mind usually, but this particular movie he was watching was most erotic. We watched together for a while, and then it became too much for me to handle. Bruce has been begging me for a while now to try anal sex, and I have always said no. But, girl, in this movie, we were watching these two guys and a girl having a threesome, and let me tell you, it got me so horny I decided to try it."

By this time, all of us were listening closely and hanging on to Nikki's every word.

As Nikki continued, she told us it took some getting used to, but it was some of the best sex she and Bruce had ever had. As Nikki finished her story, she looked at us and said, "So, ladies, fess up. How many of you have ever tried anal sex?"

The table got quiet. Everybody looked at one another and started to giggle. Carmen looked at Nikki and said, "Good girls don't tell. Well, I am of the belief that most women have tried it at least once. Don't you think, Jennifer?"

"Why am I being singled out?" I asked.

"Okay then, I have a question for you, Jen. Is it true what they say about white men?"

"I don't know. What do they say, Nik?"

"You know, they are good with oral sex, but they have little dicks."

"That is such a myth," said Virginia.

"Shut up, V. Let her answer," said Nikki.

"I can't believe that you guys buy into those kinds of myths and stereotypes. Nikki, the one thing I can say is, maybe the white men you know have little dicks, but that is a myth. You know, like they say, black men have big dicks. Honey, it's a myth," I said.

"A girlfriend of mine was dating this football player in college, and you know those little rubber things that you put on your finger to avoid paper cuts? Well, she said he was so small he could have used one of those for a condom, and to top it off, she said the brother couldn't eat coochie. Talking about your bad dates," said Carmen.

"Come on, Nikki, it's just like that porn star John Holmes. That man had the biggest penis in the free world, and he was white."

"So what do you ladies consider big?" Virginia said. "Because personally, I don't like a man who's too big. I mean, it can be so big that you can't enjoy it because it hurts so much. So, Gloria, what is your preference?"

"Any man with a pulse," said Nikki.

"Nikki, let her answer," I said.

"Yeah, Nikki, let me answer. You had your turn. Well, personally, I like a man who's about six inches. I think that is the perfect size, unless you're like Nikki and you got a pussy like the Grand Canyon."

"Come on, guys, stop laughing. That shit wasn't funny," said Nikki. "Okay, okay, everybody, let's hear from the newlywed. Beth, what do you like?" asked Nikki.

"I don't care, really," said Beth.

"You don't care?" everyone said in unison.

"What do you mean you don't care?"

"Well, if y'all must know with your nasty asses, I prefer oral sex to penetration," said Beth.

"Bitch, you out your ever-loving mind," said Nikki. "There is nothing better than a good, hard, stiff dick. Beth, you do realize you can't get pregnant from oral sex, so you gotta give up the booty sometime if you plan on having that rug rat."

"Okay, Nikki, lay off Beth," I said. "Can we please talk about something else besides sex?"

"I don't know, Jen, you're sounding a little sensitive," said Nikki.

"If you must know, Marcus has nothing to be ashamed about, because my man is packing a good eight inches, and that's all I need."

"He may not be a brother, but he has a sista singing the Campbell Soup song."

"Um, um, good," said Jen. "Carmen, you're quiet. What about Jeff with his big fine chocolate self?" asked Gloria.

"Jeff is fine. He's about average size, I guess," said Carmen. "I just wish he would switch it up a bit. He likes it doggie style most of the time, and I would like to be on top sometime too, but we're happy," said Carmen shyly.

"If you guys keep talking about sex, I'm going home to get me some dick right now," said Gloria.

"Gloria, you're like me, always got dick on the brain, but I ain't mad at you, girl. So let's order another drink. I'm ready to get my drink on," said Nikki.

The night ended early, and Carmen noticed I was quiet on the ride home. "Is everything okay, Jen?" she asked.

"Everything's great. I got my dick before I left tonight." I smiled.

Carmen laughed. "Girl, I ain't mad at you. I just wish Jeff was in a better mood. It's going on three weeks since the last time we made love. Maybe when I get home tonight, I can try to get him in the mood for a little romance. Jennifer, I envy you and Marcus relationship so much. I hope Jeffrey hanging out with Marcus will do him some good."

"I hope to hell nothing Jeff has rubbed off on Marcus," I said to myself.

As we got out of the car, I lightly kissed Carmen good night and hugged her real tight. I was worried about my friend. She was such a wonderful person, and she deserved better than Jeff.

Marcus came home early Friday afternoon so we could spend some quality time together. Dylen and I got dressed for dinner and a movie. I loved hanging out with my girls, but it was great when we spent time together as a family. While in the movie, I received an urgent text message from Carmen. She wanted me to call her as soon as I got home. The first thing that came to mind was, she had found out about Jeff, or he had hit her again. I excused myself and went to the bathroom to call Carmen.

"Hi, Jeff. It's Jennifer. Is Carmen available?"

"Jen, I think you need to get here as soon as possible. There's been a terrible accident, and she's pretty upset."

After leaving the movie, I went straight to Carmen's house. Jeff answered the door before I could even ring the bell. "Jennifer, she's upstairs," he said.

Carmen was lying on the bed, crying.

"Honey, what's wrong," I said, rushing to her side.

"It's Gloria. She's been in a horrible car accident, and they don't think she's going to make it," said Carmen.

"Do you want to go to the hospital?"

"Yes, I wanted to wait for you. She needs her girls right now."

By the time we made it to the Hennepin County Hospital, they had Gloria on life support.

Gloria had sustained multiple head injuries, a broken leg, two broken ribs, and a crushed pelvis. It was so hard seeing her like that; she looked so fragile and pale. We huddled around Donald and said a prayer. Virginia took Donald down to the cafeteria to get coffee while we sat with Gloria. Nikki leaned over and kissed Gloria on the forehead and said, "You better not die, bitch, you better not die." I just kinda laughed; Gloria would appreciate Nikki's sentiment.

Hours turned to days, days turned to weeks, and weeks turned into months. It was Halloween again, and I was getting the decorations out for Dylen. It was hard to believe that Gloria had been in the hospital for three months. Very little progress had been made in her condition, and Donald was starting to lose hope. She had been put in a medically induced coma initially to help her brain heal, but once they took her off the medication last week, the coma persisted. Halloween came and went without any change in Gloria's condition. The day after Thanksgiving, I received a call at 2:00 a.m. from Donald that Gloria had passed away in the middle of the night.

I got dressed and ran to get Carmen. We arrived at the hospital; all the girls were there. Gloria looked so peaceful. All her bruising had healed, and she had begun to look like her old self again. I leaned over and kissed her lips. "I'm going to miss you, you big flirt." All the girls took turns kissing her and saying their goodbyes. We sat with Donald for a while, waiting on the coroner to come and collect the body. The nurse wheeled in the gurney, and Donald left the room; he couldn't take it. We stood there holding one another as they took Gloria away. That night, our lives changed forever.

The days leading up to the funeral were sad. We tried to be there for Donald and one another, but it was difficult. Gloria's family and Donald had never gotten along, so everything was very tense. The funeral was scheduled for that Saturday afternoon, and with all the drama, everyone was glad to get it over with. I remember it well because it was the first weekend in December, and it was cold and wet from snow that had fallen the night before. I normally love a white Christmas, but this year would be a sad holiday for everyone. The service was lovely, and afterward, everyone went back to Donald's house for dinner to say goodbye to Gloria's family and the friends she worked with. Everyone had good things to say about our wonderful friend. She would be missed terribly by everyone who loved her, and our friendship grew stronger from her passing.

Since the accident, I'd been feeling really tired and sluggish. My periods have always been a little irregular, so I didn't really think anything until the day after Gloria died when I started throwing up. At first, I just thought it was nerves, but then I began to wonder if I could be pregnant. I went to the drugstore and bought a pregnancy test. I could hardly wait for the results, and after that minute was up, I was ecstatic. I had been struggling about what to give Marcus for Christmas, and now I had the perfect gift.

The one thing that helped me get through the days after Gloria's death was Carmen and the fact that I was pregnant. On Christmas Eve, I broke the news to Marcus over strawberries and champagne. Marcus was the happiest man on earth, and we looked forward to the New Year.

Marcus and I decided to have a New Year's Eve party. We tried to invite Donald but learned he had packed up and left town three days after the funeral. We were sad that he didn't say goodbye, but we understood his reasons for doing it.

As usual, the men hung out in their corner, and the girls mingled together, and the conversation eventually turned to Gloria. We laughed and remembered a lot of crazy moments together. We had all become such close friends, and I hoped our friendship would last forever.

Right before midnight, Marcus made the announcement about the new addition to our family. The girls were ecstatic; they knew how long we had been trying.

At two o'clock, the party started to thin out; everyone hugged one another good night, and we promised we would all get together real soon.

Our Thursday nights kind of fizzled out after Gloria's death. It just wasn't the same without her.

Friday morning, Nikki called me about a sale they were having at Gap. I knew it was a little early to start shopping for the baby, but I was so happy I said, "What the hell." She picked me up, and it seemed like we shopped for hours. I was getting tired and needed some lunch. I was dying for a taco supreme, so we decided to stop at Taco Bell. As we were pulling into the parking lot, we spotted Jeff. There was the same handsome young man I had seen Jeff with at Dayton's leaning into his car, kissing him. After the kiss, he walked over to a really nice Mercedes that was parked next to Jeff.

Nikki parked sideways, trying to block Jeff in. He spotted us and tried to pull off. Nikki jumped out of the car and started screaming, "You nasty-ass fag! How could you fuck over Carmen like this, and with a goddamn man? You dirty bastard. Get your ass out of the car because I'm going to fuck you up right here."

I jumped out of the car to grab Nikki. Just as I was about to grab Nikki's arm, Jeff jumped into the car and tried to pull off. I thought Jeff was going to run over Nikki, so I pushed her out of the way. I was so busy pushing Nikki out of the way that I did not see the right side of the bumper that slammed into me. I could hear Nikki screaming, and everything went black.

I vaguely remember waking up in the hospital four days later. I woke up staring into Dylen's smiling face and Marcus's tired eyes. "Why aren't you at work?" I asked.

He looked at me and smiled. "I took off to be by your side, silly."

"How long have I been here?" I asked.

"Almost a week," he said.

"What about the baby?"

"Don't worry about that, sweetheart," and Marcus started to cry. I held his head to my chest and asked him if I had lost the baby, and he whispered yes. "Baby, don't worry, we'll have other children."

"As a matter of fact, we can start as soon as they let me out of here." I tried to raise my head up to kiss him, but I had a terrible pain in my stomach. "They couldn't have given me a C-section. I wasn't far enough along," I heard myself saying.

"Jen, honey, listen, there was so much hemorrhaging the only way they could stop the bleeding was to do a hysterectomy," said Marcus.

"Marcus, what are you talking about? I'm only thirty-two years old, and you're trying to tell me I will never be able to have another child?"

Marcus held me tightly and tried to comfort me. I started to shake and cry uncontrollably, and Marcus called for the nurse.

"Don't worry, Mr. Covington, this shot will help her relax and, she will be able to sleep comfortably for the rest of the afternoon."

Eight days later, I was released from the hospital, and I couldn't wait to get home. When I arrived, all my girls were at the house waiting for me. The house was filled with beautiful flowers, and I tried to put on a brave face. After about an hour of socializing, I became tired and needed to take a nap. I said my goodbyes to everyone and went upstairs. Nikki came upstairs to help get me settled.

As I was getting undressed, Nikki started to cry. "Jennifer, I am so sorry this happened. If I had not confronted Jeff, this would not have happened."

"Nikki, what are you talking about? I don't remember that day, and what does Jeff have to do with anything?" I asked.

Nikki was about to go into details about what happened that day when Marcus walked into the room. "Sweetie, don't worry about anything," said Nikki. "We will talk later."

"Nikki, I think our patient needs to get some rest," said Marcus as he handed me my medication.

Nikki kissed me goodbye and told me she loved me before she walked out the door.

"Marcus, why does Nikki think she caused the accident?" I asked.

"Honey, that day is still unclear to all of us. I just know she was with you, but I still haven't gotten a lot of details about that day. I do know the police listed it as a hit-and-run, but try not to worry about it right now. It will all come back to you eventually," said Marcus.

Dylen brought me a glass of water to take my medication, and I drifted off to sleep. I woke up a little dazed and confused. It was already dark, and I had slept through dinner. I didn't have much of an appetite, but Marcus insisted that I try to force a little something down. I needed to get my strength back, so I tried to eat, but I just kept feeling sick to my stomach.

Over the next six weeks, I started to return to normal. Carmen would come over and help out during the day while Marcus was at work. Dylen loved this because she got a chance to spend time with River. Carmen told me things were getting worse between her and Jeff.

"He's spending more time working late, and he rarely makes it home before River and I go to bed," said Carmen. I asked Carmen about all the girls, and she gave me an update on everybody and their lives. I finally got around to asking Carmen about the day of the accident. "The only thing I know is that Nikki saw Jeff at Taco Bell right before the accident happened. Jen, you still don't remember?" asked Carmen.

"No, the doctor said my memory would eventually come back to me and not to worry. I wish I could remember what happened. It's like, it's right there on the tip of my brain, but something is blocking it from coming through."

"Jen, don't push it. It's just going to take some time. I am so sorry about the baby. I know how much you and Marcus wanted another child. Just don't get discouraged. You can always adopt. There are so many children out there that need a good home," said Carmen.

"I don't know, Carmen, my heart just isn't into having another child right now. I just hope Marcus can get past the disappointment of not having a son."

"I think he loves having you more, Jen," said Carmen.

After four months my life began to return to normal even though there were days I didn't think I could get out of bed. The weather was getting warmer, and I was thinking about having everyone over for a barbecue, maybe the first week in June. I needed something to take my mind off the baby and the accident.

Carmen and I got busy planning the event and calling the girls to help with the arrangements. The barbecue took my mind off my problems and Carmen's mind off Jeff. I tried to be supportive because I knew she was going through a difficult time, but it gets hard sometimes to hold someone else up when you feel like your life is falling apart.

Carmen said Jeff's mood swings were getting worse and he had shoved her a couple of times, but she was still not willing to leave him.

After two months of planning, it was finally time for the barbecue. It was a gorgeous day, and for the first time in a very long time, I was excited to get out of bed. This was also the first time Marcus and I made love in months. He was so gentle and reassuring, and I felt a tear run down his face as he hugged me. "I thought I had lost you, Jennifer," said Marcus. "I would die if anything ever happened to you or Dylen," he said through tear-filled eyes.

"I know, baby. I love you too…always, Marcus, I promise."

The barbecue started at one o'clock, and Carmen came over early to help me prepare. Jeff was to come over later with River when everyone else started to arrive. Carmen said Jeff woke up in a bad mood, but she told him that he was coming to the barbecue come hell or high water. I was proud of her for standing her ground with him.

By two thirty, most of the guests had started to arrive, and everyone seemed to be having a good time, even Jeff. The guys decided to play dominoes, the girls were playing a friendly game of gin rummy, and the kids were in the pool having a great time. The lifeguard we hired was one of the best things we could have done. The kids were safe, and the adults were left to do their own thing.

Dylen had gotten a battery-operated Corvette for Christmas, and River had gotten a baby Hummer, and they were begging to bring them out. Against my better judgment, I gave in, so Jeff went next door and got River's car so the kids could play bumper cars. Something kept telling me this is a bad idea, and then I heard a crash.

I jumped up to see what was happening. Marcus and Jeff heard the crash also and ran to see what was going on. We all arrived at the scene at almost the same time. When we got to the play area, Dylen was lying on the ground, pretending to be dead.

Marcus rushed to her to make sure she was all right. I was frozen, I couldn't move, I wasn't sure if Dylen was hurt or not. Jeff was dusting off River's clothing when I started to remember the day of the accident. "I remember I yelled."

Marcus walked over to me. "Sweetheart, you remember what?"

"I remember, you bastard. You killed my baby!" I screamed at Jeff.

Marcus brought Dylen to me and said, "Sweetheart, no, she's fine."

"No, my unborn baby. That bastard killed our son. It was Jeff who was driving the car that hit me. Nikki, tell them. Tell them!" I screamed.

Marcus looked at Nikki. "Is this true?" he said.

"Yes, it's true," said Nikki. "It was Jeff that hit Carmen that day at Taco Bell."

Marcus rushed to him. "You fucking coward, tell me what happened!" Marcus kept punching Jeff in the face as he yelled at him. Bruce tried to pull Marcus off Jeff, but Marcus was relentless.

Dylen started yelling, "Daddy, Daddy, please don't hurt Uncle Jeff!" Marcus saw Dylen running toward him and released Jeff.

Carmen came over and hugged me. "Jennifer, I am so sorry, I did not know. I swear to God I did not know," sobbed Carmen.

Marcus lifted Dylen up in his arms and looked at Jeff and said, "Get the fuck out of my yard before I have you arrested right now."

Jeff looked at Carmen. "Get my son. We're leaving," he said, storming off.

Bruce walked up and kissed me and expressed his sorrow and told me if there was anything he could do to let him know. Everyone else said their goodbyes, and I was left devastatingly imagining Jeff and his lover and the tragedy that changed all our lives forever.

Marcus said his goodbyes to the guests and came upstairs as I was putting Dylen to bed. He kissed his beautiful little girl good night and apologized to her for Daddy getting angry and shouting today. She told him she loved him and drifted off to sleep.

I was about to return downstairs and start cleaning up when Marcus grabbed my arm. "Jen, please tell me what happened the day of the accident." asked Marcus. Just as I was about to explain, the doorbell rang. It was Carmen and River. Marcus took River upstairs and laid him down in the guest room.

Marcus joined Carmen and me in the kitchen as we began to talk. Carmen looked so tired and old, like she had been up for days crying her eyes out. When I asked her what was wrong, she said that when she went back to the house to check on Jeff, he had packed his bags and left. "He left me a note saying he loved River and me but that I would leave him once I found out the truth about him and the day of the accident and he couldn't handle me knowing the truth."

"Well, Carmen, you're just in time. We are about to discuss that very thing," said Marcus.

"Jennifer, please tell us what happened that day," said Carmen.

Marcus sat next to me and held my hand as I began to tell them what I remembered.

"Nikki and I were going to Taco Bell for lunch after shopping. We were pulling into the parking lot, and I saw Jeff's Jag. There was someone standing by the driver's window leaning in, talking with him. At least that's what it looked like at first."

The room was quiet as I turned and looked at Carmen's face. "Go ahead, Jen, it's okay. I have got to know," said Carmen.

"Well, I pulled up next to Jeff, and Nikki noticed the person that was leaning into the window was kissing Jeff."

Tears began to form in Carmen's eyes. "Jen, do you know who the woman is?" asked Carmen.

Marcus looked on with anticipation as he squeezed my hand. "No," I whispered.

"Jen, speak up. I can't hear you."

"No, Carmen, I didn't know the person, but it wasn't a woman, it was a man."

"Jennifer, you're mistaken. That can't be true."

"Carmen, I'm not mistaken. It was a man that Jeff was with, and it's not the first time I've seen them together."

"What do you mean?" asked Carmen.

"I saw them together at Dayton's the day I went shopping for the black dress. Do you remember that day?"

Marcus looked like he was in shock; he didn't say anything.

"Yes, I remember that day, Jennifer. So what happened then, Jen?" said Carmen.

"Well, Nikki jumped out of the car and started screaming at Jeff. Jeff was trying to pull away, but Nikki kept banging on the hood of the car. I jumped out of the car to try to stop Nikki from making a scene. Just as I went to grab Nikki, Jeff backed out, and all I remember is his car coming toward me. The next thing I remember is waking up in the hospital."

"Jennifer, why didn't you tell me the first time you saw Jeff with this man?"

"Because it's devastating enough to find out your husband is having an affair, but to find out it's with a man? Carmen, I just didn't know what to say or how to say it. I'm sorry. I just couldn't hurt you like that."

"Jennifer, you are supposed to be my friend."

"I am your friend. That's why I couldn't hurt you. With all the problems you were having with Jeff, I just didn't think it was the right time."

"Carmen, I feel for you, I really do, but this son of a bitch killed our baby and almost killed Jennifer. He's dead if I get my hands on him," said Marcus, storming out of the room.

"Carmen, I am sorry. I did not want you to find out this way."

"Jennifer, I'm the one who's sorry. I'm sorry for all the heartache and pain Jeff has caused you and your family. Please try and forgive him. I'm sure he never meant to hurt you."

"Carmen, can you forgive him? I mean, really, he's been having an affair with a man."

"I don't know if I can forgive him, Jennifer, but he is my husband, and I just can't abandon him. I don't think I can look at him right now, but I know I can't leave him."

"Carmen, why don't you go to the house and get some clothes for you and River and just spend the night here? That way, we can sit and talk and figure out where we go from here."

Carmen hurried back to the house, while I got the kids ready for bed. I said good night to Marcus and let him know that Carmen and I would be in the den talking.

"Jennifer, I love you. I love you very much. Always remember that."

"I know you do, Marcus, and I love you too. So, baby, don't worry, we will get through this."

I sat there listening to Carmen talk about Jeff and how they first met. I tried to be comforting, but I didn't really know what to say.

"Jen, maybe that explains the mood swings Jeff's been having. Jen, do you think there was anything I could have done?"

"Carmen, you cannot blame yourself for Jeff's actions. After all, that's the thing now, or haven't you heard? You have all these brothers on the down-low because the world is so homophobic that black men are too afraid to be who they really are. So they feel they have to conform to society's bullshit standards of what a real man is. They're supposed to get married, have a family, all along trying to fight the natural urges they were born with. You still have black men thinking that homosexuality is a white man's perversion and that if they get married and play the role, somehow it changes the fact that they are attracted to men. Shit, E. Lynn Harris tried to warn sistas about brothers playing both sides of the field. Society is just not ready to see professional football and basketball players hugged up with other men. So in order for them to protect their image and their livelihoods, they live double lives. I am not condoning it, but I think I understand it, Carmen.

"So, Carmen, let me ask you a question. Were there ever any signs, maybe some that you overlooked?"

"Maybe. I don't know, Jen. I do know that he didn't like going down on me, but a lot of black men don't, so that doesn't mean anything," said Carmen.

"Honey, on what planet do black men not like eating pussy? All the black men I know will suck the chrome off a bicycle if you give them half a chance. Carmen, I can't believe you ever bought into that bullshit myth," I said flatly. "Girl, please, there are a lot of black men who may not admit they eat pussy, but believe me they do, and if they don't, there's probably something wrong with the pussy.

"Carmen, I'm sorry, that was insensitive of me to say that."

"No, Jen, I know what you meant, but to answer your question, no, there were no real signs that Jeff was seeing anyone, let alone a man. Jeff was always really into his appearance, but aren't most professional black men these days?"

"Most professional black men these days that are that into their appearance are gay," I said jokingly. "I'm sorry to make jokes, Carmen. But, girl, this is not your fault. If Jeff wanted to sleep with men, the least he could have done was have the decency to tell you and be honest about his sexuality.

"Carmen, do you realize that black and Hispanic women rank number one in new HIV/AIDS cases each year? Partly because of this very topic, men on the down-low. I remember one year I went home from college for spring break. I needed to get my hair done, so my cousin recommended this guy named Marshay. And, honey, this queen could lay some hair. Later on that night, my cousin and I met Marshay at this little hole in the wall for drinks. This little club was really smoky, so I decided to step outside for some air. Just as I was walking out the door, there stood Marshay, climbing out of the truck of this fine brother that had just tried to talk to me earlier that day in the mall. I tried to pretend I hadn't seen anything, but Marshay came up to me and said, 'Girl, that was a quick fifty. Let's get some drinks on him.' Now earlier that day, when the guy had introduced himself to me, my cousin told me that he had a girlfriend and five kids. Marshay told me that the guy in the truck was one of his regulars. So, Carmen, you see, you never can tell about people. My cousin called me two years ago and told me that Marshay died of AIDS. I wonder where that guy in the truck is now?

"Carmen, I know this may be a touchy subject, but I have to ask. When's the last time you've been tested?"

"Tested? Tested for what?"

"You know, HIV/AIDS or just STDs in general."

"It's been a while, Jennifer, but I didn't think I was in a high-risk category."

"Listen, I'm sure you're fine. Jeff wouldn't be stupid enough to have unprotected sex, would he, Carmen?"

Carmen started to cry again, and I hugged her and placed her head in my lap and rubbed her head until she fell asleep. I slipped my leg from underneath her, placed a blanket over her body, and kissed my friend good night. I went upstairs to check on the kids one more time and then snuggled next to my husband. I silently thanked God for Marcus and drifted off to sleep.

The next morning, Marcus rolled over and kissed me. He apologized for being so insensitive to Carmen and her situation. "But that faggot-ass nigga is going to pay for what he has done." I felt a tear run down his face as he hugged me and told me how scared he was of losing me. "Jennifer, I swear, if I get to that trifling nigga before the police, I don't know what I'll do."

"Marcus, I'm surprised at you. That's not a word you use."

"Honey, I'm sorry, but it applies in this case. You know when I hang out with the boys, we all say the N word, so don't be offended."

Marcus knew I didn't like that word. Being biracial held a lot of heartache and pain for me. Marcus apologized again because he knows how sensitive I am about my heritage.

"Marcus, I know you want to kill Jeff right now, but we have to be there for Carmen and River. I know we have our own problems we're dealing with, but Carmen needs our support right now."

Marcus rolled over and looked at the clock. It was eight, and he needed to call the office and let them know he would not be coming in until around noon. The firm had been very understanding and supportive after my accident and had suggested Marcus take as much time as he needed, but he insisted that he could handle work and things at home.

I got dressed and went downstairs to start breakfast. I peeked in on Carmen, and she was still asleep. Before I could get the coffee started, Nikki was calling.

"Jen, how are things, girl?" she asked.

"I'm fine. Carmen is the one who is going to need our support."

"Well, I'll round up the girls, and we can be there around one o'clock. Do we need to bring anything?"

"No, just come on over. I will make lunch for us a little later."

Carmen finally woke up and went upstairs to take a shower, while I made breakfast. Dylen and River came downstairs and decided they wanted waffles for breakfast. I always kept the blueberry pancakes on hand because they were Dylen's favorite. While the waffles were cooking, I made toast and coffee for Carmen. When she came downstairs, I told her to keep an eye on the waffles while I went upstairs to check on Marcus. I knocked on the shower door, and Marcus opened it up and pulled me inside.

"What are you doing, you crazy man? We don't have time for this!"

"Girl, get your ass in here. Big Papa needs some loving."

"You need some what?" I asked.

"You know what I want," he said mysteriously.

"No, Marcus, what do you want?"

"I want my wife, Mrs. Jennifer Covington, to love me for the rest of my life, because all I want to do is love her."

"Marcus, I think that is one of the most romantic things you have ever said to me."

"Baby, you know that you and Dylen are my world."

"I know, Marcus, but I know how much you wanted a son, and now I can never give you that."

"Jennifer, just stop worrying about that, okay? We're going to be okay. Our family is going to be okay, and if it will make you happy, I promise not to murder Jeff," Marcus said, smiling. "However, I will be reporting his black ass to the police for the hit-and-run. He cannot walk away from this without any consequences."

"Marcus, I know you're angry, but he's probably lost his family. Isn't that enough?"

"Not for me, it isn't."

Suddenly, there was a knock at the door, and Marcus and I looked at each other and laughed because we knew it was Dylen. I jumped out of the shower just as she opened the door.

"Mommy, why are you all wet? Are you taking a shower with Daddy?" she asked so innocently.

"No, sweetie, not really. I just washed his back. Now let me change out of these wet clothes, and I will meet you downstairs for pancakes," I said, staring mischievously at Marcus.

"That was close."

"Yeah, so we need to be more careful, and keep that door locked when you're trying to be all nasty," said Marcus.

"Me? That was you playing grab ass, mister, but this is to be continued later, I promise," I said, smiling.

I walked in the kitchen, and Carmen was doing the dishes. She told me she had received a call from Jeff but was not ready to face him yet. "He wants to explain what's been going on with him."

Marcus came downstairs, and I kissed him goodbye as he left for work. Carmen and I got dressed and dropped the kids off at the jump zone. We made it back to the house as Beth and Virginia arrived. Nikki and I pulled into the driveway at the same time. Virginia had stopped and picked up sandwiches from McAlister's, and Carmen made a cheese tray and a pitcher of mimosas. At first, we just sat there making small talk and exchanging pleasantries. Nikki, with her tactless self, was the first one to bring up Jeff.

"So, Carmen, has that faggot bastard called you yet?" asked Nikki.

"Come on, Nikki," said Virginia.

"Look, I'm sorry, but I'm just so upset with this whole situation."

"Carmen, how are you doing?" asked Beth as she scowled at Nikki.

"Honestly, I think I'm still in shock, and to answer your question, Nikki, yes, I have heard from him," said Carmen. "He called me this morning and told me we needed to talk."

"That is the fucking understatement of the year," said Nikki.

"Carmen, honey, what are you going to do?" Beth asked.

"It's hard to explain," said Carmen. "I'm upset about the affair, of course, but the fact that it was with another man just makes it downright humiliating. I don't understand this. I mean, if Jeff was truly into men, then why did he marry me?"

"Carmen, these are questions only Jeff can answer," said Virginia. "Carmen, look, there is so much pressure on the black man to be this macho stud or they're not considered real men. They're thrown into sports at a young age. They're not supposed to cry or have real emotions, so they are forced to hide their real feelings. There are so many emotionally crippled black men out there that it's no wonder more black women are starting to date outside their race," said Virginia.

"You know, Carmen and I were talking about that very thing last night. I was trying to explain to her that she cannot blame herself for Jeff's emotional failures or his sexuality."

"I'm not trying to be a bitch," said Nikki.

"Then don't," said Virginia.

"Anyway, as I was saying, Jennifer, you're married to a white man, your father is white, you have no brothers, so what in the hell would you know about the emotions of a black man? Excuse me," said Jennifer.

"Nikki, excuse me, but I do have black cousins, and I had quite a few black male friends in high school and college. And for your information, you condescending witch, I do read books, and I am totally aware of how difficult it is for black men to express their sexuality. In this day and age, you have a bunch of stressed-out, overworked, single black mothers who rarely get the opportunity to discuss intimate issues with their sons. So black men learn to play the game. They hide who they really are and show the world what it wants to see. So they end up leading double lives. Look at Victor who hangs out at the Gay 90s. He has a seven-year-old son from some girl he got pregnant on prom night, but half the time, he can't decide whether he wants to be Little Richard, Patti LaBelle, or Whitney Houston. So don't give me that shit, Nikki, about not being black enough," I said without taking a breath.

"I agree with Jennifer," said Beth.

"Come on, Beth, what would you know about it? You're one of the most sexually naive people I have ever met in my life," said Nikki.

"Nikki, how are you going to just lay her shit bare like that?" I said, getting very irritated.

"Come on, Jennifer, let's keep it real. We're girls, right? And if you can't be honest with your girls, then who can you be honest with?"

"I know, Nikki, but you don't have to embarrass her."

"So, Virginia, what's your opinion? We really haven't heard from you," said Nikki. "You always have something to say."

"Okay, Nikki, since you're so inquisitive about what I have to say. I understand both sides actually. I had a lesbian relationship in college, and I don't think I would have made it through emotionally without her. I had a horrible relationship with my mother, and I was shy and withdrawn most of the time. Lydia brought me out of my shell," said Virginia.

"I bet she did bring you out." Nikki smirked.

"As I was saying, before I was so rudely interrupted, I was molested by one of my mother's many boyfriends, and she knew about it but did nothing. I lived with that abuse and suffered in silence until I left for college.

"Lydia was one of the first people I met when I arrived at Howard. She was from New York, and she used to tease me about my Minnesota accent. Her mother was black, and her father was Jewish. He was from upstate New York and came from old money. So her parents were furious when Lydia came out the closet during her graduation party. Anyway, we had been roommates for about a month, and one night, we were sitting around the dorm drinking beer, and Lydia asked me if I wanted to do some coke. I did a couple of lines, and I started telling Lydia about my terrible childhood. She came over to hug and comfort me, and the next thing I knew, we were locked in a kiss. We made love for hours that first night. I think it was the best sex I'd ever had. Lydia was tender and loving and the most exciting person I had met up to that point in my life. Even though she had money, she was very unpretentious, and she cared about me like no one ever had before.

"We were lovers through my junior year, and then I fell for a study partner named Maurice Shelton. I fell for him because I didn't feel like I could be open about my relationship with Lydia. I felt like everyone would judge me. It's bad enough being a black woman in

America, but being black and lesbian was something that I was not ready to deal with. And really at that time, I wasn't sure if that was a label I wanted associated with my life.

"Lydia was understanding and supportive of my choices and the decisions I made for my life. We remained friends, and she eventually got another love interest, but we occasionally got together for drinks, and usually, one thing led to another, and we would end up making love, but she never tried to pressure me to conform to what she thought my life should be. She knew I wasn't ready to announce our relationship to the world, and she was fine with that, but I couldn't ask her to remain in the closet for me."

Everyone sat speechless for a moment.

"I think that was the most I had heard Virginia speak since I'd met her." Carmen was the first one to speak. "So, V, do you consider yourself gay, straight, or bi?"

"I don't like labels, Carmen. Besides, Lydia was more than a lover. She understood me, she was my friend. The sex was just an extra, added bonus. We send each other cards and talk occasionally during the holidays, but to answer your question, no, I don't consider myself a lesbian. Brian and I have been happily married for twelve years, and I've never thought about being with another woman or another man, for that matter. I'll always love Lydia for helping me to heal from my mother's abuse. She was the first woman in my life who ever made me feel safe and loved, and I will always love her for that."

"Damn, girl, you think you know someone," said Nikki.

"So what, Nikki, now you have a problem with me? You think less of me as a person? Is that what you're saying?" asked Virginia.

"No, I don't have a problem with you. I still love you like a play cousin." Nikki laughed. Everyone in the room laughed as well.

"Ladies, we're kind of getting off track. This is about Carmen's issues. I don't know how segued into Virginia's drama," said Nikki.

"Nikki, it's okay. This is all so educational to me," said Carmen. "I've lived a sheltered life when it comes to issues like this," said Carmen. "We had one guy like that in my high school home economics class. James was his name. He wanted to be a hairdresser. James was a very sweet guy. All the girls loved him. After all, he was just like one of the girls. I remember at a pep rally once, he walked in the auditorium in some capri pants. Everyone laughed at him. He was so embarrassed he transferred school the next day," said Carmen. "Looking back, I remember having a hairdresser in Chicago named Parris and Jeff hated him. He hated him so much he made me switch salons. He used to say that fag was always staring at him. I was pregnant at that time with River, and I was so big I couldn't drive, so Jeff had to take me. Looking back now, I'm wondering whether Parris new about Jeff. Parris would often talk about the number of athletes and professional men walking around with their trophy wives and their little boy toys on the side," said Carmen. "You know, ladies, I am angry, and you're damn right I'm hurt, but the bottom line is, I still love my husband," said Carmen.

"Carmen, are you saying you want Jeff back?" I asked.

"Maybe, Jennifer. I don't know, but I do know this: I won't get a clear understanding about Jeff or our marriage until I talk with him."

"Carmen, really, what is there to talk about?" asked Virginia.

"Virginia, what would you do if you found out Brian was on the down-low?"

"Hell, Carmen, that's a dumb-ass question. Brian is one of the most homophobic assholes I've ever met," said Nikki, laughing.

"Girls, I really appreciate all your input, especially you, Virginia. And, Nikki, baby, you need Jesus," said Carmen. Everyone had a nice laugh at Nikki's expense for once.

"All I have to say is, Carmen, this is not an issue your girls are going to be able to solve for you," said Beth.

"I agree," said Virginia. "You need to meet with Jeff and find out what the hell is going on."

While we cleaned up our mess, Carmen went into the kitchen to call Jeff. When she came back, she had the strangest look on her face.

"Sweetie, what's wrong?" I said.

"I checked my messages, and Jeff's office has been trying to reach me all afternoon," Carmen said in shock.

"What's wrong? Carmen," I said again, calling her name.

"Jennifer, Jeff is dead. They found his body in the parking garage at eleven thirty this morning with a gunshot wound to the head. They say the gunshot wound was self-inflicted. The police want me to identify the body. This can't be happening. Why would he do this? This will destroy River. Goddamn, that selfish bastard. Goddamn him," Carmen said, weeping in tears.

I called Marcus and told him what was going on and that I would be taking Carmen to the morgue.

"Jennifer, I can't say I'm sorry, but I am sorry for River and Carmen."

Carmen went home to change clothes, and I broke the news to the girls.

"Ciao, Bella, and good riddance," said Nikki. Everyone shook their heads and rolled their eyes at Nikki.

"I'm taking her to identify the body as soon as I can get changed. Virginia, can you pick up the kids for me?"

"Of course, no problem. If there is anything I can do, please don't hesitate to call me," said Virginia.

I held Carmen's hand as we viewed the body.

"You would take the coward way out, wouldn't you, Jeff? Why couldn't you have just been honest with me?" Carmen said, weeping as she touched Jeff's face. "I could have loved you through anything, but now you've taken away everything, and I'm the one left holding the bag, the one who will have to explain to our son that his father took the coward way out because he couldn't face the reality he had created for himself. Thank you, Jeff, thank you." After Carmen's emotional speech to Jeff, she dried her eyes, walked away, and never looked back.

Carmen had the funeral two weeks later. Jeff's family came down and acted like real jerks. They were cold to Carmen as though she was responsible for Jeff taking his own life. When they asked why Jeff would commit suicide, Carmen told them Jeff was having problems with his partners and had become very depressed. His family refused to stay at the house or attend the wake. After the services, they left the following Monday without ever saying goodbye to River or to Carmen.

I am all River has now, and I am to be mother and father. I can't have the nervous breakdown I have earned or deserved. So I'm doing what I always did when things got tough. I put on a happy face and rely on my wonderful friends, the people I knew I could truly count on.

Carmen asked me to go with her to the office of Jeff's attorney for the reading of the will. A good-looking tall gentleman who looked like he was barely out of law school came in and read Jeff's last will and testament. Jeff left everything to Carmen and River. He left provisions to have the house paid off and their entire credit card debit be paid in full. Carmen was not shocked that Jeff had done the responsible thing to make sure she and River were taken care of, but she was floored when she found out that he left one hundred thousand dollars to his half brother.

"Wait," Carmen said. "Jeff doesn't have a brother, half or otherwise. Who is this guy? Jeff only has two sisters."

"Mrs. Bradley, I'm just the attorney. I write up the will according to the client's wishes."

"Well, can you at least tell me the brother's name?"

"No, I'm sorry, I am not at liberty to discuss that with you. I do apologize for any misunderstanding," said the attorney.

The secretary buzzed and advised Mr. Chilton that she needed to see him right away. He excused himself and left the room. I ran to his desk and quickly riffled through the file he left on his desk. The half brother's name was listed as Darnell Sterling, and he lived in Saint Paul. I quickly jotted down the address. Mr. Chilton walked back into the office and once again apologized to Carmen for not being able to be more helpful. Carmen shook his hand and thanked him for his time. Carmen told him she would get with him later on in the week about drafting a will of her own.

After leaving Mr. Chilton's office, we drove straight to Saint Paul. I turned and looked at Carmen and said, "Honey, are you sure you're ready to do this?" I asked.

"Yes, let's go. I'm ready to meet this half brother," said Carmen.

Carmen knocked on the door. A gorgeous, coco-brown-skinned man opened the door. I recognized him as being the man I had seen

Jeff with at Dayton's and then again at Taco Bell. I could tell by the look on his face that he knew who Carmen was.

"Yes? Can I help you, ladies?"

"I'm looking for Darnell Sterling," said Carmen.

"Why are you looking for him?"

"Because my husband left him one hundred thousand dollars in his will, and I want to know why," said Carmen, becoming pissed off all over again.

The young man became nervous, and tears ran down his face.

"Can you please come in?" he said. His apartment was neat and elegant with beautiful artwork and fixtures. "I know it's early, but would you ladies like something to drink?"

"No," Carmen said. "The only thing I want to know is, were you involved with my husband?"

"We were lovers," he said as he poured himself a glass of wine.

"How long?" asked Carmen.

"I know this is difficult for you, Carmen."

"So you know my name?" asked Carmen, looking shocked and shaken.

"Yes, I know a great deal about you."

"How long?" Carmen said again forcefully.

"Two years, we were involved for two years."

"How can that be? We have only been in Minnesota for two years."

"I know. Jeff moved here to be close to me after I left Chicago," he said. "I loved him and wanted to be with him exclusively, but he did not want to leave you and River. He tried to keep his lives separate, but it became more and more difficult. When I found out that he hit you, I was furious, because I knew he was angry with me but taking it out on you. I am so sorry for that, Carmen."

"Don't speak to me like you know me. You know nothing about me."

"I know that Jeff loved you and River very much, but he loved me too."

Carmen sat there like a statue as she listened to Darnell talk. He was tormented by the double life he was leading.

"Carmen, you have to understand, I am not some scum Jeff met cruising a bar. I am an artist. I own a gallery in Chicago and one here in Saint Paul as well. That's where we met, actually, at my gallery in Chicago. I think I fell in love with Jeff the moment I saw him. We dated for a while before I found out about you, but once I realized he would not and could not ever be totally mine, I left Chicago and moved to Minnesota. Six months later, I received a call from Jeff saying he had moved here as well and he wanted to see me. After that initial meeting, things just picked up where they left off in Chicago," explained Darnell.

Carmen stood up and announced she had heard enough. She handed Darnell the attorney's business card and told him to contact the attorney if he wanted his money.

"Carmen, I don't want his money, and I am so sorry for any hurt or pain that our relationship has caused you and your family. That was never my intent. Please take it. You seem like a really decent person, and Jeff wanted you to have it. Maybe I will give it to charity or something. Who knows?" he said.

Darnell showed us the door and hugged us both goodbye. He was really sweet and endearing. Carmen and I both knew that under different circumstances, he could have been a close friend of ours. Carmen was quiet on the drive home, and all I could do was think that at least now she had closure.

Several months had passed, and our lives started to return to normal. We started to go out together again, and Beth and Richard decided to have a baby. Virginia and Brian were planning an island vacation for the first of the year, and Carmen was in therapy trying to deal with her feelings about Jeff.

The winter was cold and hard this year, and the holidays went by quickly, and we were all looking forward to 2001. Time goes by quickly when you're happy, but it's unfair how short-lived that happiness can be. Things were going well for Marcus at the office, and we were talking about adopting a baby in the spring. Marcus had made partner, and our life was going great. Two days before my birthday in March, Marcus received a phone call from his father that his mother had passed away. I started to pack, while Marcus went to the office to let the partners know what had happened and that he needed to be out of town for a few weeks. I called Carmen and asked her to water the plants and take care of Toodles while we were away. Toodles was the Shih Tzu Dylen had gotten for Christmas.

We flew in and rented a car at the airport; Marcus did not want to trouble his father. I held Marcus's hand as we pulled into the driveway. The house seemed a lot bigger than I remembered.

Dylen kept asking, "Mommy, where are we?"

"This is where Daddy grew up," I said.

David Covington still looked as handsome as the first day I met him in 1983. It had been eleven years, and he looked as though he hadn't aged at all. David hugged me and kissed me on the cheek. "How are you, my dear?" he said. "And who is this lovely young lady holding your hand?"

"I'm Dylen Covington. Who are you?"

"I'm your grandfather, sweetheart." David picked up Dylen and gave her a big hug.

"Hello, Father," Marcus said shyly.

David grabbed Marcus and hugged him. "I have missed you, son."

Marcus always loved his father but couldn't stand his mother. He resented his mother for being so controlling of him and his father.

"Well, let's take this welcome-home party inside," said David.

"Dad, what happened to Mother?"

"She was at a garden party and had a massive heart attack."

"You know Mother, she always had to be the center of attention," said Marcus. "Have you made any arrangements yet?"

"No, not really. I wanted to wait until you arrived. So why didn't you ever try to contact me, Marcus."

"The lines of communication go both ways, Dad. Plus, after receiving that last letter from Mother saying I was being taken out of the will, I just assumed that's how both of you felt."

"Son, I didn't find out about the letter until a couple of years later when I found out Dylen had been born. Son, that was your mother's doing, not mine. She was just trying to keep you under her thumb the way she had me," explained David.

"Dad, why did you let her treat you like that?"

"Son, listen, when I was just a young attorney just starting out, I went to work for your grandfather's law firm. I met your mother at one of the firm's Christmas parties. She was young, beautiful, and looking for a husband. Don't get me wrong, I grew to love your mother, but ours started out as a marriage of convenience. I got a jump-start on my career, and she married the man her daddy wanted her to, and she collected her one-hundred-million-dollar trust fund," explained David.

"Dad, was it worth it? I mean, all the hell Mom put you through?" asked Marcus. "She made you miserable, and you just took it and took it."

"Son, don't feel sorry for me. I did what I had to do, and I got you out of the deal, so to me, it was worth it. Plus, I haven't exactly been a saint either."

"What do you mean, Dad?"

"Well, I have someone in my life that I would like you to meet. She's a very special lady, and we have been seeing each other for twenty-five years. When enough time has passed, I am going to make her my wife."

"Stop being mysterious, Dad, and just tell me."

"No, you will just have to wait," said David. "We will go to the mortuary and finalize all the arrangements at eleven tomorrow, and then she will be here for dinner around six."

"Where is the service being held?"

"It will be held Saturday at St. Mark's Cathedral."

"That's nice, Dad. Mom would have loved that. The more extravagant, the better."

"Now it's time to get some sleep, son. We have a big day ahead of us tomorrow. I know you're probably tired. It's been a really long day."

Dylen had fallen asleep while we were talking, so Marcus picked her up and carried her upstairs. I walked behind them, tugging on his shirttail.

"So, hon, what do you think about your dad being a player?" I asked.

Marcus turned to me and said, "You're really enjoying this, aren't you? My dad's not a player."

"The hell he's not. Your mother's body is barely cold, and he's got a girlfriend."

"Jennifer, respect the dead. After all, she was my mother, and if you must know, smart-ass, my dad has been carrying on this affair for over twenty-five years."

"Get out, are you serious? And you're trying to tell me your dad's not a player."

"Sweetie, I'm sorry, but I don't share your amusement about this situation."

"Honey, I know she was your mother, but that bitch was worse than Cruella de Vil."

"Jennifer, I know their marriage was not based on love, but she was my mother, and I'm worried about my dad."

"Marcus, he seems to be coping pretty well."

"Let's get some sleep, baby. We'll see what's in store for tomorrow. I just hope it's not some twentysomething bleached-blond bimbo that's going to take him for every dime he's got," said Marcus.

"Marcus, your father's smarter than that, and besides, he's been dating the woman for twenty-five years, remember?" I said, laughing.

"Normally, he is, Jen, when he's thinking with the right head. Just forget it, and let's get some sleep."

Morning came way to soon, and even Dylen was sleeping in. Marguerite brought breakfast in bed.

"Hey, this is great, Marcus. I could get used to having servants. Hey, I will go grab the Smurf so we can eat," I said, jumping off the bad.

"Marcus, she's not in her room," I said, walking back into the bedroom.

"Don't worry, she's probably downstairs with Dad."

After breakfast, we got dressed and went to the mortuary. The arrangements were beautiful.

"It's going to be a lovely service, David," I said, trying to make polite conversation.

"Thank you, Jennifer."

Shelia is going to go out in style just as she would have wanted, I thought. *It's too bad she didn't get the chance to know her gorgeous grandchild.*

We finished the arrangements and headed to the Oak Harbor Country Club for lunch. Everyone was shaking David's hand and giving their condolences. On the other hand, Dylen and I were being totally ignored. You would think I was the first black to ever darken the door of their precious little club the way everyone was staring.

"Dad, maybe we should go somewhere else," said Marcus. "I don't want Jen and Dylen feeling uncomfortable."

"Marcus, I'm fine," I said.

"Son, I wish someone would say something out of line. I'm on the board of directors, and I've spent a lot of money to help build this club, and I will shut this bitch down if anyone disrespects my family."

After lunch, we went to the galleria to shop. David wanted to buy Dylen the world, but Marcus and I cautioned him about spoiling her, so after shopping, we headed home so we could get some rest before dinner. I dressed Dylen and was combing her hair when the doorbell rang. Marcus was rushing to get the door to find out who the mystery guest was.

"Hey, speedy, don't you have servants that answer the door?" I asked.

"Yes, smart-ass, but I'm anxious to see who the mystery guest is."

I hurried and put Dylen's hair in a ponytail and ran down behind Marcus.

When Marcus opened the door, there was this gorgeous, well-heeled black woman in a beautiful sundress standing at the door. Marcus grabbed her and hugged her.

"Jen, I want you to meet Helen. She is Dad's executive secretary," he said as Dylen and I caught up with him at the bottom of the stairs. "Ms. H, Dad's upstairs getting ready for dinner. What are you doing working this late? Please come in. I forgot my manners. We are just about to have dinner, but I'm sure Dad has time to see you. You want to wait in the study."

Just as Marcus was about to show Helen to the study, David walked in. He walked up to her and kissed her on the cheek and said, "Sweetheart, you look great. Marcus, Helen is our dinner guest."

I smiled, and Marcus just looked shocked. "Dad, what is going on?"

"Let's have drinks in the living room. Dinner is not quite ready," said David. David led Helen into the living room, holding her hand and smiling like a lovesick schoolboy.

Marcus grabbed me around my waist and pulled me close to him and whispered, "You're really enjoying this, aren't you?"

"Hell yeah, what are the odds of a white father and son both having jungle fever?" I said, giggling.

"Real cute, Jen, really fucking cute."

Helen was looking a little embarrassed, and Marcus and I were trying not to appear uncomfortable.

"Marcus, I am not trying to disrespect your mother by being here but—"

David interrupted, "We love each other. Helen and I have been together for a long time, and we have never disrespected your mother by flaunting our relationship in public. But after a little time passes, I do plan on making Helen my wife. Marcus, I would like your blessing, but my marrying Helen is not contingent on what you or anyone else thinks. I want your blessings, not your approval."

"Dad, as long as you're happy, I'm happy. You deserve some happiness, and if Helen makes you half as happy as Jen makes me, than you're a lucky man." Marcus stood up and hugged his dad and kissed Helen. The dinner conversation was very pleasant, and Dylen sat there playing with her lobster and was the life of the party.

We stayed in Florida for three more weeks after the funeral, hanging out with Helen and David. We all hated the day we had to leave, but it was time to get back to the real world. David and Helen announced they would be coming to Minnesota for the holidays, and Dylen was ecstatic. We kissed them goodbye and boarded our flight.

I snuggled close to Marcus, while Dylen slept on the flight home. I looked at my handsome husband and said, "You know,

Marcus, I'm going to really miss your dad and Helen, but most of all, I'm going to miss the servants."

"Oh, I'm so sorry, Cinderella, but it's back to reality for you," Marcus said, smiling.

Marcus took an additional week off work to help me get settled back in to my normal routine, and I couldn't help but be a little concerned that he didn't cry at his mother's funeral. The disturbing part was, he seemed okay with the fact that he wasn't very emotional about his mother's passing.

The following day, I called Carmen to let her know I was back in town. She told me River had really missed Dylen and had fallen totally in love with Toodles.

"Look, what you did, Jen. Now I'm going to have to get him a dog," said Carmen.

I just laughed and told Carmen that after breakfast, we would be over for a visit. Dylen couldn't wait. She was so excited she barely touched her breakfast. When Carmen came to the door, she looked horrible.

"Girl, what in the world is wrong with you?"

"Jen, I've had this flu for over a month now, and I just can't shake it."

"You know what, I will take River for a couple of days and give you a chance to rest, and I'll make some soup and bring it over."

"That sounds great, Jen. I could really use the rest."

I packed River a bag and dropped him and Dylen off at the house with Marcus and went shopping for ingredients to make soup.

When I took the soup over to Carmen, I found her on the bathroom floor throwing up.

"Girl, where in the world did you pick up this flu bug from in May?"

"Well, River and I went swimming about a month ago, and I stayed in the pool too long and got a chill. River had the sniffles for a couple of days, and then he was okay, but me? I can't seem to shake this crud. Not to mention I've been really depressed for the last couple of weeks, and I really haven't been eating. But, girl, I will be fine."

"Carmen, I'm sorry I haven't been here for you. But, honey, what made you depressed?"

"I got a letter from Jeff's attorney a couple of weeks ago, and he informed me that Darnell had not cashed his check. He picked it up from the office but didn't cash it."

"Carmen, what is so strange about that? Darnell told you he didn't want the money, so maybe he burned the check. Who cares anyway?"

"Mr. Chilton told me his phone number is no longer in service and he has been unable to reach him. I have tried several times, and I haven't been able to reach him either."

"Carmen, maybe he moved back to Chicago?"

"I don't think so, Jen. I have this feeling that something is seriously wrong. I need to go check on him when I'm feeling better."

"Carmen, I will drive you there myself when you're feeling better, sweetie, but this obsession with this guy is starting to worry me."

"It's not an obsession, Jennifer. The truth is, I've been talking with him on a regular basis, trying to understand what Jeff was going through living this double life. I feel close to Jeff when Darnell and I talk. We both loved him very much."

I nursed Carmen back to health, and when she was finally ready, we went to visit Darnell. We dropped the kids off at the Drop Zone and decided to make a day of it.

"Jen, I know something's wrong, and I'm worried. I tried calling the gallery, and they just keep saying he's unavailable and then his cell being turned off. I'm telling you, something's wrong."

"Carmen, maybe he just doesn't want you contacting him anymore. Maybe it's just too painful and he just wants to be left alone. After all, he is grieving too."

"Jennifer, he has no reason to hate me. I thought we were becoming friends."

"I didn't say he hated you, sweetie. I just think you're overreacting. It's not like you know this guy."

"Jen, I just need to make sure that he is okay."

We got to Darnell's apartment and knocked on the door. No one answered, so Carmen started to knock so loud that the next-door neighbor came out. She was a nosy little lady holding a cat. "Can I help you ladies?" she said.?"

"No, I don't think so," said Carmen.

"Then get the hell out of here. We don't like Jehovah's Witnesses knocking on our doors," she said.

"We're looking for Darnell," I said, irritated at the woman for upsetting Carmen.

"Who?" she said loudly. "Oh, you mean the black fellow that used to live there before Ida Goldstein moved in. Honey, he's dead."

"Dead?" said Carmen.

"Do you know what happened to him?" I asked.

"All I know is, one of the other neighbors told me that they found him dead about three weeks ago."

"Thank you for your time," I said. "We are sorry we disturbed you."

"Jennifer, what do you think happened? Do you think he was really that distraught over Jeff that he killed himself?"

"Who knows, Carmen?"

We turned to walk back to the car and saw two queens coming up the walk.

"Are you looking for that pretty boy that used to live in 112?" they asked.

"Yes, so what?" said Carmen.

"Child, he had the package, and UPS did not deliver it."

"What the hell does that mean?" asked Carmen, irritated and angry.

The other queen started singing "Waterfalls" by TLC.

I grabbed Carmen by the arm and pulled her to the car. "Look at me, Carmen. Bitch, don't go getting any ideas. They could be wrong," I said in shock.

"We both know what they were talking about, Jennifer. AIDS."

"Yes, but he could have gotten it after his relationship with Jeff, or those queens could have been lying. Have you been tested since you found out about Jeff?"

"No, I haven't."

"Carmen, think about it. Jeff would not have jeopardized your life by having unprotected sex. Regardless of his other life, I do believe that he loved you. We'll go back to the house, call your doctor, and get you tested as soon as possible. You'll see, Carmen, there's nothing to worry about."

"I'm not worried, Jen. I'm just sad about Darnell. He seemed like such a nice person, and no one deserves to die alone."

As we picked the kids up and headed home, I could tell Carmen was worried even though she tried to appear upbeat. I took the kids to the backyard to play while I got started on dinner. Carmen called her doctor to make an appointment for Thursday. He told Carmen it would take at least seven to ten days to get the results back. I felt so sorry for her. Today was Tuesday, May 15, and she would have to wait ten more days before she would find out if HIV would change her life forever.

That night, I told Marcus what was going on. I explained to him that I needed him to watch the kids tomorrow because the girls were meeting at Carmen's house. She needed our support, and we had to be there for her. Marcus was always so supportive, and I knew I could always count on him to have my back.

Nikki was the first to arrive.

"Who the hell called this meeting of the cackling sisters in the middle of the week?" she asked. "What the hell is going on now?"

"Well, Nik, if you sit your skinny talking ass down, you'll find out when everyone else arrives," I said.

"Drop dead, heffa, and I'm not skinny. As a matter of fact, Jen, you and Carmen need to bring your asses back to Pilates class because you're starting to get a little pudgy," said Nikki.

Carmen tried to smile. I just gave her a little hug and scowled at Nikki.

"What's going on divas?" asked Nikki. "Carmen, you and Jen are acting weird."

"We would rather wait until everyone's here."

"Hell no, I can't wait. Someone is going to tell me what the hell is going on right now," said Nikki.

"Jennifer, will you tell her while I get some glasses? I'm sick of hearing her bitching and griping."

"Nikki, we just found out yesterday that the man Jeff was having the affair with may have died of AIDS."

Just as I finished telling Nikki, Carmen walked back into the room. Nikki had tears running down her face, and she hugged Carmen and apologized for being such a bitch. While they were talking, I went to answer the door, and in walked Virginia and Beth. They saw Nikki and Carmen hugging and immediately asked what was going on.

"Hey, why don't we all just sit down and relax?" I said.

"This must be serious," said Beth. "Will someone tell us what the hell is going on? Because if Nikki is crying and if that cynical bitch is crying, it must be bad."

Carmen stood up with Nikki holding her hand. Carmen's voice started to shake and crack as she began to speak. "Jennifer and I found out that the man Jeff had the affair with may have died of AIDS." The room was so quiet you could hear a pin drop. "I have an appointment scheduled for Thursday, but it will be about two weeks before I get the results back."

"Carmen, you have got to be terrified," said Beth.

"Girls, at this point, we are not exactly sure about anything, so don't jump to any conclusions, okay?" said Carmen. "I just wanted my girls to know because I am going to need your support, but I don't want your pity. So let's get a card game going because I'm ready to kick some ass."

"You guys get started, and I will make some apple martinis, and we will just pray that that lying, cheating bastard had enough sense to wear a condom," said Nikki.

"Nikki, don't start that. Carmen doesn't need that right now," said Virginia.

"We're all upset about this situation, and your bullshit doesn't help," I said.

"Jen, why do you always have to be the sanctimonious one?" said Nikki. "Everyone doesn't have your perfect little life, Jennifer!" Nikki shouted.

I stood up angrily. "You fucking bitch, how dare you talk to me like that? I have more reason than anybody to hate Jeff. He killed my baby, and thanks to him, I'll never be able to have another child ever!" I said hysterically. "But this is not about Jeff, and it's not about me. This is about Carmen, and everyone gets that except you Nikki."

"Jen, I'm sorry. Honey, I forgot. My bad," said Nikki. Nikki grabbed me and hugged me.

Virginia looked at Nikki and said, "You're such a pillowcase, Nik. Why don't you do all of us a favor, take a Valium, and shut up?"

"Beth, you're awfully quiet. Are you okay?" asked Carmen.

"I'm fine," said Beth. "I'm just so frightened for you. I mean, this could happen to any one of us. You want to believe that your man is straight and he's not cheating on you, but you just never know. Isn't that all you hear about these days? Men playing both sides of the field? A girlfriend of mine spent two months with her sister in Atlanta a year ago. She said she met some of the finest brothers on the planet, and mostly, all of them were gay or bisexual. She told me if you move to Atlanta and you want a straight black man, then you better take him with you, because you definitely won't get one once you arrive."

"Girl, you tripping. I heard that Atlanta is the new black mecca," said Nikki.

"It is mecca if you're a gay black man looking for another gay black man." Virginia laughed.

"Ladies, let's not lose sight of why we're really here," I said. "Carmen, are you okay? We're not trying to make light of the situation."

"No, it's fine, Jennifer. I appreciate all the support," said Carmen. "I'm still hurt about the whole situation because I loved Jeff so much. I just always assumed I was the only woman in his life."

"You were...the only woman sweetheart. Remember he liked men," said Nikki.

"You just couldn't pass up saying that, could you, Nikki? You can be such a cunt sometimes. How can you be so cruel about Carmen's feelings?" said Virginia.

"She's our friend, and you talk to her like that. How can you be so heartless?" I asked.

"Jennifer, please, why are you getting so bent out of shape? Now have I said one thing that wasn't true? I mean, let's get real for a second here. Carmen's husband slept with men. All I have to say is, get tested and move on with your life, because regardless of the results, your girls are going to be here for you no matter what, and Carmen I put that on everything I love," said Nikki.

Virginia looked at Nikki. "Girl, you are so special. Better yet, you need Jesus and a hug, 'cause you are dealing with a whole lot of demons."

We all looked at one another and burst out laughing. We spent the rest of the evening laughing and talking. There was an occasional tear, but for the most part, we had a really good time. At the end of the night, we all went our separate ways knowing tomorrow could possibly change our lives forever.

I thought Thursday would not get here fast enough. I drove Carmen to the doctor because she was too nervous to drive herself. It seemed like an eternity before her name would be called. I sat quietly, holding her hand, trying to put on a brave face. I had a knot in the pit of my stomach that just wouldn't go away. This had been the longest ten days of our lives.

The girls and I spent the next two weeks trying to keep Carmen occupied. The days were long, but the nights seemed even longer. Marcus tried to be supportive, and I appreciated all his love and affection, but somehow it just wasn't enough. Men could never truly understand the effects of betrayal and how it hurts a woman. Carmen was going to have to deal with the effects of Jeff's betrayal probably for the rest of her life however long that was, because today she would receive her test results.

I sat there thinking about last night. I had woken up somewhere around 5:00 a.m., and I was exhausted; I had tossed and turned all night. Marcus said he would stay home with the kids; he knew Carmen would need company regardless of the results.

Nikki and Virginia arrived at eight o'clock, and Beth called to say she would meet us at the doctor's office. I could tell everyone was scared, and I tried desperately to hold back my tears. We tried to present a unified front for Carmen, but she seemed calmer than all of us. She was humming and quite cheerful. She looked at me and said, "Jen, don't worry, everything is going to be okay." I kissed her and held her tight. I wanted this moment to last forever. This was probably going to be the last time I'd see my best friend completely happy.

The appointment was scheduled for ten o'clock, and we arrived at 9:45 a.m. Beth was there waiting for us. We sat down and tried to carry on polite conversation, but it was very difficult. While I was sitting there, going over the morning's events, the nursed called Carmen's name.

"Good morning, ladies. You certainly look like you're a festive-looking group," said the doctor. "Are you all coming back with the patient?"

"Yes," Carmen said, "if that's okay with you?"

"No, I don't mind at all," said the doctor.

The nurse brought in some extra chairs, and we all sat down.'

"Carmen, I know you probably came to me because I was Jeff's physician, and I don't have a problem with that at all as long as you know I can't discuss his medical history with you."

"That's fine, Doctor. I just want my results, okay?" said Carmen.

"I understand, Carmen, and it pains me greatly to have to tell you that you tested positive for the AIDS virus," revealed the doctor.

I heard Nikki whisper "That queer son of a bitch." Beth and Virginia started to cry.

"Dr. Reston, my name is Jennifer, and I have a question, if you don't mind?"

"No, go ahead, as long as it's okay with Carmen."

"Dr. Reston, I don't understand a lot about AIDS and HIV, but what determines the difference?"

"Once the T cells fall below two hundred, you are considered to have full-blown AIDS."

"Carmen, do you have any questions?" asked the doctor.

Carmen was quiet.

"How much time does she have, Doctor?" I asked.

"I can't give a definitive answer to something like that. With today's medications, people are living a lot longer with HIV/AIDS. Carmen, are there any questions that I can answer for you? I know this news is devastating, but AIDS is no longer the death sentence it used to be. Here is my card. If you have any question, please do not hesitate to call me, but in the meantime, I need you to schedule an appointment for a complete physical so we can get you started on medication. Just keep in mind that it is manageable and there are new treatments all the time," said the doctor.

A single tear ran down my face as I squeezed Carmen's hand. Carmen rose from her seat and shook the doctor's hand. "I'll be in touch," she said politely and headed for the door. We all followed her to the receptionist's desk, where she scheduled an appointment for the following week.

The ride home was quiet. Carmen suggested we stop for lunch. We sat in the restaurant barely speaking. "Hey, guys, look, I'm not dead yet, and I am not going to live as though I am, and I don't want you to either. Life goes on, and so shall we, so let's eat," said Carmen.

The drinks came, and everyone started to loosen up. Carmen and I ordered apple martinis. Carmen took a sip and turned to Beth. "Hey, girl, taste this. Doesn't it taste funny?"

Beth pulled away hesitantly. "Carmen, I don't think it's a good idea for us to drink after you anymore," said Beth.

"Why not?" asked Nikki.

"You know, Nik, the AIDS thing," Beth said.

"You stupid cow, how are you going to sit there and say that stupid shit in front of Carmen? You can't catch it that way, you dumb bitch," said Nikki.

"No, Nikki, don't be upset with Beth. I know she's probably scared. Hell, I'm scared. I wasn't thinking when I asked you to taste my drink, Beth. I know things have to be different, but I don't want to be treated like a leper," said Carmen.

Carmen was right though; some things would change, but I didn't want her to be treated like a leper, especially not by her friends. Society would do that enough. Carmen made it through lunch with style and grace even though I saw her tear up occasionally.

June 24, 2001, changed our lives forever, and in the weeks that followed, we were all tested and received a clean bill of health. Carmen started on her treatments and her alternate lifestyle. The doctor had advised Carmen against drinking alcohol and advised her to get plenty of rest. We still had the occasional girls' night out, but Carmen was often missing from the group.

I talked to Marcus about the girls and me taking a trip to Alamogordo, New Mexico, to visit my father. He had a ranch out there, and it had been a while since I had seen him. Marcus was totally supportive as always and agreed to keep the kids.

I called Dad, and he was ecstatic about me and my friends coming for a visit. My father lived outside White Sands, New Mexico, on a beautiful ranch. He had retired from the air force and decided to make his home in New Mexico because he enjoyed the serenity of the desert.

My father was still a bit of a mystery to me. He and my mother had a love affair while he was stationed at Carswell Air Force Base in Texas. My mother had stayed in Fort Worth after graduating college and went to work as a civilian on the air base. My mother had an affair with my father for eight years, and I was the result of their love. The only thing I knew about my father was his name and that he was Italian. He came to my high school graduation, and after that, we kept in limited contact. He always sent cards for my birthday and for Christmas, and I always sent him pictures of Dylen.

I called the girls once I had made all the arrangements, and everyone was excited, even Beth. Beth was still being a little standoffish toward Carmen, but I hoped this trip would bring us all closer together. I was going to miss Dylen and Marcus, but I was excited about seeing my father.

A car met us at the airport. It was over-an-hour drive from El Paso to Alamogordo, and everyone decided to take a quick nap. I was concerned about Carmen; she was putting up a brave front, but she looked really tired, and she wasn't her usual upbeat self.

We arrived at 2:00 p.m., and Dad greeted us with flowers and champagne. God, it had been such a long time since I had seen my father. He had started to turn gray around the edges of his hair, but he was still quite handsome. Hiking kept him young, he said, so he was still in really good shape for a man in his midfifties.

The girls were excited to meet him, especially Nikki. She turned on the old charm and was smiling and giggling like some adolescent schoolgirl.

My dad set us up in a cabin that held five with an adjourning sitting room and a hot tub. The ranch was gorgeous. I could understand why my father had fallen in love with this place.

After a long nap, we all freshened up and went for dinner and drinks with my father.

My dad was playing hostess when we arrived, and we were given the VIP treatment. The restaurant had a jazz club, so we decided to hang out a bit after dinner and listen to music.

People started to look and whisper at all the attention my father was showing us. They probably thought he was some old perv making a fool out of himself over a bunch of young black women. This one old gal was staring so hard she dropped her shrimp.

Nikki turned around and said, "What the fuck are you looking at, Grandma? White men have been fucking black women since slavery, and truth be told, they have always preferred our pussy to yours."

Everyone at the table burst out laughing.

"Nikki, be nice," I said.

"No, Jen, I'm serious. That bullshit really gets on my last nerve. It's the twentieth century. Get over it already. You want to know what else gets on my nerve?"

"No, but I'm sure you're going to tell us," said Virginia.

"I hate it when you go in the bathroom behind somebody and they got FPS," said Nikki.

"Nikki, what the hell is FPS?" asked Virginia.

"FPS is funky pussy smell," said Nikki.

Everyone burst out laughing again.

"Girl, you are crazy," said Carmen.

Beth chimed in, "Nikki, you are such a pillowcase."

"What the hell is a pillowcase?" asked Carmen.

"It means the bitch needs help because she is certifiable, but of course, we have suspected this all along," said Virginia.

"Beth, why could you just say that?" asked Nikki. "Oh my god, Beth, you are just so weak," said Nikki. "Anyway, Jennifer, damn all that, I am more interested in whether or not your father ever remarried," asked Nikki.

"What does it matter, Nikki? Because you're married, remember?" said Virginia.

"Girl, Mr. Farillo is fine as hell, if y'all haven't noticed. Plus, I've always liked older men. And, girl, your dad is ripe for the picking," said Nikki.

"Nikki, don't be so disrespectful. You're talking about Jennifer's father," said Virginia.

"Shit, old men need pussy too," said Nikki.

"I'm sure Bruce would be interested to know about your love for older men," said Virginia.

"Yeah, Nikki, quit acting like a common tramp throwing yourself at Mr. Farillo like that. You're making a fool out of yourself," said Beth.

"Whatever. I'm here to have fun for two weeks, and I'm going to have fun," said Nikki.

"I know we're here for fun, but we can still act like ladies and not tramps," said Carmen.

"Tramp? Whatcha call me, tramp?" said Nikki as she broke out with her rendition of Salt-N-Pepa's song "Tramp."

We all laughed and shook our heads at Nikki. Nikki was always good for a laugh, and laughter was exactly what we needed. We hung out until midnight, then it was time to call it a night.

My father had a whole list of activities scheduled for us, but we decided to just lie by the pool and drink margaritas. Nikki continued her excessive flirting with my father, and we continued to ignore her. I became more concerned with Carmen's appearance. When we were getting dressed last night, I noticed a lesion on the back of her neck. I didn't want to say anything and embarrass her in front of the others, so I didn't mention it.

We had lunch served by the pool, where we continued to sip our drinks and enjoy one another's company.

"Jennifer, honey, why is it you never told us you were a rich half-breed? Excluding Marcus's money, of course," said Nikki.

"First of all, Nik, I'm not rich. My father is. Second, I've never liked the term 'half-breed.' I'm biracial or mixed, take your pick, but like I told you before, stop calling me a half-breed."

"Jennifer, why are you so sensitive about your ethnicity?" asked Nikki.

"I'm not, but I'm not a dog, so stop all the breed shit, okay?"

"Nikki, you always do this. We're having a good time, and you start acting like a bitch," said Virginia.

"You know, I'm really tired of you guys always ganging up on me. I was just playing with Jennifer, damn," said Nikki.

"I know, Nikki, but you have a tendency to take things too far," said Carmen.

"Whatever," said Nikki. "I'm here to have a good time, and if you ladies can't take a joke, then screw you," she said, jumping into the pool.

Virginia stood up and said, "Nikki, you never acted like this when Gloria was alive, and tonight, your head is going to look a hot mess for jumping in that pool."

Nikki gave Virginia the bird and kept swimming.

"I really don't know what possessed that girl to get all her hair cut off anyway," said Beth.

"Her head is going to look like a fucking Q-tip tonight at dinner," said Virginia. "We're going to have to either look at her nappy head or look at some damn do-rag on her head all night, and that is not a pretty sight."

"Virginia, I like her hair short," said Beth.

"Okay, Ms. Thang, if you like it so much, cut yours off."

"I don't think so," said Beth.

"Just like I thought. You know Richard would kick your butt if you came home with your hair cut short."

"I don't know what it is about black men and long hair. When I met Marcus, my hair was short, and he didn't have a problem with it. I've been contemplating cutting it again," I said.

"Honey, we all know white men are different," said Beth.

"Look at Bruce Willis when Demi Moore shaved her head for GI Jane. I don't care how much money you offer a black woman—she won't shave her head. Hell, you can barely get a black woman to shave her cat," said Virginia. We all started laughing.

"What are you laughing at?" said Nikki, getting out of the pool.

"Nothing," Virginia said.

"Yeah, whatever. Y'all don't have to share with me, but would someone please order another round of drinks?" said Nikki with attitude.

A couple of hours later, we decided to go horseback riding before dinner. I noticed Carmen was sweating and looking glassy-eyed. "Hey, girls, you go ahead. I think I'm going to take a nap," said Carmen.

"Virginia, you, Nikki, and Beth go ahead. Carmen's not feeling well. I'm going to go get her some hot tea and just sit with her a while."

When I got back to the room with the tea, Carmen was in the bathroom throwing up. I ran to help her from the floor, and she felt like a rag doll, and she was burning up with fever. When I checked her fever, it was 105.

I got Carmen in to bed and called for the doctor.

"Carmen had developed an infection," the doctor said. He hooked her up to an IV because she was dehydrated and gave her a cocktail of antibiotics.

I lay in bed beside her and held her until she fell asleep. Carmen slept for hours shivering and shaking. When she finally woke up three hours later, she was sick to her stomach. She tried to get out of bed and fell to her knees. I thought she had passed out, but she started to laugh.

"Carmen, sweetie, are you okay?"

"Yes, Jen, I'm fine. I didn't realize it had gotten dark outside."

"Carmen, what are you talking about? It's still light out. Are you talking in your sleep?"

"No, Jennifer, something is wrong. I can't see. It's all dark."

I helped Carmen sit up on the side of the bed and called for the doctor.

The doctor came back and examined Carmen again. "Carmen, this is not uncommon in AIDS patients. Usually, the blindness is temporary, but there is no way to tell how long it will last," said the doctor.

I silently cried for Carmen because she rarely cried for herself.

"Jen?"

"Yes, Carmen?"

"I'm scared," she said. "This is the second time this has happened."

"Carmen, why didn't you tell me?"

"I didn't want to worry you," she said. "One day, I was in the shower, and I got soap in my eyes. I just thought it had something to do with the soap."

"How long did the blindness last that time, Carmen?"

"About twenty minutes. I just sat in the shower and let the water run down my face until it went away."

"Carmen, I am so sorry for you, sweetie."

"Jen, I'm just scared if one day this happens while I'm driving and Rivers is in the car with me," Carmen said with tears running down her face. "I don't mind killing myself, but I don't want to hurt my son."

"Listen, Carmen Alexis Bradely, stop being so stubborn. If you need anything, to go shopping or whatever, I'm here for you and River. Do you understand me?"

"Yes, Jen, but I'm not afraid for me. I don't want my little boy to be an orphan. I miss Jeff so much, Jen. In spite of all the pain and heartache he has caused me, I still miss him terribly. We had always talked about growing old together, walking in the park with our matching jogging suits the way you see old people do. I thought we would be together forever."

"We all think that, honey. Otherwise, what would be the point of getting married and sharing your life with someone? Carmen, can I ask you a question?"

"What is it?"

"How long have you had the lesions?"

"Almost six months now. When I first got them, I thought it was some type of melanoma, you know, skin cancer."

"What is your doctor saying about the lesions?"

"There's nothing he can say. I have some antibiotic cream that I put on them, but they are just a part of my life now."

"Carmen, listen to me, people live a long time with AIDS these days. You just need to take your medicine, eat right, and have faith. Please tell me you're not giving up. Promise me, Carmen. You can beat this thing."

"Jen, I would love to promise you that, but I can't. I'm so tired, Jen."

"I know, Carmen, but just think of River and all the people who love you. Just lie down and sleep, and I'll go to dinner with the others and have some soup sent out to you. I won't stay out late, okay? I'll be back around ten."

"Jen, just don't worry about me. I will be fine alone for a few hours. I need the sleep anyway."

The rest of the girls got in about eight thirty.

"Hey, let's eat. I'm starving," said Beth.

"What's going on with Carmen?" asked Nikki.

"She's okay, just a little headache. I have someone bringing her some soup."

We dressed and went to dinner, but I wasn't very hungry. I had a small salad and a glass of wine. I couldn't stand watching my dad flirt with Nikki, so I went to my room.

I wasn't jealous or anything; I just wished my dad seemed as interested in getting to know me as he did Nikki. I knew nothing was going to happen, because in spite of all her flirting, Nikki was all talk; she loved Bruce. I think my father was just infatuated with the idea of having a pretty young girl flirting with him. I decided to let them have their fun and left.

When I got to the room, Carmen was still asleep. The soup had not been touched, so I decided to wake her up so she could eat. As the soup warmed in the microwave, I helped Carmen to the bathroom. Her vision had partially returned, but things were still a little blurry. Carmen ate her soup, took her medication, and went back to sleep. I took a quick shower and called Marcus before getting into bed. I lay next to Carmen as she slept. She was very restless, and I was sad because all I could do was hold her.

The next morning, I woke up, and everyone was in bed except for Nikki.

"Virginia, wake up," I said, shaking her. "Where is Nikki, V?" I asked her. "Didn't she come home with you guys last night?"

"Yes, she came home. I was preparing for bed, and she was putting on her bathing suit. She said she was going to get in the hot tub."

I walked out to the hot tub, and I saw two wineglasses but no Nikki.

I could feel my face turning red. If this trifling bitch slept with my father, I am going to kick her ass from here to Minnesota. I stormed back into the room and shouted, "Where the hell is Nikki? Where is that bitch?" I shouted.

"I'm in the bathroom. What do you want?" she said.

"Where did you sleep last night?" I demanded.

"In my bed. Where else would I sleep?"

"Your bed is made, Nik."

"What are you talking about?" I asked. "It's made because I made it. I got up and went jogging, made my bed, and got in the shower. What the hell are you tripping about, Jen?"

"Who did you have drinks with in the hot tub last night?"

"I don't know, some chick in the bungalow down the hill. We killed a bottle of wine while she complained about her husband, and then I went to bed. You thought I was with your father, didn't you?"

I was embarrassed, but I managed to say, "Yes, I did think you were with him."

"Jen, what's going on with you? I'm just having fun with your dad. I like talking to him, and he gets to masturbate thinking about my fine black ass."

"Eew, way too much information," I said as I cringed.

"Look, Jen, Bruce is the man I love, and even though I talk a bunch of crap, my husband satisfies me. Plus, truth be told, Bruce gets off hearing about my little escapades with other men."

"What other men?"

"No, Jen, not real men. It's just a fantasy thing we do where I tell him about me going into a bar and picking up some stranger and flirting with him while sitting at the bar with no underwear on, and I let him finger-fuck me."

"So what you're trying to tell me is that Bruce is just as big a freak as you are, huh, Nikki?"

"Well, they say birds of a feather," said Nikki as we hugged each other and laughed.

"Hey, look, maybe I've been coming on a little too strong with your dad, so I will just back off so you guys can spend some time together."

"No, it's okay, Nikki. I know my father loves me."

"Jen, listen, I don't mean to change the subject, but is Carmen okay? I don't like the way she has been looking lately."

"Nikki, it's tough. She loved Jeffrey, and now she's stuck raising a child on her own. She's sick, and she's scared. The inevitability is death, and it's coming quicker than she would like."

"That coward ass Jeff, how dare he leave her here to deal with all this bullshit on her own?" said Nikki. "I think if he wasn't already dead, I'd kill the son of a bitch myself."

"Hey, Nik, you big freak, let's wake everybody up and go eat some breakfast. I will see if Carmen is up to it."

Carmen was feeling better, and her sight was pretty much back to normal. The headaches and nausea were almost gone, and she had her appetite back. I wasn't very hungry, so I hung out by the pool while they had breakfast. I needed to spend some time with my father, and I saw him relaxing on the patio of his bungalow.

"Hey, Dad, can we talk?"

"Sure, honey, I'll have some breakfast brought out to us."

"No thanks, just coffee for me."

I sat there and watched my dad reading the sports section while I pretended to read the arts and leisure section. He was so handsome. It was easy to see why my mother fell for him. I remember whenever my grandmother got angry with me, she would always say, "You look just like your damn daddy." I don't know if I actually looked like him or if I just looked white and that reminded her of him. Other family members said I looked like my mother, just lighter. I never really got to know my mother and don't remember very much about her except she was beautiful. While I was sitting there, pretending to read, my father looked up.

"Honey, you sure you don't want breakfast?" he asked?

"Yes, Dad, I'm sure."

"So, Jennifer, tell me why you're staring at me while you pretend to read."

"I was thinking about you and my mother."

"Sweetheart, I was sad when I heard she had passed away."

"Did you love her, Dad?"

"Yes, very much."

"Will you tell me about her? After she dropped me off in Arkansas, I rarely saw her."

"Didn't your grandmother ever talk about your mother?"

"No, not really. I think she resented the fact that she dumped me off on her."

"Honey, I'm sure it was more complicated than you were led to believe."

"I just can't see the woman I loved doing something like that."

"When I met your mother, I was stationed at Carswell AFB in Texas. She was a computer analyst that worked in the command center. I was in a very dysfunctional marriage and had been miserable for years. I wanted children, and my wife didn't. She was so wrapped up in her career that she forgot about family. My wife and I met at Officer Training School. I was promoted through the ranks quicker than she was as most men are, but she resented that, and then she started to resent me as well. The only thing that was left of our marriage was for us to sign the paperwork. We were so busy that we just never got around to it.

"When I met your mother, she was a breath of fresh air. She was drop-dead gorgeous, and I loved her Southern accent. People used to tell her that she should have been a model because she was so exotic-looking, but your mother was always shy about her beauty though. It was difficult for her to think that a white man from Massachusetts could find a black girl from Pine Bluff, Arkansas, beautiful. Yvette always looked at her beauty as a curse, not a blessing. We didn't talk about her childhood much, but it couldn't have been one that reinforced beauty as an asset," my father said, strolling down memory lane.

"Please, Dad, if her childhood was anything like mine, I see why she was so messed up. My grandmother was only interested in three things: the money you sent her, me not getting pregnant before I graduated high school, and getting the hell out of her house. She didn't mistreat me, don't get me wrong. She was just so unattached to everything. So I can see why my mother was so shy."

"Jennifer, it was so much more than shyness. I courted her for about six months before she agreed to an official date. I picked her up for dinner at her apartment one night, and she was the most beautiful thing I'd ever seen, black or white. She had on a pink dress with the back out. I was so surprised she would wear something so daring, and she even had on makeup. Up to this point, she had only seen me in my uniform. She looked at me and said, 'Colonel Farillo, you clean up rather nicely.'

"'Thank you Ms. Burton.'

"'You can call me Yvette,' she said.

"'And you can call me Francis or Frank,' I said.

"'What kind of name is Francis for a man?'

"'It's actually short for Francisco. My family's Italian, in case you hadn't guessed. Are you making fun of me, Ms. Burton?'

"'Yes, I am, Colonel.' She laughed. I loved her laugh. That was one of the most beautiful things about your mother."

"Francis, get to the good stuff," I said, laughing.

"Okay, but that's Dad to you," he said jokingly.

"Okay, Dad, tell me more."

"There's not a whole lot to tell, really. We dated for four years, and then I got a change of duty assignment and was sent to Bitburg, Germany. I tried to get her to come with me, but she wouldn't. I did my four years in Germany and came back to the States. I tried to contact her when I returned, but she wouldn't return my calls. I wanted her to come to New Mexico with me, but I wasn't able to reach her. I only had six more years left in the military, and I wanted to settle down and have a family. We did talk about it once, but she said her family would never approve of her marrying a white man," he said with disappointment in his voice.

My father started to look sad, and I was hating myself for bringing up such painful memories, but there is such a gap in my life, and I needed answers.

"Dad, I'm sorry if this is painful for you, but I just feel like I need to hear it."

"Don't worry, Jennifer, I buried this pain a long time ago. I never remarried after my divorce, but your mother was the love of my life, my soul mate. I could think about her sometimes, and I knew at that very moment, she was thinking of me too. Sweetheart, you were not planned, but you were conceived out of love. Once I found out about you, I wanted to be a part of your life. Your grandmother didn't think it was a good idea, but I was not about to abandon you."

"Of course, Grandma didn't think it was a good idea. She would lose out on the money you were sending if you decided you wanted to raise me. So instead of doing what was best for me, she did what was best for her, and I was left wondering if my father loved me or not. I used to think you didn't like me or love me because I was mixed. I thought maybe you didn't want a half-breed daughter, you being a good Catholic boy and all."

"Sweetheart, I didn't find out about you until your mother passed away. I guess your grandmother needed another source of income, since your mother was no longer around to send her money. Every time I asked her about visiting you, she would say that it wasn't a good time and she didn't want to confuse you about who I was."

"Dad, I've always been confused about everything. When I used to tell the Italian kids at my school I was half Italian, they would call me eggplant or mooli. Then the black kids, even my cousins, would call me half-breed. Marcus was the one person who made me feel totally accepted and loved. I even contemplated not having children because of what I went through as a child, always wanting to belong but never belonging, not even in my own black family. Dad, do you think your family will accept me?" I asked.

"Of course, baby, I send them copies of the pictures you always send me of you and your family. Sweetheart, there are a lot of Italians and Sicilians that are darker than you are. You're my daughter, and for that reason alone, they will love you. We Italians love our own through thick and thin. In fact, I am planning a family get-together next summer, and I would love it if you and your family would join us. I would love for them to meet my gorgeous granddaughter. You have aunts, uncles, and cousins coming from all over Palermo, San Vito, New York, and Boston coming to the family reunion, and they are going to love my little *bambina*.

"Sweetheart, I hope this talk hasn't upset you about your heritage even more. Your mother loved you very much, I'm sure. That's just the type of woman she was, and if ovarian cancer had not taken her from us, I am sure she would have been right here with us today.

"I tried to contact her once I found out she had cancer, but again she didn't respond. I actually went back to Texas to find her in 1975. I ran into her best friend, Susan Bridgeport, and she told me that Yvette died in 1972. She and I had drinks, and she told me about you. I took the next flight to Arkansas to find you. I went to your grandmother's house, and she would not allow me to see you. I gave her all my information and told her to call me if you ever needed anything. I even sent her a credit card so she could buy the things you needed. It broke my heart leaving that day, but your mother had turned over custody to her, so there was nothing I could do. Yeah, I could have taken her to court and fought for custody, but I couldn't see putting you through that.

"After leaving the house, I walked past a park, and I saw this beautiful, dark-headed little beauty that was the spitting image of my mother, Isabella, with a little bit of Yvette thrown in for flavor. My mother has a wedding picture of her and my dad on their wedding day, and it could be a picture of you standing there. I would love for you to meet your grandparents."

"I will someday, Daddy, I promise," I said, tearing up.

"Hey, look, it's almost noon. We have been talking for hours."

"I am so happy to find out that you didn't abandon me, Daddy."

"Jennifer, I am glad you feel better, baby, and I would never do anything to hurt you. You're my little *bambina*, so if you're done with twenty questions, let's get some lunch. Hey, Jennifer, you think Nikki is still in her bikini?"

"Daddy, that's not funny. You better not sleep with her! She's just playing around because she loves to be the center of attention."

"Baby girl, don't you think I know that? I just like making her feel good. Plus, the girl is nuts," he said, laughing. "So, Jennifer, how much longer are you going to be here?"

"We'll probably leave on Friday. Carmen's not feeling well, and I miss my husband and my daughter. Maybe you could come back with me and spend some time with my family."

"Jennifer, are you sure?"

"Yes, Dad, we would love to have you."

"If you can give me a week, that would be great. I'm meeting a friend in New York on the eleventh, and after that, I will come straight to Minnesota, if that will work for you. Now can we eat? I'm starving," said Frank.

Nikki, Virginia, and Carmen were already having lunch when we arrived.

"Where's Beth?" I asked.

"She's on the phone arguing with Richard. He's really being a dick," said Nikki. "He wants her to come home. He is way too controlling for me. I asked Beth if she was okay, and she told me to mind my own business." Nikki shrugged. "Child, I just looked at her and said, 'Tina, you and Ike go right ahead, but don't call me when he is trying to make you eat the cake, Anna Mae,' Nikki said, laughing.

"Nikki, do you always have to get in everybody's business?" said Virginia.

"You are my girls, so your business is my business," said Nikki.

I sat next to Carmen and leaned over to ask if she was okay.

"My sight's a lot better," she said. "But I'm good, Jen, don't worry."

"Just remember, we're in this together, girl."

Carmen squeezed my hand tightly and said, "I'm counting on it, Jennifer."

While Nikki was busy entertaining my dad, I decided to go check on Beth.

"Hey, girlfriend, are you joining us for lunch or what?"

"Jennifer, I'm not hungry. I'm just frustrated with Richard, and I don't know what to do."

"What's his problem?"

"He's just missing me, that's all. This is the first time since our marriage that I have been away from him for this long."

"Does he not trust you?" I asked.

"No, Jennifer, it's not that. Of course, he trusts me. I think he's just being a brat, you know, used to having someone there to cook for him, pick up the laundry, you know, that sort of stuff. Richard is the kind of man who likes everything in order, everything on schedule, and me being gone has thrown that out of whack for him."

"I'm not trying to be in your business, Beth, but how do you live like that?"

"Jennifer, Richard is a wonderful man. He gives me everything I want. I've never had a man treat me like a queen before."

"Beth, but you give up so much to have those things, like who you are and the things you want for your life."

"Jennifer, you can't possibly understand because you're married to a white man. Things are so different for black men in today's society."

"What the hell does color have to do with anything? I'm sick of you guys thinking my life is easier and simpler because my husband is white. Yes, Marcus has money, and he comes from money, but he gave up his family to be with me when his mother disowned him. The stares we get from blacks and whites for being married tell me that times haven't changed all that much, we are still resented because of it. So, Beth, don't tell me how easy my life is.

"I've dealt with this crap all my life, and now my daughter's going to have to go through the same nonsense, never being black enough or white enough. The really sad part of it is, if I had married a black man, my child still would have been mixed because I am. So see, there's no way she will be spared from the small-minded people of the world," I said, annoyed. "I would love to be able to spare her, but I can't. The only thing I can teach her how to do is cope and pray for the small-minded people who are going to treat her differently."

"Jennifer, I'm sorry. I didn't know that you were really this sensitive about your racial heritage," said Beth.

"Beth, I know you guys don't mean anything when you call me a half-breed, but it still hurts. I heard this crap all my life, and I just wish I didn't have to hear it from my friends," I said sadly.

Beth hugged me and apologized again. "Do you forgive me, Jen?"

"Of course, I do, Anna Mae Bullock."

Beth started laughing. "Richard and I are okay, and there is absolutely no comparison between him and Ike Turner. I personally think the brother has OCD," said Beth. "Jen, you remember the movie *Sleeping with the Enemy*? That is Richard all the way. Don't get me wrong, he has never hit me or anything like that. Shit, the nigga's not crazy, but he is a bit anal about the way he likes things. Now let's go get something to eat before lunch is over and Nikki has your father stretched out on a table trying to jump his bones."

As soon as we walked into the dining room, Nikki started. "So, Beth, what flight are you leaving on today? Because you know once Richard puts his foot down, you jump at his every command."

"Well, unfortunately, Nikki, everyone doesn't lead their man around by his dick the way you do," said Beth. "Bruce would put on a dress if you told him to."

"You go, Beth. Stand up for yourself, girl," said Virginia.

"You're damn right he would, and if you must know, he has already, and my panties too," said Nikki proudly. "Maybe if you and Richard's tight ass would play dress-up sometimes, he wouldn't be so fucking anal," said Nikki.

"Well, ladies, this is my cue to leave," said Frank.

"Daddy, you don't have to leave."

"Yes, I do. Please excuse me, sweetheart. I have some business I must attend to, but I will catch up with you later. Maybe we can get together later when you ladies are a little calmer."

"Look, you guys, we got one day left here, so let's try to really have fun," I said. "My dad is going to take us to the Officers Club for dinner and dancing tonight, and I think we need to relax and pamper ourselves."

"I mean, if we can get along long enough, Nikki," said Virginia sarcastically.

"Why are you singling me out?" said Nikki.

"Nikki, you are the number one instigator of bullshit. Over half the arguments we get into are started by you," said Virginia.

"Oh, so it's 'gang up on Nikki' day. Okay, that's fine, because just like I dish it out, I can take it. So if you girls think you can stand me long enough, I suggest we go chill out by the pool. Sounds like a plan to me. Plus, drinking makes me more tolerable, wouldn't you say, Beth?"

"Yes, Nikki, I think it does," Beth said sarcastically.

As we sat by the pool, I couldn't help but think of the things my father and I talked about. I wish I had gotten the chance to know my mother. I couldn't wait to meet my dad's family. I needed a family connection, and Italians always seemed so loving; at least in the movies they did. My mother's family is so disconnected from one another it's hard to tell they are even family. I think I'll plan a get-together for my dad's visit. As I sat there planning the menu in my head, I started thinking about the last holiday I spent in Arkansas.

"What are you thinking about?" asked Beth.

"I was thinking that maybe I will plan a dinner party for my dad's visit, and I was also thinking about the last time I saw my mother's family."

"How long has it been?" asked Beth.

"It was when I was in college. I decided to take Marcus to Arkansas to meet my family. It was Labor Day weekend, and my family was having a big picnic. The holidays usually start out fun. The kids play badminton or croquet, while the adults play cards, dominoes and drink way too much. When Marcus and I arrived, the barbecue was already in full swing. We walked into the backyard, and everyone turned around and looked at us. I could see the shocked look on their faces, but it was confirmed when everyone started to whisper. Marcus could tell that I was uncomfortable, and I felt him squeeze my hand for support. We walked around and spoke to everyone, and I politely introduced him. I overheard my aunt Ruby Ann saying 'I can't believe she brought that white boy here. That's just so typical of Jennifer. She never wanted to acknowledge her blackness anyway.'

"I pretended I didn't hear her, and we found a table near my cousin Trisha and her husband, Ty. Trisha said, 'Don't let Aunt Ruby get to you. You know how she is when she's had too much to drink, which is often. You know she has been like that since we were little.' Trisha and I were the same age and had been really close when we were growing up, so I tried to take heed to what she was saying.

"After a couple of hours, people started to loosen up, and Uncle Don asked Marcus to play cards. Marcus was pretty good at spades. He used to play all the time with his roommates in college. He and Uncle Don lost the first game, and of course, Aunt Ruby blamed Marcus. 'Don, I told you, don't know white boy know how to play this game,' she said.

"Marcus just smiled and said, 'Aunt Ruby, give me a chance. I'm pretty good. Some of the brothers taught me my first year of college, so we'll win the next game, no worries.'

"'I'm not your goddamn aunt,' she said, slurring her words.

"'Ms. Ruby, have I done something to offend you?'

"'Your very presence offends me, white boy. My sister Yvette always thought she was betta than the rest of us mere Negros and had to go out and get her a white man. Then she has the nerve to get pregnant and have his bastard child.'

"'Aunt Ruby, what have I ever done to you?' I asked. Trisha tried to grab me as I got up to confront her. 'No, Trisha, I want to know. What did my mother or I ever do to make you hate us so much, you bitter black bitch?'

"'You don't belong here, you never belonged here,' she said.

"Marcus grabbed my arm and said, 'Baby, let's just go. It's obvious we're not wanted here.' We left, and I've never seen that side of my family again. I sent flowers to my grandmother's funeral when she died in 1997, but I thought it best I not attend."

"Oh my god, what a horrible story," said Beth.

"Marcus and I made a pact that day to always be there for each other. We knew we did not have our families to depend on, so that day, we left the picnic and drove to Branson, Missouri, and got married."

"Jennifer, after that story, girl, I need a drink," said Beth.

"Hey, bartender, what goes with a blue motherfucker?" asked Nikki. "I need a shot of something."

Virginia turned and looked at Nikki and said, "I know what goes with a blue motherfucker"—she paused—"an angry black bitch named Nikki."

Beth fell out of her chair laughing.

"Fuck you, Virginia," said Nikki.

"Real snappy comeback, Nik," said Beth.

"Ladies, I'm not feeling any love right now. Remember, we promised we were not going to do this our last day here," said Carmen. "Yeah, but you have to admit that 'black bitch' line was priceless" said Carmen, giggling.

"Shut up, Carmen. You're always cosigning for Virginia. Plus, it wasn't that funny," Nikki said.

"The hell it wasn't," I said. "Every time I think about it, I want to laugh. It serves you right, Nik. You're always ragging on other people, but you can't take it when someone does it to you."

"Bartender, are we going to get those drinks or not?" asked Nikki.

"Yes, ma'am," he said.

"Nik, don't take your frustrations out on that poor guy just because you're angry."

"Damn all that, I'm thirsty."

We spent another two hours at the pool and then headed to the salon to get our hair and nails done.

At eight o'clock, Dad met us in the lobby and escorted us to the car he had hired to take us to the Officers Club. It was elegant and very formal. My father was greeted as though he was still in the military. We were seated in the ballroom because they were having some type of formal military ball. The officers were dressed in their formal uniforms, and the wives had on gowns. We had some very handsome single officers who invited us to dance. After we danced, Dad invited them to join our table. He explained to them we were all married and in New Mexico on holiday. They were perfect gentlemen, and at the end of the night, they kissed our hands and said good night.

Daddy walked us to our bungalow and kissed us all good night and said, "I'll see you girls around ten for breakfast, and then a car will take you to the airport around two p.m., so be ready, okay? Ladies, I would just like to say that I have really enjoyed your visit, and I look forward to seeing you again in a couple of weeks."

"Are you coming to Minnesota?" asked Nikki.

"Yes, I have a meeting in New York, then I'll be coming out your way for a couple of weeks. So, ladies, sleep tight, and I will see you in the morning."

Ten o'clock came quickly, and we were all scrambling around, trying to pack before breakfast. Carmen was looking a little flushed even though she kept telling me she was fine. I really hated saying goodbye to my father, but after breakfast, we hit a couple of souvenir shops and were rushed to the airport.

"Jennifer, don't cry, sweetheart. I promise I'll just stay in New York a couple of days and then I'll be in Minnesota in no time," he said.

"Don't worry, Frank, we'll take good care of your little girl," said Carmen.

He kissed us all on the cheek, and he left to catch his flight.

The plane ride home was pretty quiet. Everyone read or slept. Carmen laid her head on my shoulder and napped a little. I was really worried about her. She told me she was just tired from all the excitement of the trip, but I knew it was more. She tried too hard to hide the truth, and I kept wondering why she wouldn't let me help.

The plane landed, and I saw Marcus, Dylen, and River. The kids ran to hug Carmen and me, while Marcus just stood there and smiled.

"My god, you're beautiful," said Marcus. "I missed you so much. Hey, ladies, how was the trip?" asked Marcus.

"Great," said Virginia. "It was just what we needed."

"Do you girls need a ride home?"

"No," said Nikki, "I have my car, and I will give Beth and Virginia a ride."

"So Bruce let you drive the Jag," said Marcus.

"Let hell, this jag is mine. Do you know how many blow jobs I had to give Bruce before he agreed to buy me that damn car? His car my ass. I don't know what you think this is, Marcus," said Nikki.

"I'm sure he enjoyed every one of them, so it was worth it, I'm sure," said Marcus. "Remind me not to kiss Nikki goodbye anymore," said Marcus, laughing.

"Marcus, you stop that. You know you don't want to get in a pissing contest with Nikki," I said, laughing. "Let's just go," I said as we said our goodbyes, hugging and kissing one another.

River and Dylen were really chatty on the ride home, but it seemed to brighten Carmen's spirits. She even had a smile on her face. It made me happy to see her smile. When we arrived at the house, River wanted Dylen to come to his house.

"No, honey, maybe she can come over tomorrow. It's been a long trip, and your mother needs her rest."

"No, Jennifer, it's fine, really. I want to be able to spend as much time with them as possible. Go home and spend some time with your husband. I'm sure you two can find something to do while you're home alone."

Dylen was happy to spend the night with River, and she ran upstairs and collected her things.

"Can I at least get a kiss before you leave, young lady?" I said, smiling.

"Yes, Mom, I'm sorry." Then she gave me a quick kiss, and she was gone.

Marcus saw the look on my face and said, "Face it, Jen, our baby is growing up."

"Yes, I know, but I just enjoy her so much."

"Well, why don't you spread a little of that joy my way right now."

"You bet. Let me take a quick shower, and I am all yours, baby."

I've always enjoyed our lovemaking. Marcus is very meticulous and gentle. Every time he kisses me, it's like being kissed for the very first time. I lay there and daydreamed while he rubbed oil over my moist body. Then he turned me over on my stomach and started to massage my shoulders. He moved to my thighs and gently spread my legs and entered me from behind, moving slowly as he kissed the back of my neck, in and out, as I felt his hardness caress the inside of me. I was so wet and hot, and I begged for more. I felt his strong, muscular thighs banging against me, and I was in heaven. I missed him so much while I was away, but the homecoming was great.

He stopped for a moment to turn me over. He said he wanted to watch my face as I had my orgasm.

It seemed we made love for hours before coming together. It was the most beautiful feeling in the world. As we lay in bed next to each other, he kissed me over and over, telling me how much he loved me.

"Baby, did you enjoy your visit with your father?" he asked.

"I did very much," I said. "I hope you don't mind that I invited him to come and visit."

"Of course, I don't mind, Jennifer. Don't be silly. I am looking forward to meeting the man who created such a beautiful human being," said Marcus.

"I can't wait for you to meet him. He would have come with us, but he was flying to New York to meet an old military buddy. His friend works at the World Trade Center. How cool is that? We will have to go and see that place one day," I said.

"I hear it is one of the most beautiful pieces of architecture in the world. Maybe next summer, we can take Dylen. You can even check with Carmen to see if she and River could join us," Marcus suggested.

"Marcus, that is a great idea," I said.

Marcus kissed me on the forehead, and I laid my head on his chest, and a sense of peace came over me before I drifted off to sleep.

The week after returning home from vacation went by quickly. I couldn't believe my dad would be here in the next couple of days. River and Carmen came over for Sunday dinner, and we sat around and looked at pictures from our vacation.

Carmen and I decided to give the kids a break from homeschooling and let them hang out with us for the day. I had planned the dinner party for Saturday. Daddy would be flying in Tuesday, and I wanted to have everything done before it was time to pick him up.

I fixed an early dinner and sent Dylen to bed. She had been a handful all day, and I was ready for some quiet time of my own. Marcus was working late at the office, and I decided to soak in the tub and go to bed early myself. Tomorrow would be a busy day, and I was so tired that I barely heard Marcus slip into bed. He snuggled closed to me, and I went back to sleep.

The phone woke me from a deep sleep and a wonderful dream.

"Hello, who is this?" I asked through a sleepy haze.

"Jen, it's Carmen."

"Carmen, what's wrong? Are you and River okay?" I asked, trying to sit up in bed. "Carmen, why are you crying? What's wrong? Carmen, answer me, damn it."

"Jennifer, River and I are fine. Jennifer, why are you guys still in bed? It's almost nine o'clock."

"We just decided to sleep in late, Carmen, but you still haven't told me what's wrong."

"I need you to turn on the television. There has been a terrible explosion. There are so many people dead."

"What are you talking about? What explosion, and who's dead?"

"Jennifer, someone flew a plane into the World Trade Center. Turn on the TV, please."

"Marcus, turn on the TV. Hurry up."

Marcus hit the button on the remote, and the scene on the television looked like Armageddon. The reporter was describing the second plane hitting the tower just as we tuned in.

"What was once thought to be an accident has turned out to be an attack," said the reporter.

"Carmen, hold on, I have another call coming in."

"Jennifer, it's Nikki. Are you watching the news? Girl, this is devastating."

"Yes, Nik, we just turned on the TV. Carmen called and woke us up. Marcus, what time is it?"

"It's about nine ten a.m."

"Nik, hold on, let me get back to Carmen." But Carmen had hung up. "Nik, hold on, the doorbell's ringing. "What the hell is all the freaking commotion this morning?" I said, answering the door. "Nikki, it's V and Beth. Let me call you back. Hey, what are you guys doing here?" Just as I was about to invite them in, I saw Carmen and River coming across the yard. "Everyone come on in," I said. By the time I had returned to the phone, Nikki had also hung up. "What is going on here?"

"We're concerned about you, of course," said Virginia.

"Me?"

"Jen, your dad, did you forget he went to New York?"

"Oh my god, I forgot. When Carmen called, we were still asleep."

"Wasn't his meeting at the World Trade Center?" said Virginia.

"Yes, but it's so early he probably hadn't made it there yet," I said. I grabbed the phone and tried to call his cell phone. "All circuits are busy now" is all I kept getting. I hung up and tried again and again, but still nothing. I ran into the family room, where Marcus was sitting. "What are they saying now?"

"Baby, this is bad. It's really bad. It's not just the towers. They just reported that flight 93 was hijacked. This is a terrorist attack against the United States. What about your dad? Were you able to reach him?"

"No, all the circuits are busy." Tears began to roll down my face. Beth walked over to me and held my hand.

"He probably can't get a line out either," said Virginia.

"The television coverage was hard to watch. How could someone be so heartless and kill all those innocent people?" said Carmen.

I tried to be strong and hold back the tears, but I broke down.

"I'll make some coffee," said Virginia.

"Carmen, come with me. We'll make the kids some breakfast," said Beth.

Carmen took Dylen and River into the kitchen for a bowl of cereal.

"Why is my mother crying?" said Dylen.

"Some bad men did a really horrible thing to some nice people, and Mommy is just upset," said Carmen.

"Was it the building my grandfather went to visit?" said Dylen.

"Yes, how did you know that?"

"Because I had a dream about Grandpa and he told me he loved me but he had to go back into the building to try to save some of the people who were hurt. He told me he was sorry he wouldn't get a chance to see me but for me to take care of Mommy because he loves her very much."

I was standing in the doorway and overheard what Dylen said to Carmen. I grabbed Dylen and hugged her tight. "Dylen, what did Grandpa look like?"

"He was very pretty, with a white light that looked like angel wings. Mommy, don't be sad. You will see him again, he promised."

I broke down and sobbed uncontrollably. Marcus tried to reassure me, but I knew in my heart that my father was gone.

Everyone called in to work just so they could stay by my side. We were all glued to the TV, trying to get updates. The death tolls continued to mount, and all I could do was sit and hold the phone.

Nikki had arrived, and she sat with me and tried to comfort me, but it was no use. I just couldn't believe God would let me get close to my father and then just take him away from me. I was so deep in thought that when the phone rang, it startled me so bad I dropped it. It was Brian trying to reach Virginia. She had left her cell phone at the house, and he was calling to see how much longer she was going to be. Virginia took the phone into the other room, but you could still hear her and Brian arguing.

"I'm sorry if you are a little inconvenienced by sitting with the baby, but your bitch is going to have to wait for you. Being with my best friend is a hell of a lot more important than you and your mistress getting together."

"V, is everything okay?"

"Yes, Jen, sweetie, everything is fine."

We all continued to sit by the phone and the TV way into the night. Carmen and Beth went to pick up food for dinner, but I couldn't eat. Around 10:00 p.m., everyone went home and promised they would be back tomorrow. Marcus and I went to bed around midnight, but I couldn't sleep. We kept the TV on for any late breaking news, but it was just pretty much all the same.

Three days had passed, and still no word. Marcus had gone into the office, and I was making coffee when Virginia and Syble arrived. It had been so long since I had seen her.

"My god, Virginia, she is getting so big. She was an adorable little girl with big brown eyes and rosebud lips. Virginia, just put her down, and I will get some of Dylen's old toys for her to play with. Virginia, what is going on with you and Brian?"

"Nothing's going on with me," she said.

"Why didn't you tell us you and Brian were having problems?"

"My problems are nothing compared to what Carmen is going through and now you. I'm just tired of being disrespected. This bitch was bold enough to call our home one morning at five a.m."

"Virginia, are you joking?"

"No, I'm not, and when I asked who was calling, she said Valerie. I woke up Brian and told him Valerie was on the phone, and he told her he'd be right there. When I asked him about it, he said Valerie was the woman he was going to marry once our divorce was final."

"Wait, V, when did you guys file for divorce?"

"The day after that bitch called my house. I guess I shouldn't call her a bitch since I don't really know her, but in my eyes, she became a bitch the moment she called and disrespected me and my house. Jennifer, don't be sad for me," said Virginia, hugging me tightly. "Our marriage has been over for a while now. After Syble was born and I was struggling to lose the weight, Brain changed. He didn't come out and say it, but he was ashamed of me. We rarely had sex anymore, and the only time we ever went out in public together was when we came to your house," Virginia said sadly. "Jennifer, I don't want anything from him other than for him to take care of his financial obligations when it comes to Syble."

"Virginia, I just wished you had told us. So when is the divorce final?"

"October 17. I am not going to contest it as long as I get the house, one of the vehicles, and one hundred thousand dollars. He had agreed to pay fifteen hundred dollars a month in child support. So, Jennifer, I will be okay."

Just as I was pouring a second cup of coffee, Carmen and the kids walked in.

"Good morning, Mommy," said Dylen.

"Dylen, are you ever coming home? I don't want you getting on Carmen's nerves."

"I'm not. She loves me, don't you, Aunt Carmen?"

"Yes, baby, I love you very much."

Beth and Nikki came over and brought lunch, and we camped out in front of the television as usual when the phone rang.

"Jennifer Covington, please?"

"Jen, phone," said Nikki.

"Yes, this is Jennifer. Who's calling?"

"My name is Rosa Sanchez, and I am the manager at the Waldorf Astoria. Frank Farillo checked in three days ago, and we have not heard from him. We found your name in his address book that was on his nightstand as an emergency contact. We have notified the police, but I wanted to contact you to see if you wanted us to send his things to you."

"Ma'am, when did my father leave the hotel?"

"We know he had breakfast around 7:30 a.m. on September 11 and he asked the doorman how far the World Trade Center was from the hotel. A taxi driver remembers dropping him off around eight a.m. It's been three days, and with everything that has happened, Mrs. Covington, I just thought you should know."

"Thank you, Ms. Sanchez. I appreciate that. My husband and I have been trying to get a flight to New York, but nothing is flying into the airport at this time. Ms. Sanchez, I can give you a credit card, and if you could overnight the items to me, it would be greatly appreciated."

"I will be happy to send it to you free of charge, ma'am."

"What about the police?"

"They came and took a report, and I was told I could send the items to the next of kin."

"I appreciate you so much for doing this, Ms. Sanchez."

"Jennifer, what's wrong?" said Nikki.

I told them what Ms. Sanchez had told me, and everyone became quiet.

"This is a nightmare. This is a fucking nightmare."

"Jennifer, sit down," said Carmen.

"I'll call Marcus," said Virginia.

"How could this happen? Somebody is going to have to explain to me how this could happen in America. This is not fucking Afghanistan!" I screamed. "How could an unidentified plane be allowed to fly in our airspace with no one knowing about it until it's too late? My dad served his country and never got a scratch, and he comes home, where he is supposed to be safe, and he dies because of some asshole named Osama bin Laden. It's not fair that his life is over. It's not fair that all those innocent people had to die, and for what?"

"Jennifer, calm down. You're going to make yourself sick," said Virginia.

Marcus walked into the room and hugged me.

"Jennifer, I am so sorry, baby, but there is still a chance. Maybe he's just hurt and he is in a hospital somewhere in New York. We'll call every hospital in New York if we have to," said Marcus.

"We'll start right now. We'll all help, Jennifer. Just don't give up," said Carmen.

It was impossible to find anything out at the hospitals. Everything was still a mess. The body count increased every day, and they still had people trying to move rubble to get to people, so Marcus was right; there still might be hope. The only thing that kept me from believing that was Dylen's dream about her grandfather. My mind wanted to believe that, but my heart was telling me that he was gone.

On the fifth day, the devastating news came. There was a knock at the door at 9:30 a.m., September 17, 2001. Marcus answered the door to find a police officer standing there. He informed us that he had been informed by the New York police that my father's wallet had been found in a pile of debris. A card with the name of the hotel he was staying at while in New York was also in his wallet. When the

New York police phoned the hotel, they found out that Frank Farillo had not returned since 9/11.

"Officer, was his body found?" I asked.

"No, ma'am. Mrs. Covington, you have got to understand this is not a normal situation."

"Officer, just say it," said Marcus.

"There are body parts all over the place, according to everything we've been told. They did find a partial torso where the wallet was recovered. Do you know if your father had any identifying marks on his upper body?"

"I'm not sure, Officer. It's complicated." And I walked away.

Marcus escorted the officer to the door, and I heard him say that I had just gotten the chance to really know my father about three weeks ago and I didn't really know a lot about him.

"I understand," said the officer. "And I am so sorry for your loss," he said.

"Jennifer, are you okay? Honey, just talk to me. Don't you dare shut me out."

"I'm not, Marcus. I'm just thinking."

"Thinking about what?"

"Could God be this cruel? How could he bring my father back into my life only to take him away?"

"If God was cruel, Jennifer, he wouldn't have given you that time with him at all. He would have just taken him. You were blessed you got a chance to spend time with him and find out about the other part of you, the part you never knew."

"Marcus, I have to tell them, I have to tell his family."

"I know, sweetheart, but not tonight. You are going to go upstairs, take a hot bath, and get some rest before you collapse. Carmen left you a couple of Valium to help you sleep. Dylen is fine. She went home with Carmen. I am going to fix you a little something to eat, and then I am going to hold you until you fall asleep."

I don't remember falling asleep, but when I woke up, it was noon the next day. Nikki and Beth had stopped by but did not want to wake me. Virginia had come over and was sitting downstairs with Carmen.

"I think it's your father's things."

I grabbed the box and ripped into it with a pen that was lying on the coffee table. As soon as the box opened, I could smell his scent. He smelled like Ralph Lauren Polo. I loved that smell. My eyes started to water, and Virginia held my hand.

"Jennifer, you don't have to do this right now," she said.

I picked up my dad's shirt and held it close to my heart and remembered him hugging me goodbye—not realizing that it was the last goodbye.

My father's address book was lying on top, and I opened it and found my grandmother's name. Her name was Isabella Farillo.

"I bet they don't even know."

"Who, Jennifer?" said Virginia.

"My grandparents, I bet they don't even know my father is dead. I have got to tell them."

"Jennifer, I thought you had never met them," said Virginia.

"I haven't, but they still have to know, and I think I need to be the one who tells them." I picked up the phone and dialed the number. I'm glad Carmen and V were here to support me. I dialed the number slowly, praying no one would answer the phone, but someone did.

A lady with a thick Italian accent said hello. I heard her yelling to someone named Lucilla not to let the sauce burn.

"I'm sorry. How may I help you?" she said.

"I'm calling for Isabella Farillo."

"Look, lady, I don't know what you're selling, but I ain't buying. I don't need insurance or a vacuum cleaner, and I don't want to change my long-distance service, so thank you, but no thanks."

"No, Mrs. Farillo, my name is Jennifer Covington, and Frank Farillo was my father."

Everything went quiet, and then I heard her scream for Rudy, Marco, and Maria. "Where's your father? Francis's little girl is on the phone."

I was surprised she knew who I was.

She said, "Jennifer, I'm your grandmother."

"Yes, I know."

"I am so glad you called, sweetheart. We are so excited about finally getting to meet you. Francis said he was going to have you call us," she said. I could hear whispering and laughter in the background. "You have a big Italian family that can't wait to meet you."

I heard a big booming voice in the background. "What's everybody doing? And who is Isabel talking to, Mussolini?"

"No, Angelo, it's Frank's little girl on the phone," I heard her say.

"Is this a bad time?" I said.

"No, honey, your grandfather's just walked in, and stop calling me Mrs. Farillo, it's Grandma."

"Is Francis with you, honey?" she asked.

"No, you see, that's why I'm calling. There's no easy way to say this, but the authorities think my father was killed on 9/11 in the World Trade Center bombing," I said.

The phone dropped, and I heard screaming and yelling in Italian. A lady picked up the phone and introduced herself as my aunt Lucilla. "What's going on? Mother just got upset and dropped the phone. I can't understand what she's saying when she's upset like this. Can you tell me what happened?"

"My father's wallet was found in the rubble and debris at the World Trade Center in New York. He was going there to meet a friend on the day the towers were bombed."

"Did they find a body?" she said.

"No, not really. They found part of an upper torso, but not a complete body. They also found several other body parts near the same sight, but they are not sure if they belong to my father. I have to fly to New York next week for a DNA test."

"Wait, Jennifer, my father wants to speak with you."

"Hello, Jennifer, this is Angelo Farillo, your grandfather."

"Yes, sir," I said.

"Is there any way they could be mistaken?"

"Yes, I guess. The wallet they found wasn't taken off the torso. It was just found next to it. He could have dropped it in all the commotion."

"I just don't believe my Francis is gone." I could hear the sadness in his voice as he tried to be optimistic and fight back the tears.

"Look, we would like to go to New York with you next week, if that's okay. My husband and I are going to fly out on Monday. If you don't mind, we can fly to Boston and leave from there. That way, you get to meet my husband and my daughter, Dylen."

"We would love that, especially at a time like this. I will call this afternoon to make plane and hotel reservations. Look, I understand you don't know us, but you're the only thing left of our Francis, and it would be great if you stayed with us."

"We would love to. I will call you later with the flight information, Mr. Farillo—I mean, Grandfather."

"Okay, sweetheart, we will look forward to seeing you and your family. I think I need to go see after your grandmother."

I called Marcus so he could book the flight and schedule the time off work. Carmen and Virginia helped me pack. I was so thankful for my friends. I would miss them while I was away. I was still worried about Carmen and concerned about Virginia and her situation.

Nikki came over at five and brought food. I tried to eat, but my stomach was in knots. I was excited about meeting my dad's family, but I just wished it were under different circumstances. While I was upstairs taking a nap, Nikki knocked on the door.

"Hey, girl, I hope I'm not disturbing you. I just wanted to let you know how sorry I am about your father. He was a very special man, and we all adored him very much. I must tell you, though, if he were just a few years younger and I weren't married, you'd be calling me Mommy. Oh yeah, I would have fucked him, honey," said Nikki.

I couldn't help but laugh. Nikki could be a pain in the ass with her bad attitude, but she had a way of making you feel better through laughter. As she lay on the bed beside me, I put my head on her shoulder and cried myself to sleep.

The next morning, we left for the airport. Marcus had been told to arrive early because check-in would take about an hour. Once we arrived at the airport, we were practically stripped, searched like common criminals. Every airport we arrived in was the same thing. I suddenly felt like I was in a Third World country trying to get out.

We finally arrived at the airport, and we were exhausted. Dylen was cranky and complaining about everything. Marcus kept telling her we were going to eat as soon as we got to Grandma's house, but that was not good enough for her; she was ready to eat right now.

"Dylen, look, I know you're tired, but so are we, so quit being a brat and pick up the damn suitcase. Remember, you're the one that wanted to bring all this junk, and the sooner you grab your stuff, the sooner we can get out of here."

We finally collected our bags and were trying to get a taxi when we noticed a crowd of people holding a sign that said The Farillo Family. A heavyset lady walked up to me and kissed me on both cheeks and called me her little *bambina*.

"You look just like my Francisco," she said. "I would know you anywhere. You have the Farillo Italian beauty like all the Farillo women. Angelo, come look at Frank's *bambina*." My grandfather had tears in his eyes as he hugged me.

The rest of the family started to crowd around us and introduce themselves. People were looking at us, trying to figure out if there was a celebrity around.

"Mrs. Farillo, you didn't have to come to the airport to meet us."

"No, *bambina*, it's Grandma. You're Frank's baby, so that makes you my baby."

After hugging my grandmother, my grandfather, half a dozen aunts, uncles, and not to mention a ton of cousins, we all got into the cars and headed to the house.

We arrived at what could only be described as a family reunion at best. There were relatives and more relatives and more food than I had ever seen at a family function. The amount of food they had cooked was incredible. Every Italian delicacy you could imagine had been cooked. My grandfather had the house built in the early eighties, and it was gorgeous. All the rooms were master suites with their own bathrooms. I was physically and mentally drained, but I knew we were expected downstairs for dinner.

"Jennifer, I want you to know, sweetheart, we all love you," said my grandmother. "We've known about you since your father found out, and I just want you to know that he loves you very much." I noticed my grandmother would not speak of my father in the past tense. I guess if she refused to think of him that way, then maybe he wasn't gone. "I hope that you and Frank will get the chance to spend more time together. I may seem like a silly ole Italian woman to you, but he is my son, my firstborn, and I am not ready to give up on him yet."

"We will leave on Tuesday and fly to New York and stay with your great-uncle Matty and his family. Then on Wednesday, we will meet with this medical-examiner person and will see that this body they found is not my Francis," said my grandfather. "I think we will find him in a hospital hurt somewhere, but not dead."

Dinner was wonderful, and we all had a great time. Dylen loved being the center of attention. We were all treated like they had known us for years. Marcus and I ate too much and drank way too much, but the love we felt from everyone was indescribable.

The next morning, we woke up to a house full of people fixing breakfast. There were always a lot of people around for mealtime, we soon discovered, but it was good. It was very good to feel loved. I think my father would have enjoyed us meeting everyone.

We arrived at JFK to another mob of Italian relatives. It felt like déjà vu. We went through yet another meet and greet of uncles, aunts, and cousins. As excited as everyone was, no one was looking forward to tomorrow.

My grandmother and grandfather gave blood and hair samples. We were told it would be twenty-four hours before we got the results. We had another huge dinner that night and then left to go visit ground zero. After laying flowers near the site, we went to mass. I got the chance to meet Monsignor Ryan. He would be the one to preside over my father's ceremony if the results proved to be a positive match. Monsignor was a wonderful man, and dinner was more pleasant with him around. We all retired early that night. Everyone was both mentally and physically drained from the activities of the day and was nervous as hell about what tomorrow would bring.

We had breakfast and sat around waiting to be called about the test results. Around 11:30 a.m., the call came. We said a prayer before leaving, and my grandmother was confident that the results would come back a negative match. We were all waiting in the lobby when the doctor came in and asked for the Farillo family. About twelve people stood up.

"I need just the immediate family," he said.

I was allowed to go back with my grandparents for the test results. A thin-lipped, greasy-looking man came out to deliver the news. This guy had the bedside manner of a mass murder. He came in without any hesitation and said, "The tests are conclusive. The DNA matches the remains that were found at the site." My grandmother broke down.

"Sir, will we be able to take the remains that were found and give them a proper burial?" asked my grandfather.

"Sure, whatever we have, it's yours. We have no need for it now that a positive identification has been made."

Marcus held me as I cried.

"Do you think you could be a little more sensitive to the people who have just lost their son and father?" said Marcus.

"Excuse me?"

"Yes, sir, I'm speaking with you. You're rude, insensitive, and you're an asshole. My wife just lost her father, and you act as though you deliver the results of an SAT score or something," said Marcus. "Now get your ass out of my sight before I kick your bony ass."

My grandfather made a phone call to have the remains picked up and taken to the funeral home. Isabella held my hand the entire way home. It was as though she could feel my dad through me. Two days later, we had a memorial ceremony for my father, and a couple of hours later, we boarded a plane to Boston with his ashes. Isabella wanted to have a formal ceremony with military honors in Boston and then have the ashes scattered at his ranch in New Mexico. Our lives were changed by 9/11 forever, but not only ours; everyone in the country had changed, and as a nation, we would never be the same. I felt like we had been gone forever.

Dylen couldn't wait to see River, and I couldn't wait to see my girls. Marcus complained that he had put on fifteen pounds eating all that rich Italian food, and he couldn't wait to get to the gym.

The next couple of days were difficult readjusting to life in Minnesota. Carmen came over for cake and coffee, and she looked terrible.

"Carmen, I am so sorry for neglecting you."

"Jennifer, you didn't neglect me, and your father was just killed. Girl, I'm okay. I don't look so hot on the outside, but I am really okay," she said.

"So, Carmen, how is everyone else doing?"

"Well, Nikki is being Nikki. Richard is on Beth about having a baby, and Virginia is just acting weird. I know there is something going on, but she won't tell me what it is. She will when she's ready. So, Jennifer, you know what it is?" asked Carmen.

"Yes, she told me before I left to go to Boston. But, Carmen, it is not my business to tell you. V will tell you when she's ready."

"Okay then, let's get them over here so we can all sit down and catch up. Don't worry, I called before you got here, so they should be here."

Before I could sit down, the doorbell rang.

Nikki was the first to start. "Jennifer, are you okay, girl?"

"Yeah, I'm fine. It's just gonna take some time. Carmen, are you okay? Child, you look like shit," said Nikki. "Carmen, don't be offended. You know I sometimes speak before I think."

"Nikki, it must be exhausting being a bitch 24-7," said Virginia.

"Virginia, it's okay. I'm used to Nikki by now, and I know I look like shit. Thank you very much, Ms. Nikki," said Carmen. "If you must know, I have been fighting a fever the last couple of days, and I'm just kind of drained."

Nikki went over and kissed Carmen on the forehead and apologized for being insensitive. "Beth, you pregnant yet?" asked Nikki.

"Can we at least get through the door and have a seat and maybe a drink before you start giving everyone shit, Nikki?" said Beth. "But the answer to your question is no, but I assure you, when it happens, you'll be the first person I call. You know, the truth is, I don't really want a baby yet. I thought I did for a while, but I realize now I was only doing it because it's what Richard wants. When we were in New

Mexico, I had a lot of time to think about it, and I don't want to be pregnant. I don't want to get fat and lose my figure."

"Beth, you can lose the weight after the baby comes," said Carmen.

"Look at Virginia. She didn't lose the weight, and I remember what she looked like before she got pregnant. She was beautiful," said Beth.

"How dare you, Beth. I happen to think I'm still beautiful. No, I didn't lose all my weight right away, but I'm healthy, and I'm working on it every day," said Virginia.

"Virginia, I know you work out almost every day, but it doesn't seem like it's doing any good," Beth said fretfully. "I know you're still beautiful, but you could be so much more beautiful if you lost the weight and you were thin again."

"Come on, guys, let's change the subject. It seems like it's been so long since we sat down and talked. Let's not fuss," said Carmen.

"No, wait," said Virginia. "Let's hear what Beth has to say since her marriage is so fucking perfect."

"I'm just saying, Virginia, maybe that's why Brian's having an affair, because you're overweight."

"How dare you put my shit out there like that, you anorexic bitch! Yes, Beth, I know about your little eating problem. I know the symptoms because my sister died from that shit. Beth, you rarely eat, and you always go to the bathroom right after you eat. What, did you think people wouldn't notice? Beth, you're right about one thing: my husband is leaving me. But it is more complicated than just the weight, and maybe you would realize that if you had a real marriage."

"Beth, you need to put that shit on pause," said Nikki. "That throwing-up bullshit is for white women. Sistas don't do that shit. See, I knew there was something going on with you, but I just couldn't put my finger on it. At first, I just thought you were just one of those salad-eating bitches."

"Nikki, I don't need this shit from you, because if you keep talking, I'm going to lay all your shit bare," said Beth.

"What the fuck are you talking about?" said Nikki.

"Are you sure you want to do this in front of everybody?" said Beth. "You're always so quick to judge everyone else, but you never take a look at the shit you're doing wrong."

"Whatever," said Nikki.

"You know, Nikki, that is your answer for everything," said Virginia.

"Look, Virginia, I didn't mean anything by what I said. I know you have been trying to lose the weight, and you've come a long way, but I'm afraid that I will have a difficult time as well, and I just don't think I can handle that in my life right now," said Beth.

"Beth, I understand how you feel," I said. "The night I went into labor with Dylen, I weighed in at 208 pounds. I thought I would never be thin again, but I worked at it, and I would give anything to be able to have another child."

"Jen, I know, sweetie. I'm sorry," said Beth.

"Beth, I would do anything to be able to keep weight on my body," said Carmen. "Between diarrhea and the vomiting, I can't keep weight on. I'm beginning to look like a damn skeleton. So please stop doing this to yourself. We will help you. Anorexia is a serious illness. It's not just physical, but it is also a mental illness that needs to be addressed."

"Damn right, 'cause any bitch that would stick her finger down her throat to induce vomiting needs to have her fucking head examined, because that shit is stupid as hell," said Nikki.

"Nikki, you evil bitch, but since you want to go there, then let's go there," said Beth. "Jennifer, I think you need to know that Nikki fucked your father. Our last night at the ranch, she sneaked out of the room when everyone was asleep, and she fucked your father. I caught her sneaking back into the room, and she admitted to me that she had been with Frank."

"Nik, is that true?" said Jennifer. "After you told me all that crap about how much you loved Bruce? And then you cheat on him? How could you do that?"

"You just couldn't resist, could you? You know what I think? I think you wanted to know what it was like to be with a white man so badly that you would have fucked the Pillsbury doughboy."

"Virginia's right. You are a scandalous cunt. Now get the fuck out my house, you bitch."

"Jennifer, let me explain what happened," said Nikki. "It wasn't just sex. I connected with your father in a way you couldn't possibly understand. I think I fell in love with him the first night we arrived. I don't know if it was just the need for an older man's approval, because I never knew my father or what, but Frank was special."

"Nik, that wasn't love. It was lust, and he was my father," I said. "That alone should have made him off-limits."

"Jennifer he's a man first—was a man."

Before I knew what happened, I slapped Nikki in the face.

Carmen grabbed me. "Jennifer, it's not worth it. You have so much more you need to be concerned with. Sweetheart, just let it go," she said.

"You have tainted the memory of my father, Nikki, and I don't want you in my house or in my life. Just get out," I said, trying to fight back the tears.

Marcus walked in. "Ladies, what is going on?"

Nikki grabbed her jacket and left.

"I think it's time for all of us to leave," said Virginia.

"Are you all right, Jen?" said Carmen.

"No, I'm not. I've just lost my father and one of my best friends, Carmen. I may never be all right again."

"Baby, what's wrong?" said Marcus.

"Nikki slept with Frank."

"What?" asked Marcus.

"While we were in New Mexico, she slept with my father, and I don't think we're going to be friends anymore." I kissed Beth and Virginia goodbye and went to my room. I loved my girls, but after today, I didn't know if our friendship would ever be the same.

Beth and Virginia called several times over the next couple of weeks to make sure I was okay, but I still was not ready to see anyone. Marcus and I spent a lot of time with Dylen. We felt like since 9/11, we had been neglecting her. We had become so wrapped up in adult life she was on autopilot. She didn't seem to mind, though. She spent just as much time at River's as she did at home. Carmen enjoyed spending time with her and River, so I felt a little less guilty about neglecting her.

October 17 finally arrived, and it had been a month since I had spoken with Nikki. Virginia called me and asked if I would still go to court with her.

"Of course, I will. You're my friend, aren't you?"

The proceedings were bland. The judge read the order, and both parties agreed, and the divorce was granted. Brian was granted visitation; V got her one hundred thousand dollars, the house, and child support. Afterward, we met Carmen for lunch to celebrate.

Virginia was very calm, not at all upset that her marriage had just ended. *Shit, I would have been a basket case*, I thought.

"Virginia, are you okay?" Carmen asked.

"Yes, I am fine," Virginia said with conviction. "I must tell you, though, that I have already met someone and we've been dating for about three weeks now."

"Who is this dark horse?" I asked.

"Well, I'm not ready for you guys to meet Jorden yet. I need to see where this is going first, if anywhere."

"Okay, but can we at least get some details?" I asked.

"Not yet, Jen. I don't want to jinx it."

"Okay, I won't push it this time." I laughed.

"Has anyone heard from Nikki?" asked Carmen.

"She's called me a couple of times, but I haven't taken the calls," I said.

"Jennifer, I know what she did was foul as hell, but she's our sister. We have been through so much together, and that's not a bond you can easily break," said Carmen.

"I'm just not ready yet." I smiled half-heartedly. "Not to change the subject, but how's Beth doing, by the way?"

"Well, I spoke to her last week, and she and Richard have agreed to go to counseling," said Virginia.

"That's wonderful. I'm happy for them. I haven't wanted to say anything, but I guess I might as well tell you guys some great news."

"Okay, spill it, girl," said Virginia anxiously.

"My father left the ranch in New Mexico to me. Marcus is going to take a month off, and we're meeting my grandparents there for a memorial service for my father, and we're going to lay his ashes to rest. Brandon Longfeather, who runs the ranch, had a memorial statue of my father made. We're going to bury his ashes. I want you guys to join us. All expenses paid. It's going to be over the Thanksgiving holiday, and all my Italian family is going to be there. I just would like for us to go back to a place that was happy for all of us. You're invited to bring your husbands or significant others along also. Come on, guys, please say yes. This last month has been extremely difficult on all of us, so let's go and have some fun."

"Is Nikki invited?" asked Carmen.

"Not on your life. It's going to be difficult enough going back there and having all those memories of my father. I just don't want to think about them together, okay?"

"Just think about it, okay?" said Virginia.

"Go home, V, and talk it over with Jorden, and I'll call Beth and invite her and Richard. Since you're not that excited about us meeting your new friend, this would be the perfect opportunity," I said. "By the way, V, what does Jorden do for a living?"

"Jorden's a lawyer."

"What's his last name? Marcus might know him," I said.

"I doubt it, Jennifer. Jorden just moved here from New Orleans. Jennifer, I don't know if I'm ready to introduce Jorden to everyone yet. This trip is about closure for you and your family, and I just want to be there for you. I don't want to be worried about someone else and their feelings and whether they're getting enough attention, so maybe next trip," said Virginia.

"Okay, V, but you have to promise we will meet him soon. I will give you a call later and let you know about Beth."

Everyone was excited about going back to the ranch. We didn't want to be hassled with airport's security or any of that because things were still crazy from 9/11, so we decided to rent an RV. Marcus and I went to RV City, and I was really impressed. Some of these things were better and bigger than my first apartment. The one we decided on accommodated twelve people easily. It had three bathrooms, four bedroom compartments, and the seats reclined into cots. It had a full kitchen with a refrigerator and hot tub.

Since we had so much room, Marcus decided to invite his father and Helen. We hadn't seen them since Marcus's mother passed away. It would be great to see them again, and Dylen said she missed her grandfather. David had called to say he and Helen had gotten engaged. After 9/11, they decided that with everything going on in the world, life was too short, so why wait? They had already waited twenty-five years, and now they just wanted to be together. David had wanted to come to Minnesota when Marcus had told him about my father, so it would be perfect to have them along on this trip.

We decided to leave on November 15 so we could get there the week before Thanksgiving and get everything set up before my grandparents arrived. David and Helen were flying in, in a couple of days before so we could spend some time with them before leaving. Marcus and I went shopping to stock the camper, and we advised everyone to bring anything special they might want in addition to what we were buying.

Dave and Helen arrived at 5:30 p.m. the day before the trip, and Dylen was excited to see them again. She always loved being the center of attention. I looked at her running from Marcus to Dave, and suddenly, I felt very sad. I tried to hold back the tears, but I couldn't, so I excused myself to the bathroom. I felt sorry for all the people who died on 9/11 and for the loved ones they left behind. As I walked to the bathroom, the realization that I would never see my father again hit me very hard. Marcus followed me to make sure I was okay.

"Jennifer, are you okay?" Marcus asked.

"No, I'm not, but I will be," I said as I walked away.

The two weeks I spent with my father was the best time of my life. Just seeing Marcus and his father together just became too overwhelming. I returned to the table, and Helen looked at me.

"Jennifer, baby, it's okay that you become overwhelmed sometimes. This tragedy has hit us all pretty hard. There are so many people who are going through the same things you're feeling right now.

Give yourself some time. It's barely been two months. Just relax and stop trying to be Superwoman," said Helen.

"Jen, sweetheart, are you okay?" asked Marcus again.

"Yes, I'm fine." And I leaned over and kissed his cheek.

We finished dinner and headed home. I was emotionally drained, but I had promised Carmen we would have coffee and cake when we returned from dinner. She was dying to meet Marcus's parents.

Carmen was already at the house when we arrived.

"Everyone, come on in, and we'll have some cake and coffee and call it a night. I know we have a big day ahead of us tomorrow."

I went into the kitchen to help Carmen and was met by a conversation I was not ready to have.

"Jennifer, look, I know you don't want to talk about Nikki, but I miss all of us hanging out together, and sooner or later, you are going to have to deal with the issue of Nikki and your father. You're trying to be strong for me and Virginia, and it's just too much. So go to New Mexico and bury your father's ashes, and remember, you're burying his ashes, not your memories and certainly not your love for him. Just don't let what happened between your father and Nikki taint your memories of him and let it destroy your friendship with Nikki. Plus, just think about it. One of your father's last wishes could have been to get him some young black poononi before he died, and look, his wish came true."

I looked at Carmen and burst out laughing. "Maybe you're right, Carmen. Who am I to step on a man's last wish? But why did it have to be that tacky tramp?"

"I know, Jennifer, but it is what it is. So call her and invite her on this trip with us."

"I can't, Carmen, not right now, but I promise as soon as we get back, I will call her."

"Good enough. Now let's go get some cake."

After everyone left, I cleaned up the kitchen, while Marcus put Dylen to bed. It had been a really long day, and I was exhausted. I still had not been sleeping very well, and I wanted to get some rest before we left tomorrow. Marcus lay beside me and held me as I fell asleep. I don't think I could have made it without him. He was my rock.

Marcus and I woke up around seven o'clock so we could get an early start. Helen and Dave were already in the kitchen fixing breakfast. The driver was supposed to arrive at eight, and we wanted to have the RV already packed before he arrived. The kids were busy entertaining David and Helen, so I went upstairs to find Carmen. I walked into the room, and I could hear Carmen in the bathroom throwing up.

"My god, girl, are you okay?" I asked.

"No, Jen, I'm not. I have been throwing up blood all night."

"Get dressed. I'm taking you to the emergency room. You need a doctor."

"No, I don't, Jen. I need a priest."

"Why a priest?"

"Because I feel like I'm dying."

"Carmen, don't you do this to me. I can't take this right now. Please don't give up," I said as I started to cry. "You'll get past this. I will help you get past this, I promise. Just don't give up. Marcus, I need you upstairs right now!" I called out.

Marcus ran upstairs. "What is so urgent?" he asked, running into the bathroom.

"Look, baby, I need to get Carmen to the emergency room, but I don't want to excite everyone, okay? If the kids ask, just say we went to the store."

I called Carmen's doctor and told him we were on our way to the emergency room, and he agreed to meet us there. We arrived at the Hennepin County emergency room, and they called Carmen back right away. We were grateful for her doctor phoning ahead, because you could die waiting to be seen in the emergency room. The nurse came in and took some blood, and the doctor had instructed them to run some tests before he arrived. It seemed like hours before the doctor arrived to give Carmen the results of her test. He told Carmen she had ruptured the lining of her esophagus and that's why she was throwing up blood. He explained to her that the same thing happens to women who suffer from anorexia. She was running a temperature, so he gave her antibiotics and medication for the nausea. He wanted to admit her, but Carmen refused to stay. So the doctor medicated her and sent her on her way.

On the ride home, I kept starring at Carmen as she tried to sleep.

"Jennifer, will you please stop staring at me?" said Carmen. "I'm fine. The doctors told me a while back that this would happen because of all the excessive vomiting. Now let's suck it up and put on a happy face so the kids won't know anything is wrong."

Even though Carmen was trying to put on a brave face, I could tell she was really scared.

We arrived at the house to be rushed by Dylen.

"Mommy, what did you buy me at the store?"

"Nothing, sweetheart. We got medication for carsickness just in case we need it on our long trip."

"Is that the only reason you went to the store?" asked Dylen.

"Dylen, not now. Go upstairs and get your stuff so we can get on the road."

"Don't snap at me. All you do is cry and yell at me."

"Dylen, that's enough," I said, walking upstairs.

"What's wrong?" Dylen asked River.

"Mom's in another one of her moods, so let's just go get in the camper so we can get the best seats."

Everyone had arrived and boarded the camper. Carmen was in the back lying down, and Virginia was checking on her.

"Jennifer, is Carmen okay? She doesn't look very well," asked Marcus.

"Marcus, I really don't think she has much time left, and I can't handle losing my best friend right now."

"Jennifer, you can't give up on her. People are living so much longer these days with AIDS than ever before, and Carmen has a lot to live for. She's just going through a rough patch right now."

The kids entertained themselves with video games, while the women played cards, and the men watched sports. Driving cross-country was amazing. We were all getting along so well, and I enjoyed how attentive Richard was to Beth. I guess the therapy was working for them.

The second day into the trip, Dylen started to cause problems. She and Helen were playing UNO, and Dylen was being a sore loser. I started to hear this big commotion, and Marcus and I jumped up to see what was going on. Dylen was screaming and yelling at Helen.

"Hey, hey, what is going on?" I said.

"Well, Mom, Grandma Helen is cheating. Just because she won, she doesn't want to play anymore."

"Well, Dylen, you can't make her play if she's tired."

"Yes, I can, because I'm gonna put that old bird out of her misery."

"Dylen, don't speak to Helen that way. You better apologize now, young lady," I said with a tone in my voice that meant business.

"No, Mommy, because she is a cheater."

Marcus grabbed Dylen and gave her a quick swat on her behind. Dylen started to yell as though someone was killing her. River jumped up and started to yell at Marcus. Carmen walked in.

"What in the hell is going on?" she asked.

"Carmen, it's just a big misunderstanding. Dylen was being disrespectful to Helen, so Marcus spanked her, and River came to her defense. It was kind of cute, actually," I said, smiling. River was just like a big brother coming to her rescue.

"River, you can't speak to Marcus that way. He's Dylen's father, and he has the right to spank her."

River walked up to Marcus with his little head down and apologized.

Marcus shook his hand and smiled. "At least I know you got her back," said Marcus.

Dylen continued to act like a brat and ran to her cabin and slammed the door. David decided to go back and talk with her.

"I think it's time for a lunch break. I think everyone is starting to get cabin fever," I said.

When I walked past Beth and Richard, I heard Beth say "Are you sure you want one of those?"

Richard started to laugh. "Well, you got to take the good ones with the bad, I guess."

I smiled as I kept walking past them.

We arrived at the ranch at 1:30 p.m. the next afternoon. Brandon and his staff were great. They got everyone settled in their bungalows, and we all decided to take a nap. I went in to talk to Dylen, and she apologized for being mean to Helen. It was really sweet seeing Dylen be so humble. All I could do was kiss her and tell her how much I loved her. I watched her lay her sweet little head on her pillow and close her eyes.

Marcus and I took a long, hot shower and decided to take a nap. Everyone was up at six and getting dressed for dinner when I heard a knock at the door. I thought it was maid service, but then I heard a very distinctive Italian accent.

"Honey, it's for you," said Marcus.

I walked out of the bathroom and saw my grandparents standing in the doorway, smiling.

"What are you guys doing here so soon?" I asked. "I didn't expect you until the week of Thanksgiving."

"Surprise, sweetheart," said my grandmother. "Marcus chartered a plane so we could be here early."

"Who are 'we'?" I asked.

People started to pile into our room. My grandfather looked at me and said, "All of us. Your Uncle Matty and his family. Aunt Teresa and her family. You want me to go on? It's about fifty of us that made the trip."

"I hope it's okay, Jennifer. We just wanted to be with you. It's our first holiday without Francis, and we just wanted to be with his little *bambina*," said Isabella.

I looked at Marcus. "Honey, I can't believe you did all this for me."

"Yes, Dad and I set it up. He has a friend who's a pilot, so it was easy, really. Jennifer, I know you have been so sad since your father's death. I just wanted you to be happy for the holidays."

"How long are you going to be able to stay?" I asked.

"We're going to be here with you until the New Year comes in," Angelo said.

"Angelo, I hope this isn't an intrusive question, but can you afford to be off work for so long?"

"Jennifer, how many times do I have to tell you to call me Grandfather or Grandpa?"

"Okay, Grandpa."

"Jennifer, don't worry, sweetheart, we have means, and we just received a check from your father's attorney for a great deal of money, so don't worry about us," he said. "So we're going to let you finish dressing, and we will meet you for dinner in an hour."

I just looked at Marcus in amazement and smiled.

"Jennifer, I never want you to be unhappy," he said. "So just enjoy your new family—I mean, our new family." He smiled.

Surprisingly, everyone got along. The men played lots of golf, the kids rode horses, and I worried about Carmen, which had become my full-time job.

I loved hearing all the stories of my father growing up in Boston, about my grandparents moving to the United States from the old country, and about all my cousins in Brooklyn and various other areas of New York.

Blacks and Italians have always had their share of problems, but I was glad that my dad's family had accepted Dylen and me. My grandmother told me that they were concerned when my father told them he was in love with an African American girl.

"Italian men have always been attracted to black women," said Uncle Carmine. "It's because they're so wild and untamed, not like good Catholic girls."

"Carmine, hush. You've had too much vino," said grandmother.

"Jennifer, I apologize. I meant no disrespect," said Uncle Carmine.

My grandfather came over and said something to Uncle Carmine in Italian. I could tell my grandfather was upset, and Uncle Carmine apologized again and kissed me on the forehead.

"We love you, Jennifer. You're a part of us, and anyone in this family who does not recognize that will no longer be a part of this family."

Everything was awkward for a moment until the band started to play traditional Italian music and everyone got up to dance. David and Helen were having a ball, and Richard was being overly protective as usual. He kept Beth under his thumb and was upset when one of my cousins asked her to dance. I went over to Beth to make sure she was okay. She had had too much to wine and was flirting with my cousin Tomas.

"Beth, what are you doing?" I asked.

"I'm having fun, girl. Italian men are some of the sexiest, romantic men on the planet, and I'm about to dance with Tomas."

"Yeah, Beth, but you know how Richard is," said Carmen, who had strolled over and joined the conversation.

"I think you've had a little too much to drink and maybe you need to lie down," said Carmen. "Jennifer, I'll walk Beth to her room, and then I'll come back and help you get everyone settled."

"Settled? Settled? Are you serious? Please. These people look like they are going to be here until sunrise at least."

"Isabella—I mean, Grandmother—I'm tired. You guys are welcome to stay up as long as you like, but I'm exhausted. You have access to everything. The staff is here at your disposal, but I must get Dylen in bed."

"I know, sweetheart, but I'm enjoying her company so much. She asked if she could stay in our room tonight, and I told her she could if that's okay with you."

"Grandmother, of course, she can. I will ask Brandon to send a cot to your room, okay?" I kissed her good night and made my way to my bungalow.

When I made it to the room, Marcus was already lying down. I crawled into bed beside him.

"Hey, you, are you asleep?"

"No. Why? What do you have in mind?"

"Why don't we make mad, passionate love and then fall asleep?" I said.

"Why don't you kiss me passionately, we go to sleep, wake up in a couple of hours, and then I give you the fuck of your life? Then we can go back to sleep and sleep until noon," said Marcus.

"Sounds like a plan." So I kissed my husband and fell asleep. It was the best sleep I had had in weeks. We didn't have sex, but we did sleep until noon.

After waking up, Marcus and I took a quick shower and walked out by the pool. Richard and Beth were in the pool playing.

"Hey, I thought black women didn't like to get their hair wet," said Marcus.

"Dude, the only reason she is in the pool is because I pushed her in the pool," said Richard. "Plus, you can get Beth to do almost anything after a couple of drinks."

I walked over to where Carmen and the kids were sitting.

"Hey, what's going on with Beth? Carmen, she doesn't usually drink this much."

"Jen, I was thinking that same thing last night after she had her third glass of wine. She always had less to drink than any of us. Where's V?"

"Oh, she will be right back. Syble wanted to get in the pool, so she went to braid up her hair or something. Thank God, I don't have to deal with that drama," I said jokingly.

"What are you talking about? You're good at combing Dylen's hair."

"There's not a whole lot to do since she wears it either down or in a ponytail most of the time. Carmen, has Virginia said much to you about Jorden?"

"No, not really."

"I asked Marcus if he knew of this person, and he said no, but Virginia said he just moved here from New Orleans. I'm thinking that maybe he's married since she is being so secretive."

"You think so, Jen?"

"Girl, who the hell knows? I'm dealing with enough of my own. I don't need to get wrapped up in someone else's drama."

"Jen, I'm going to take your grandfather into town. He wants to visit your father's vineyards," said Marcus. "You didn't tell me he owned a winery."

"That's because I didn't know, but okay, I'll catch up with you at dinner."

"Speaking of dinner, the cook told me that your grandmother has taken over the kitchen and is teaching him how to make genuine Italian food," Marcus said, laughing.

"Jennifer, where is Marcus going?" asked Virginia.

"The men are going into town."

"What happened to Beth?"

"Nothing. She went in to dry off and change. She'll be back," I said.

"So let's dish some dirt until she returns."

"Virginia, how many times have you called Jorden since you've been here?"

"Only a couple. Why?"

"So is this getting serious or what?" asked Carmen.

"I'm not sure yet, but possibly," said Virginia. "We're not going to talk about Jorden, though. I want to talk about something more important."

"What's more important?" I asked.

"There are a couple of things, actually. First, what the hell is going on with Beth? I don't think I've ever seen her drinking so much," said Virginia. "I sat with her and Richard last night, and it was embarrassing the way she was flirting with your cousin Tomas. I mean, the man is fine, don't get me wrong, but I couldn't believe she was so open with that shit."

"Virginia, are you serious?" I asked.

"Hell yeah, girl, she better hope Richard doesn't tighten that ass up."

"Virginia, something is definitely going on, because I caught her drinking out of a flask even though the bar is fully stocked," said Carmen.

"You know, like she's hiding the fact that she is drinking or at least how much she is drinking."

"Jennifer, I didn't really want to say anything, but I think Beth has an even more serious problem."

"What kind of problem?"

"I think Beth is doing coke."

"Cocaine?" asked Carmen.

"Virginia, why would you think something like that?" I asked.

"You remember the day Dylen caused the scene and then we stopped to get food? Well, Beth said she left her purse. I went back to get Sybil's medication, and I saw Beth tooting."

"Virginia, are you serious? Because if that is the case, then I have to say something. She's our friend, and that shit is real bad, but not only that—how could she bring that shit with her? What if we got stopped by the police and searched?"

"Jen, don't say anything, not yet," said Carmen. "Let's just see how the rest of the vacation goes. If her behavior is still sporadic, then we'll talk with her."

We all agreed not to spoil the trip, but I couldn't help but think we were making a big mistake.

We decided to have a traditional Thanksgiving dinner, and Beth, Carmen, Virginia, and I decided we were going to cook. We had given the staff the weekend off after they went shopping for everything we needed. Some of the housekeeping staff remained, but we were pretty much on our own as far as meals were concerned until Monday morning. My grandmother was happy about that since she loved to cook. She'd already taken over the kitchen duties since her arrival, but we were determined to cook an old-fashioned Southern Thanksgiving dinner.

We were up all night cooking, and Beth kept sneaking off to the bathroom, and we just kind of looked at one another whenever she pulled a disappearing act.

I was the first to comment. "Beth, why are you spending so much time in the bathroom? You can't be throwing up because you're not eating anything. Why is that, Beth?" I asked.

"Yeah, Beth. Why aren't you eating?" asked Virginia.

"Because I'm not hungry, that's why."

"Is it because of that shit you keep shoving up your nose?" said Carmen.

"What are you talking about?"

"We know about the coke," I said.

"You don't know shit, Jennifer."

"We know more than you think we do," I said. "We're not stupid, but go ahead and play these little games, but I'll tell you this: do not bring that bullshit back on the RV with you. Are we clear?" I said, more pissed off than ever. "You're not going to get the rest of us in trouble with that shit."

"Just mind your own business, Jennifer. I don't tell you how many Valium to take, so don't try to tell me how to run my life."

"You know, Beth, you always do that. You can never be real about your shit. You always have to bring up what everybody is doing wrong. Just be real about your shit for a minute," said Virginia.

"It's my life. I can do what I want."

"You're wrong, Beth. We love you, and we're just being concerned about you and your health," I said.

"What you need to be concerned about is that turkey you're burning up in the oven, Jennifer, with your microwaving ass," said Beth.

Everyone could not help but laugh. It actually seemed like old times.

Thanksgiving Day was a day to remember now that I think back on it. My grandmother was a little upset that she was not allowed in the kitchen, but she enjoyed the food anyway. After dinner, we had mass and a memorial ceremony for my father. Everyone enjoyed the service, and there was a huge party afterward thrown by Brandon and the staff members who had stayed behind. The party lasted until midnight, but I was determined to leave early and spend some time with my husband.

I passed the gazebo and saw Richard standing there, talking with my cousin Juanita. They both had a look on their face as if they had been caught doing something wrong even though it appeared they were having an innocent conversation.

"Richard, where is Beth?" I asked.

"I'm not sure. I came outside looking for her when I bumped into Juanita."

I went to the bungalow to see if Beth had gone to bed early, but I still could not find her. I went to Carmen's room hoping she was there, but still no Beth. Carmen and I went to Virginia's room, but she was in bed asleep with Sybil.

"Jen, you don't think she sneaked off somewhere with Tomas, do you?"

"No, I saw Tomas at the party when I was leaving."

"Why are you so worried about her, Jennifer?" asked Carmen.

"I don't know. She just seemed really stoned after the memorial service, and at the party, she had a lot to drink. Let's go out by the pool. She may be sitting out there. Who knows? Maybe she fell asleep out there."

The pool area was dark, and she didn't answer when we called, but as we got closer, I could see something in the water from the glow of the lights around the pool. I had walked ahead of Carmen and Virginia, and the closer I got, I could see it was a body in the pool. I yelled to the others to call for help as I dived into the water. I struggled to bring the body to the edge. Virginia jumped in to help me. We pulled and pulled until we got the body out of the water. We turned Beth over and started CPR. We had no idea how long she had been in the pool, but we took turns trying to resuscitate her.

Marcus was the first to arrive then Richard.

He took Beth up into his arms and screamed, "Wake up, baby! Please wake up! I love you, Beth. You can't leave me. I won't let you leave me."

Marcus tried to pull Beth away from Richard. "Man, look, we have to keep trying to resuscitate her. Let her go, damn it!"

Richard let go, and Beth's limp body fell to the ground. This time, Marcus took over the breathing, while I tried to pump the water from her lungs. I could hear my grandmother praying and other people around us talking, but I was determined not to let Beth die. We worked on her for what seemed like an hour, and then I heard her cough. She started to spit up the water, but we knew she was not completely out of the woods yet. By the time the paramedics arrived, Beth was breathing but had a very weak pulse. They put an oxygen mask on her face and transported her to the local hospital.

We arrived at the hospital, and Richard informed us there had been no word. Richard was pacing the floor, and Marcus was trying to keep him calm. The doctor came out and wanted to speak with Richard in private. Richard advised him that it was okay to speak in front of us. The doctor informed Richard that Beth and the baby were doing fine.

"Baby? What baby?" asked Richard.

"I'm sorry, sir, I thought you knew. Your wife is about twelve weeks pregnant," he said. The doctor questioned Richard about Beth's eating disorder and asked if he knew of any reason Beth would try to commit suicide.

"I just recently learned of the eating disorder, but we have been going to counseling, and I thought things were getting better," said Richard.

After the doctor left, Richard turned to us. "So how long have you ladies known Beth was pregnant?" he asked.

"Richard, we didn't know," I said.

"Do you think she tried to kill herself, or was this an accident?" he asked.

"Richard, we don't know," said Virginia.

"Don't lie to me, Jennifer. She tells her girls everything," said Richard.

"Richard, not this. She didn't even tell us this," said Carmen.

We could tell Richard was upset as he turned and walked away. I turned and hugged Marcus and started to sob in his arms when Carmen and Virginia came over to hug me.

"Jennifer, I wanted you to know that I called Nikki. She and Bruce will be here tomorrow," said Virginia.

The nurse came out and said that Beth would like to see us. We walked into the room, and Beth looked so old. Beth was the darker sista of the group, but right now, her skin was ashy and white, and her eyes were red and tired. Richard was sitting on the edge of the bed, holding her hand. Tears were rolling down his face, and he looked scared. We walked over to the bed, and I kissed Beth on the forehead.

Richard looked at her. "Why would she do this? Were you trying to kill yourself and the baby?" he asked somberly.

"What are you talking about, Richard? I didn't do this on purpose. The last thing I remember is sitting by the pool and then waking up here. And what are you talking about? What baby?" asked Beth, looking confused.

"Beth, the doctor said you're twelve weeks pregnant," said Richard.

"Are you serious? I'm pregnant? Are you sure?"

"Yes, we're going to have a baby."

There was a knock on the door, and Marcus walked in.

"Is this where they moved the party? I just wanted to come in and check on the little mermaid," said Marcus, smiling. Beth started to laugh. "Plus, I hear congratulations are in order." Marcus shook Richard's hand and kissed Beth's.

"Thank you, Marcus, for saving my life!"

"Hey, Virginia and Jen had done most of the work by the time I arrived on the scene. So the credit, if any, goes to them."

"Thank you, girls. I love you very much," said Beth.

"We love you too."

The nurse came in and told us it was time to say good night; only Richard was allowed to stay. The rest of us were quiet and somber on the ride home, wondering what tomorrow might bring, but tonight we had comfort in knowing our best friend was alive and safe.

Nikki arrived the next day, and she wanted to go straight to the hospital. Beth was looking a lot better, but she was still not out of the woods yet.

We stayed with her while Richard went to the ranch to shower and change. It seemed like forever since I'd seen Nikki, and I tried, for the sake of Beth, to be cordial, but it was difficult. Nikki was happy and surprised to hear about the pregnancy, but like the rest of us, she was shocked and wondered if Beth had really tried to commit suicide or if this was truly an accident. Even though we wondered, we knew we would never ask.

After spending a week in the hospital, Beth was finally released. My grandmother decided to throw her a welcome-home dinner. My grandmother just loved having a reason to cook. Christmas was coming soon, and I was missing Minnesota. I missed the snow and was getting really tired of the desert. Minnesota during the holidays was magical. The snow reflecting off the Christmas lights was always beautiful.

Everyone was bummed out about Beth and wondered if we should shorten the trip, but since Christmas was only two weeks away, we decided to tough it out and have a good time.

We got the kids together and decided to decorate the ballroom. All the kids were gathered around, but I could not find Dylen. She loved to decorate. I couldn't imagine her missing all this.

"River, have you seen Dylen?" I asked.

"Yes, ma'am, she went to her room. I think she was crying."

"Do you know why?"

"No, she was playing with some of the other kids, then she just left."

When I walked into the room, I could tell she had been crying. "Baby, what's wrong?" I asked.

"Mario kept saying I was a mooli."

"Do you know what a mooli is?" I asked her.

"No, Mommy, I don't."

"Then, baby, why are you crying?"

"Because I think it is something bad, because everyone started laughing at me. Then Giorgio said I was food," said Dylen with tears in her eyes.

"What?" I said, trying not to laugh. "What kind of food did he call you, baby?" I asked.

"He called me an eggplant. Mommy, why would he call me food?"

"Sweetie, they are just being boys. Boys just play like that with girls sometimes. You know sometimes in the movies people use the *N* word, right? Well, sometimes Italian people use the words *mooli* and *eggplant* to refer to black people."

"Mommy, why are my cousins being mean to me?"

"Kids can be mean sometimes, baby, but that doesn't mean they don't like you."

"River is never mean to me. He is like my brother."

"Yes, I know, but you have known River for a long time, and you haven't really known your cousins that long. Your cousins have probably heard someone say those mean words and they just don't realize how mean and hurtful those words can be to black people."

"Are you guys okay?" I heard Marcus say as he knocked on the door.

Dylen ran to Marcus and started to cry again.

"Hey, what's wrong with Daddy's little girl?"

"Mario and Giorgio called me food."

"What kind of food?" Marcus said, laughing.

"They called me an eggplant and a mooli."

"What! Jennifer, they actually called my baby that foul shit? Those little Italian bastards!"

"Marcus, calm down. Don't say those types of things in front of Dylen."

"The hell I can't. They think they can call my baby that kind of crap and get away with it."

"It's obvious they have heard someone else say that bullshit. Listen, Marcus, just calm down, and we'll go and talk with my grandparents. Since we're talking about kids, Marcus, we have to face the reality of the situation."

"What reality?"

"That Dylen is going to have to deal with this kind of racial bigotry from people of all races. We can't always be there to protect her, Marcus, no matter how much we want to. Take it from me, I know from experience, and she will have to develop a tough skin like I did."

"I understand that, Jennifer, but not from family. She shouldn't have to put up with it from family."

"Baby, sometimes family can be the cruelest. I can't tell you how many times I was called a high yellow heifer or a half-breed by family members. The only thing we can do is show her we love and support her and teach her about racial tolerance."

"That's all fine and well, but we need to speak with your grandparents about what's going on right now."

I tried to calm Marcus down, but nothing I said was working.

"Grandma, Marcus and I need to speak with you and Grandpa."

"Jennifer, is anything wrong?" said Angelo.

"Yes, I'm afraid so."

Dylen was standing there, holding her father's hand, and looking scared.

"What's wrong with the little *bambina*?"

"Some of the kids were calling her a mooli."

"Who said those foul things to my granddaughter?" yelled Angelo. "Come to Grandpa, *bambina*, and tell me who said mean things to you."

"It was Giorgio and Mario," said Dylen in a little baby voice. "Grandpa, they called me a vegetable."

"What does she mean vegetable?" said Grandpa.

"They called her an eggplant," I said.

"Cecilia, go and get your cousins right now," he said. "Better yet, get Lucilla and tell her to get everyone together in the dining room." My grandfather's thick Italian accent came out when he was excited or angry.

We walked into the dining room, and everyone was seated as though they were waiting on dinner.

"Shut up, everyone," said Grandpa with fire in his eyes. My grandfather was so upset he started speaking in Italian. "Anyone in this room who has a problem with my Frank's family has a problem with me. It has been brought to my attention that Dylen was called a mooli and an eggplant by Giorgio and Mario, and I want to know where they would get such language. We don't use racial slurs in this family. This family is not above any race of people, and I'm sure Francisco is turning over in his grave that someone insulted his family. We came here to honor his memory, and you insult his family. I am the head of this family, and this type of behavior will not be tolerated. We came to this country long ago as strangers in a new land. Jennifer and her family came to us as strangers, and now they are a part of us—not only by blood, but by love and commitment."

Giorgio and Mario were the twins of Carlo and Marrisa, Uncle Matty's daughter. Uncle Matty stood up and begged forgiveness for his daughter's children. Marrisa also gave us her apology and made the twins apologize to Dylen. Everyone could tell Marcus was visibly upset, but at least he knew this type of behavior was not something that was tolerated by my dad's family and that my grandparents supported and welcomed us into their family. Dylen seemed happy around her cousins once again, and Marcus was content with the apologies we received that evening from everyone.

Christmas finally came, and we had a big celebration. I still had not had a chance to be alone with Nikki, and I tried to avoid it as much as possible. Beth and Richard returned to Minnesota after she was released from the hospital. I was worried about her; no one had been thoroughly convinced that the near drowning was an accident.

The days following Christmas, Dylen returned to her usual high-spirited self, and I was ready to start the New Year. Friday came quickly, and we loaded up the RV and headed back to Minnesota. I would miss my grandparents dearly, but they promised they would come during the summer for a visit. Brandon was left in charge of the ranch, and I promised him I would keep in touch. Marcus had set up the paperwork for an equal partnership between Brandon and myself, but I would maintain controlling interest. Marcus set him up an account to help keep up with the revenue, and I was confident that he could handle it. He was always responsible for the ranch in my father's absence, so he was the perfect choice to turn things over to, so we headed home.

Everyone was pretty exhausted for the ride home. The kids seemed to sleep the entire trip. Helen and David just cuddled together and talked like two schoolkids. I tried to sleep but was unable to, so I read a magazine and watched Marcus sleep. My husband was so handsome, and I thanked God every day for his love and devotion.

I noticed Carmen on the phone giggling and smiling like a lovestruck schoolgirl. I eased to the back and sat down beside her.

"So what are you smiling about?" I asked.

"It's your cousin Baltazar."

"Who?"

"Your cousin, silly. Remember we sat next to each other at dinner the other night?"

"Oh, okay, so what's that about?" I whispered.

"Don't worry, Jennifer, he knows my situation. We just decided to be pen pals or whatever. Actually, he wants to come to Minnesota and visit me. So if you finished with the third degree, can I get back to my conversation, Ms. Thang? I will give you all the details later." She smiled.

As I walked back to my seat, I couldn't help but think it will be great to have my entire Italian family in Minnesota next year. I finally had a family, and I loved it.

Whew the ride home finally came to an end on December 29, 2001, I could have kissed the ground; I was so happy to be home. Marcus and David helped the driver unload the RV, and I helped Carmen take her luggage to the house, with River and Dylen bringing up the rear, complaining the entire way about how hungry they were.

"Mom, can I spend the night with River?"

"No, Dylen, you guys have been together nonstop for the last two months. Besides, your grandpa David is leaving tomorrow."

"Jen, it's okay with me if you don't mind," said Carmen. "I'll bring her over after they eat dinner and get a bath so she can say good night to her grandparents."

"Okay, that's fine, Carmen, if you're ok with it. But, Dylen, you need to come to the house and get clean clothes and unpack your suitcase before you go over."

Marcus ordered Chinese food, so we had an early dinner and turned in. David and Helen had an early flight the next morning, and everyone was exhausted. I took a long, hot bath and tried to relax. Marcus took a shower and went to lie down. I thought he would be asleep when I finally got out of the tub, but he wasn't. He had opened a bottle of wine and had lit some candles and was lying on the bed with a smile on his face. People had often told me that Marcus resembled Brad Pitt, and in the candlelight, he was gorgeous.

He did remind me of Brad Pitt with his dirty-blond hair and strong jawbone.

Marcus had gotten his hair cut short before we left, and with his well-toned, tanned body, he did bear a striking resemblance to Brad Pitt. He lay there looking sexy with a smirk on his face and a devious look in his eye.

"What are you up to?" I said.

He pulled the covers back and said, "I am up to about seven inches, if you're interested."

I tried to act coy and ignore his hard-on by asking him if he was hungry. "Would you like something to snack on with the wine?" I asked.

"Yes, as a matter of fact, I would, Mrs. Covington. I would like your pussy on a platter."

I let my towel fall to the floor. "Well, Mr. Covington, your wish is my command."

We had fooled around a little while we were on vacation, but I missed our intimate moments like this. By the time we were done, the blankets were on the floor, and we were soaking wet with sweat. We grabbed the covers and curled up in front of the fireplace.

"Jennifer, I love you," he said. "I really do love you, and I want to spend the rest of my life making you happy."

"Baby, what's wrong?" I asked.

"Nothing, sweetheart. I was just thinking about Richard and Beth. You and Dylen are my whole life," he said as he laid his head on my stomach and drifted off to sleep.

I said an extra prayer that night, thanking God for all my blessings, before I too fell asleep.

The next morning, we took Helen and David to the airport and went to Starbucks for coffee. We sat and talked while we read the paper. Marcus turned and looked at me suddenly.

"Baby, what would you like to do for New Year's Eve?" he said.

"I was hoping for some quiet time with my husband."

"Well, that was the answer I was hoping for. I need some alone time with my family. We rarely see Dylen anymore. She is always with Carmen and River. Is River her only friend?"

"No, of course not, but that's the one she prefers to spend most of her time with. You see, that is one of the problems of being homeschooled."

"Marcus, don't worry, though. Dylen has very good social skills. Besides, Carmen and River are at our house just as much as she is at theirs."

"I guess you're right, Jennifer, but it just seems as though the three of us never spend any time together anymore—you know, just us. I would like for us to go away for a long weekend real soon. She's growing up so fast, and I feel like I'm missing valuable time with her. She's already eight, and the next thing we know, she will be leaving for college," he said.

"Baby, don't you think you're exaggerating just a bit?" I said, laughing.

"Jennifer, do you ever think about having another baby?" asked Marcus.

"All the time, baby, but I try not to dwell on it."

"Honey, let's give some serious thought to adoption. There are a lot of kids that need good homes."

"Marcus, are you serious?"

"I would love to. When can we contact an agency? I'll make some calls next week and try to set something up."

"Marcus, how do you think Dylen will react?" I asked.

"I think we need to talk with her and get her thoughts. You know she's been an only child for a long time, and this will be a huge adjustment for her."

"I know, Marcus, but I think she will be excited about the idea. Well, why don't we go to Carmen's and pick her up and surprise her with a trip to Mall of America?"

"That sounds like a great idea," said Marcus.

As usual, our threesome turned into a foursome. River wanted to come along, and we didn't have the heart to say no. We invited Carmen, but she said she wanted some alone time. I told her that if the kids were getting on her nerves, we would take them for the day.

"No, girl, of course not. Dylen is great, and we love having her around. She's the sister River will never have, and he would be lost without her in his life. So don't you dare stop letting her come over. Besides, we have big plans for New Year's Eve," said Carmen.

"You guys are welcome to join us if you like."

"No thank you, Carmen. I think we are going to have some plans of our own," said Marcus.

"Okay, so we are going to the mall, so you can do whatever. By the way, what are you doing?"

"Phone sex, Jen. Honey, it doesn't get any safer than that. And, child, your cousin got game."

The kids were excited about the mall and headed straight for Camp Snoopy. We gave them money and picked a designated spot to meet in an hour. Dylen had gotten a cell phone for Christmas so she could phone us if there were any problems. We stopped by the toy store and bought the kids a couple of presents so they could open them tonight, and I got Carmen a bottle of Champs-Elysées by Guerlain. That's her favorite perfume, and I knew she would be pleased. I also picked out a Prada bag that she admired so much the last time we had gone shopping. Marcus had gone to Victoria's Secret, so I knew what I was getting. I purchased him a Rolex watch that he had been wanting but kept putting off. We were getting close to the one-hour mark to meet the kids, so I left Bloomingdale's to find Marcus. There was also a pro golf shop nearby, so when I didn't find Marcus at Victoria's Secret, I knew where he was.

Just as I was walking past Neiman's, I spotted Nikki walking toward me. I couldn't duck into another store because she had seen me.

"Let her keep going, let her keep going," I kept saying to myself.

Nikki made a beeline straight for me. I can't believe this bitch is going to walk right up to me.

"Hello, Jennifer, we need to talk," said Nikki.

"Nikki, this is not the time or the place for a talk."

"I know, but when, Jennifer?" she asked. "I need a definite date. You can't continue to avoid me."

"You got a lot of nerve. You're not in the position to demand anything from me."

"Hey, ladies, you're getting a little loud," said Marcus. "And this is not the place to air your dirty laundry."

I turned to walk away, and Nikki grabbed my arm.

"Jen, I'm sorry I slept with your father."

A lady turned and looked at Nikki.

"Bitch, what the fuck are you looking at?" said Nikki. "You need to take your ugly ass to the Estee Lauder counter and get a makeover."

I just shook my head and laughed to myself. Same old Nikki. I got to admit, I did miss her bluntness and quick wit. She was by far the most tactless person I'd ever met in my life, but she's real—real bold, real tacky, and a real bitch. But what you see is what you get.

I finally conceded and said, "Okay, Nikki, I will call you the first of next week."

"Okay, Jen, that's fine, but believe me, if I don't hear from you by the first of next week, I will be at your fucking house knocking at your door, okay?" Nikki turned and looked at me. "Jen, I am so sorry for hurting you. Please forgive me. Happy New Year's, Marcus. I love you guys." And then Nikki turned and walked away.

We picked up the kids and took them to Carmen's for the night.

"So how was it?" I asked.

"Are you kidding, girl? I smoked a cigarette after that phone call."

"Hussy, you don't smoke."

"I know, but if I had one, I would have smoked it. Your cousin is an excellent orator, and I bet he can suck a mean pussy too."

"Okay, girl, I will take your word for it, and I will see you tomorrow. That's just way too much information for me," I said, laughing. "Happy New Year, Carmen. I love you."

She blew me a kiss and closed the door.

When I walked into the house, Marcus met me in the kitchen and ushered me upstairs.

"Go get in the tub and relax. I ran you a bath complete with rose petals and wine. I'll let you know when I'm ready for you to come down."

An hour later, Marcus came upstairs and told me it was okay to come down. At the top of the stairs, there was a trail of rose petals that led all the way down the staircase to the living room. The room was beautiful. It looked like Marcus purchased every rose in Minnesota. The room was like something out of an Arabian movie—giant pillows everywhere covered in multicolored silk scarves with candles lit everywhere. The room took my breath away.

"Sweetheart, when did you have time to do all this?" I asked.

"While we were out shopping, I stopped at the store next door to Victoria's Secret, and they do romantic parties, so while you were upstairs taking your bath, my little elves came in and hooked me up. Welcome to paradise, my love," said Marcus.

"Baby, you are so sweet, and I love the way you look in your silk pajama bottoms."

I almost had an orgasm looking at my handsome husband's gorgeous body standing there shirtless. I had to admit, Marcus did resemble Brad Pitt. That was one of the first things that attracted me to him, but at this moment, Brad Pitt was the last person on my mind. The only thing that was on my mind was the LD. "And for those of you ladies who don't know what that is, that is the long dick," I said to myself and smiled.

Marcus walked over to me and held out his hand. He led me across the room and positioned me on the pillows near the fireplace and got down on his knees in front of me. He pulled a box out of his pocket and proceeded to ask me to marry him again. Tears came to my eyes as he pledged his undying love for me. The ring was a four-karat diamond surrounded by emeralds. He took my wedding ring off my finger and put the new one in its place.

"Jennifer, you are the air that I breathe, my reason for living, and my life is incomplete without you. I wake up sometimes in the middle of the night, and I watch you sleeping so peacefully, and I thank God for you and Dylen. I want you to marry me all over again. This time, we will invite our family and friends. It will be the way you always dreamed it would be."

"Yes. Marcus, I will marry you again, but when do you want to do this?"

"Whenever you want, sweetheart, and you can spend as much as you want to have your dream wedding." Marcus got up and poured two glasses of champagne, and we made a toast to the rest of our lives together.

That night, our lovemaking was incredible, and I fell in love with Marcus all over again. His gentle touch, his soft lips, and the hard firmness of his body made me melt. Feeling his lips on my breast made my head spin, then he flipped me over onto my stomach. I felt him kiss the nape of my neck, and his tongue slid down the small of my back. I gasped for air as he entered me from behind and rocked my world. That night was magical, and I wanted it to last forever.

The sunlight coming through the curtain woke me up. I was curled up in Marcus's arms like a newborn baby. I rolled over and pushed my butt up against him. I could feel his hardness against my back.

"Hey, you, is that a pickle in your pocket, or are you just happy to see me?"

"Well, honey, since I'm not wearing any pants, I must be happy to see you."

"I think I can do something to make sure you're just a little bit happier," I said as I slid underneath the covers. I felt Marcus's body tense as my lips slid across his hard dick.

I had two orgasms before the third was interrupted by the phone.

"Who is this?" I said, picking up the phone.

"I want to talk to my daddy," I heard a little voice say.

"Okay, hold on."

"Daddy?"

"Yes, sweet pea."

"Daddy, I need five hundred dollars."

"What?"

"Marcus, what's wrong?" I said.

"Nothing, Jen. Sweet pea, what do you need it for?"

"Carmen is taking us shopping today, and I want to get something for Mommy's birthday."

"Okay, Dylen, but why so much?"

"Aunt Carmen said that Mommy wants a purse by somebody named Marc Jack or something like that."

"You mean Marc Jacobs?"

"Yes, Daddy, that's it. Aunt Carmen is going to put in one thousand for her and River, and I have to pay the rest. So, Daddy, please say yes. Can I have it? It is going to be from the three of us."

"Marcus, what is going on?" I asked again. "What is she saying?"

"Jen, go get in the shower. This is between me and my daughter. Dylen, that will be okay. Just come by before you leave, and I will make sure you have everything you need."

"Marcus, what was that all about?" I asked again.

"Dylen is planning a shopping trip with River and Carmen for your birthday present, and she needed some money. She is being all secretive because she wants it to be a surprise," he said.

"What are they getting me?"

"I didn't ask, so stop asking me."

"Why are they shopping so early? My birthday is over a month away."

"Jen, I don't know. Now bring your fine ass over here and finish what you started before we were interrupted, or go in the shower. Carmen said they would be here around one o'clock, so we have plenty of time."

After I satisfied my husband one more time, I took a shower and cooked brunch. As I was cooking, I started daydreaming about the wedding. Maybe it would be silly to get married again. We had been married for ten years, and Dylen was turning nine in April, so what would be the point?

"My god, how time flies," I said, thinking to myself.

We had been in Minnesota for almost six years. Six years and so much had happened in our lives. I was in such a daze I didn't hear Marcus when he walked into the kitchen.

"Baby, I'm so sorry, I didn't mean to startle you, but I think you forgot something." And he placed the ring on my finger.

I kissed him deeply and just looked at my wonderful husband. It made me sad to think I could not give him the one thing that he so desperately wanted: a son. I snapped back to reality when I heard the doorbell ring and the pitter-patter of feet coming toward the kitchen. Dylen ran in and jumped in her father's arms.

"Hi, Daddy," she said, laughing.

Marcus took Dylen and River into the study to give them the money, while Carmen and I talked.

"So how was the party last night?" asked Carmen.

"Wonderful. Look what I got," I said, showing her my new ring.

"Oh my god, Jen, that ring is beautiful. Girl, what did you ever do to deserve that, I wonder," Carmen said, smiling.

"Carmen, you are so nasty. Well, enough about me. Carmen, how are you feeling?"

"I'm good, Jen. Really, I am. I'm having fun with my new pen pal."

"Please don't tell me you're communicating with some fool you met on the internet?"

"No, girl it's your cousin Baltazar."

"I hope you're okay with that."

"Why wouldn't I be?"

"Well, you know you did go ballistic on Nikki," Carmen said, laughing.

"What about, you know, your condition?" I said.

"Oh, don't worry, I told him about my condition, remember? He was very sympathetic and supportive. He told me one of his fraternity brothers died of AIDS a year ago, so he's aware of all the bullshit I've been going through, and it helps to talk to him about it," said Carmen. "All the time we spent together at the ranch was nice. It's great having someone to talk to, you know, besides my girls. There were nights I couldn't sleep, and we would take long walks together. He would hold my hand. And, Jennifer, he wasn't afraid to touch me. Do you know how great that felt? To be touched by someone who knows my condition and is not afraid? I thought the romantic part of my life was over, but now I'm beginning to have those feelings."

"Carmen, I don't know what to say. I mean, have you talked about sex with him?"

"Yes, sort of. I'm not sure if you know it or not, but he is in his second year of residency, so he is well aware of all the risks. He even tried to kiss me, but I wouldn't let him. I don't want the possibility of infecting someone else on my conscience."

I was floored by all this. I never thought of Carmen being romantically involved with anyone either. I love Carmen; she's like my sister, but Baltazar is family, and I didn't want to see him hurt or risk his life in such a way.

"Jen, are you listening to me?"

"Yes, I am. I just drifted off for a second. I was thinking about the wedding," I told her as I lied to my best friend.

"What wedding?"

"Oh, I forgot to tell you, Marcus asked me to marry him."

"What? Jen, am I missing something?"

"That's right. I'm sorry I forgot to tell you. When Marcus gave me the ring last night, he asked me to marry him. The first time we got married, we eloped. He wants to get married with all our family and friends."

"How romantic is that," said Carmen. "Jennifer, I know you're probably worried about your cousin, but I like him, and I wouldn't do anything to jeopardize his life. I promise I will not let this get out of hand. I wouldn't want to put another human being through what I have to go through every day."

"So, Carmen, has Jennifer told you the great news?" Marcus said, handing Carmen a check.

"Yes, she has, and I am so happy for you both."

"Hey, Carmen, double or nothing if you tell me what you're shopping for," I said.

"Never mind that. Jen, you're just going to have to wait and see. Now go start planning the wedding of the century, and the kids and I are going shopping."

"So what does Mrs. Covington want to do today?"

"Well, first, we need to clean up this mess."

"No, don't worry about the house. Rena is coming over today, and she'll take care of it. So go get dressed, and let's spend the day together. We'll grab some lunch and then go buy some bridal magazines. By the way, Marcus, when's your dad getting married?"

"They are flying to Jamaica in August, so what we're doing won't interfere with any of their plans."

"Are we not invited to Jamaica?"

"Yes, we are, but it is supposed to be a surprise, so act surprised when Helen asks you to be her maid of honor."

"I will, Marcus, don't worry," I said.

We did a little shopping and met Carmen and the kids for dinner and a movie. All through dinner, Carmen kept texting on her cell phone. She was acting like a lovesick schoolgirl. It was cute to watch her.

Marcus looked at me and said, "What's that all about?"

"I will tell you later," I said.

As we were walking out of the movie, Dylen spotted Virginia and Syble. "Hi, Aunt Virginia, we went to see *A Bug's Life*," said Dylen. "What did you guys see?"

"*Osmosis Jones*," said Virginia.

"How was it?" I asked.

"It was funny," said Dylen.

I noticed Virginia was acting a little strange. She was looking around like she was hiding something. Just as I was about to ask if she was okay, a manly-looking woman walked up and put her arm around her.

"Sweetheart, aren't you going to introduce me to your friends?"

"Marcus and Jennifer Covington, this is my friend Jorden Parrish. This is my dear friend Carmen and her son, River, and this precious little busybody is Dylen."

"It's great to finally meet all of you," Jorden said. "I have heard so much about you."

Everyone was in shock and tried to regroup, but the awkwardness was very noticeable.

Marcus shook her hand first. "Well, Jorden, I hear you're an attorney? What firm are you with?"

"I have a private practice, personal injury mostly. Jennifer, I was told that you are a nonpracticing family attorney. And, Carmen, you're a teacher?"

"Yes, a nonpracticing teacher," Carmen said sarcastically.

"I'm sorry, ladies, I meant no disrespect."

"Sure, you did," said Carmen, and she walked away.

"Well, it was nice to meet you," said Marcus. "I'm sure we will meet again since Jennifer and Virginia are best friends."

"It was nice meeting all of you as well," said Jorden.

"Jen, I'll call you later on in the week. Maybe we can get together for lunch soon. I have missed you since New Mexico," said Virginia.

"Okay, V, just call next week."

Virginia kissed the kids, and they walked away.

"What the hell is going on with Virginia?" Marcus asked.

"I'm not exactly sure. She's been talking about this Jorden person for over a month now but hasn't really wanted us to meet, and now I know why."

"Jennifer, did you know Virginia was a lesbian?"

"Mom, what's a lesbian?" asked Dylen.

"Dylen, be quiet."

"But, Mom, isn't that when two ladies kiss?"

"Dylen, how do you know that?"

"I heard someone on TV talking about Ellen and her girlfriend."

"Dylen, we will talk about it later. Let's just get home so you can get in the tub and get in bed, young lady."

"Mom, can River stay over?"

"Yes, if it's okay with his mother."

We dropped Carmen off and took the kids home so they could shower and get ready for bed. The holiday break would be over next week, and they needed to get back on a schedule.

Marcus could tell I was stressed, so he brought up a bottle of wine.

"Jen, what's going on?" he said.

"I'm not really sure. Virginia told us about this lesbian relationship she had in college, but she said it was just a phase."

"Guess not," said Marcus jokingly.

"Marcus, don't be like that. This relationship can't be serious."

"Well, Jen, it looked pretty serious to me."

"You're to blame for this," I said.

"Me?" said Marcus.

"No, not you. Men, I mean. In the eighties, all men talked about were threesomes, and women gave them what they wanted. Then women realized that women ate their pussy as good as men or even better than some men. So now they are getting the same pleasure without all the other bullshit."

"Jennifer, that's ridiculous."

"I know, Marcus, I'm just joking, but you do have to admit, a lot of men are losing their women to other women."

"Honestly, Jen, why do you think that is?"

"I'm not really sure, but I think for years, people have been denying their feelings, and now it's more acceptable, so people don't feel the need to hide their feelings anymore."

The following week, Marcus set up an appointment with an adoption agency. The requirements were outrageous.

"Marcus, now I understand why there are still so many kids in the system," I said.

"Personally, I don't want our personal lives put under a microscope," said Marcus.

"Maybe we should just find another way," I said sadly.

"Jen, I know that you think I'm not happy because we can't have any more children, but I'm content. I just want you to be happy. We can look into other avenues if you like, but if it doesn't happen, I just don't want you to be upset," Marcus explained.

"I don't want to talk about it anymore, Marcus. Let's just change the subject. Did I tell you about Carmen and Baltazar?"

"No, what's going on? I did notice when we were at the ranch that they were getting pretty cozy," said Marcus.

"Well, she told him about her condition, and he doesn't mind. Right now, they're just taking it slow."

"What do you mean slow? How else can they take it, Jen? Let's be serious, I love Carmen too, but the fact is, she has AIDS, and I don't want her to be hurt. What kind of relationship could they possibly have?" said Marcus.

"All I know is, right now they're having some pretty hot phone sex, and he wants to come to Minnesota once he takes the boards and gets his medical license."

"I called my grandmother to make sure he was on the up-and-up. I didn't want him trying to latch on to Carmen because of her money. According to Grandma, when his fraternity brother got sick, Baltazar was right by his side until he died. I think it's endearing he wants to be Carmen's friend."

"Well, Jen, if they are having phone sex, it sounds like he wants to be more than just a friend."

"Well, I'm glad Carmen has a male friend. It will help keep her spirits up," I said. "You know, a man finding her attractive is good for her."

"I got an idea. Why don't we invite Carmen and the kids to a movie?" Marcus asked.

"If you wouldn't mind, honey, I was going to invite Carmen and Virginia to dinner. We haven't really talked since our vacation, and Virginia's got a lot of explaining to do about Jorden," I said.

"That's fine, Jennifer. Whatever. I can take the kids to the video store and maybe order a pizza. You girls could probably use some alone time," Marcus said caringly.

"You bet we do. I'm ticked at Virginia for letting everyone think Jorden was a man. We are her girls, we're supposed to share these kinds of things."

"It doesn't appear so in this case now, does it, Jen?"

"What do you mean, Marcus?"

"Look at the situation with you and Nikki."

"Marcus, that situation is totally different. That was just Nikki being trifling."

"Okay, Jen, if Nikki was trifling, what do you call Frank? And don't get angry, I'm just playing the devil's advocate here. Think about it. You're ready to write off your friendship with Nikki, but you are not ready to lay any of the blame on your father. He was, after all, an active participant."

"I know, Marcus, but I tried to explain before being cut off."

"No buts, Jennifer, I think you should bury the hatchet and give her a call. That's just my opinion, Jen. Take it for what it's worth."

I thought about what Marcus had said as I dressed for dinner. Maybe I was being too hard on Nikki.

We decided to meet at the Macaroni Grill for dinner. Virginia and Jorden were already there waiting when we arrived.

"Jen, I didn't know she was coming," said Carmen.

"Neither did I. Hi, Virginia, what made you decide to bring a date to girls' night out?" I asked. "No disrespect, Jorden," I said giving her a half-hearted smile. "These dinners are just for the girls. Spouses or significant others don't normally attend."

"None taken, Jennifer. Look, Virginia, I'll swing by and pick up Syble and maybe take her to a movie, okay? So you girls enjoy your evening, Jennifer," said Jorden, glaring me down.

"What the fuck was that, Jennifer?" asked Virginia. "How could you talk to her like that? I have never seen you be such a bitch to someone."

"Ladies, lower your voices. Everyone is looking at us," said Carmen. "Can we order some drinks and just calm down?"

"Look, Virginia, I don't have a problem with Jorden. I'm just curious why you let us believe Jorden was a man."

"I wasn't sure if the relationship was going anywhere, and I didn't want you guys to think I was going through some kind of phase just because my marriage had just broken up. I actually met Jorden six months ago at the gym. We became instant friends, and I was attracted to her physically. I started to think that maybe what I went through in college wasn't a fling and what I felt for women scared me, so I rushed into a marriage with a man I didn't love. After all, that's what my family expected: career, husband, and then a family. The truth is, I've always been attracted to women."

"Virginia, we don't have a problem with your preference. At least I don't," said Carmen. "My only issue is why you felt the need to hide it from us."

"I guess I was a little afraid, because you know how vicious Nikki can be."

"Oh my god, she is going to have a field day with this one," I said.

"Speaking of Nikki, Jennifer, when are you going to squash this feud you have going on with her? Life is too short for this shit," said Virginia.

"I'm dealing with my feelings, and I plan to call her next week for lunch so we can talk."

"You don't have to wait until next week," said Carmen.

"What do you mean, Carmen?"

"She and Beth will be here in about ten minutes."

"What? Carmen, please tell me you didn't invite her."

"When I called to invite Beth, they were together, so I had to invite her too."

"You better get your game face on, kid, because here they come," said Virginia.

"How are my divas doing?" asked Nikki.

Everyone hugged Beth and told her how happy we were to see her. We had not seen her since she left New Mexico.

Nikki hugged and kissed Carmen and Virginia. "Hi, Jennifer," she said shyly.

"Hello, Nikki," I said, forcing a smile.

"Sit down, ladies. Let's order some drinks and appetizers," said Virginia.

"Beth, honey, how are you doing?"

"I'm great, actually," said Beth. "Richard and I are still in therapy, and the baby is fine. I'm starting to eat more, which is a big struggle, but I want a healthy baby, and I'm willing to do whatever it takes. Richard has started to buy things for the nursery already. He's so excited," said Beth, laughing. "Jennifer, I just want to apologize for what happened at the ranch. I swear, I was not trying to kill myself. I had too much to drink, and I remember sitting out by the pool. The next memory I have is waking up with everyone standing over me and my chest hurting."

"Beth, we are just so glad you're okay," I said.

"We lost Gloria, and it would have been devastating to have lost you too," said Carmen.

"So, Nikki, it's your turn. What have you been up to?" said Virginia.

"Well, Bruce and I are fine."

"Did you tell him about you and Frank?" said Virginia.

"Why would I do some stupid shit like that? I didn't tell Bruce, and I'm not going to tell him," said Nikki. "I mean, girl, please, why should I tell him? Men cheat all the time, and the only time they confess is when their asses get caught. Isn't that right, Jennifer?" Nikki said sarcastically.

"Nikki, that was really low," said Carmen. "We're here trying to mend the relationship between you and Jennifer, and your pissy little comments aren't helping."

"Okay, Jennifer, what is your issue with me and your father?"

"I want to know the real reason you did it, Nikki. Did you just use Frank because you were curious about white men?"

"Jen, is that what you really think? Do you think I'm really that fucking shallow? Okay, you want the truth? Here it is. Bruce is going to be a father, but I'm not going to be a mother," Nikki said sadly. "That night, when I was in the hot tub, Bruce called. He told me that he had been seeing an intern from his office, and she told him that she was pregnant. She had threatened to call me, so he wanted to beat her to the punch.

"After I left the hot tub, I went out by the pool, and Frank happened to come by. We sat and talked, and he told me about your mother and how she was the love of his life. We sat there talking, and we bonded. After our talk, he walked me to my room. We were saying good night, and he hugged me. The next thing I knew, we were kissing.

"I didn't pursue him out of curiosity or some type of game I'm playing. He gave me what I needed, and I guess I did the same for him. Your father told me he had not been with a woman in five years, so this wasn't something he did lightly, Jennifer, and I honestly don't know what I would have done that night if your father had not been there for me. That could have been me floating in that pool, and I thank Frank every day for being there for me. He was a remarkable man and one of the most interesting people I have ever had the pleasure of meeting. I am glad I had the chance to bring some joy to his life before he died, and I won't apologize for that, but I am truly sorry I hurt you, Jennifer."

At that moment, I couldn't do anything but cry. I cried for Nikki's pain, and I cried for my father's pain of losing the only woman he had ever truly loved. Everyone sat there in awe as tears flowed down Nikki's face. Nikki was always such a closed, cynical person, and to see her emotions exposed like this left everyone silent.

Beth was the first one to break the silence. "Nikki, what are you going to do?"

"I don't know. I love my husband, but a baby? I hate that son of a bitch for not using protection. I guess it could have been worse. We could have ended up like Jeff and Carmen," she said sadly.

"How long has this affair been going on?" said Carmen.

"I don't know. He said 'For about two months.' He said when he tried to end it, she told him she was pregnant. He offered to pay for an abortion, but the little gold digger said she wouldn't. Bruce even offered the little bitch two hundred and fifty thousand dollars, and she still said no."

"So what does she want?" Virginia asked.

"I really don't know."

"Have you guys discussed the plans for saving your marriage? Because I have plenty of room if you need a place to crash," said Carmen. "You know it's just me and River, and you're more than welcome."

"No, Carmen, but thanks. I'm not letting this skanky bitch run me off. Bruce and I have been talking, and I really don't know what's going to happen, but I got some really expensive jewelry for Christmas," said Nikki.

"How can you joke about this? I would be a wreck if Richard cheated on me."

"Beth, I'm all cried out. I can't scream anymore, I can't cry anymore, I'm just empty inside. I just wanted to set things right with you, Jennifer. I never meant for you to get hurt, and I am willing to get down on my knees and beg your forgiveness."

I could see the hurt and the pain in Nikki's eyes as she tried to fight back the tears. "Nikki, I'm sorry too. I'm sorry for the way I treated you. I guess I overreacted a bit," I said.

"Yes, girl, you were a bit hard on a sista." Nikki laughed. "I think it's probably every man's dream to get some pussy before they die," said Nikki.

"No, Nikki, actually, I think every man's dream is to die inside some pussy," said Virginia. "Nikki, you are just as tacky as ever."

"I know, but that's why you love me so much," said Nikki. "Seriously, I haven't decided what I'm going to do yet. I know Bruce loves me. He always said we were going to grow old together. That's one reason why he didn't make me sign a prenup."

"Why would he make you sign a prenup?" asked Carmen.

"Girlfriend, Bruce is worth over sixty million dollars," said Nikki. "He signed a twenty-five-million-dollar contract when he went to the NFL. He only played three seasons before he got hurt, but he was smart enough to make it a condition of his contract that if he got hurt within the first five years of his contract, he would keep half of his signing bonus. He walked away from the NFL with fifteen million dollars guaranteed. After he retired, he opened his public relations firm."

"No wonder this little hussy is trying to trap him," I said.

"Hell, Nikki, girl, you are set for life if you divorce him," said Beth.

"Beth, I don't want his money. I want my man, and this little tramp is going to try to get rich off Bruce's hard-earned money."

"Nikki, my advice to you would be to stand by your man. Look at Marcus and me. Don't let one mistake—even though it is a big-ass mistake—don't let it ruin your life," I said, thinking back on Marcus's transgressions. "If you truly believe in your marriage and your man, then, girl, you need to stay in there and fight."

"You're right, Jennifer, and if it means being a stepmom, then I'll have to learn to change diapers. It does hurt me though that I won't be the one to give Bruce his first child. When Bruce was first drafted, I became pregnant, and I didn't think we were ready, so I had an abortion. We have tried since then to get pregnant but haven't been unable to conceive. According to the doctor, Bruce has a low sperm count, but I guess one of his little soldiers became a good swimmer after all," said Nikki. "Well, on that note, ladies, I think it's time for us to call it a night before we get put out this joint."

We kissed each other good night, and I was happy that our friendship was once again intact.

On the drive home, Carmen seemed really quiet and withdrawn.

"What's wrong, Carmen? And don't say 'Nothing.' I know you," I said.

"Jennifer, I try so hard not to dwell in self-pity, but it does get difficult at times not to. I sat there tonight listening to everyone talk about their love lives, and what do I have?"

"You have a wonderful son and great friends who love you," I said.

"It was a rhetorical question, Jen. I am thankful for the blessings I have every day, but I miss real intimacy. I've actually thought about contacting some of the chat lines that are for people living with HIV and AIDS, but I don't think I would be able to get into a real relationship with someone I met that way. What would we do? Sit around and see who dies first? Jennifer, don't worry, I'm fine, but if you don't mind, please allow River to spend the night. I could use some alone time."

"You got it, friend."

I walked Carmen to her door and kissed her good night. I was so sad for my friend.

"No one deserves this...Damn you, Jeffrey, damn you to hell for killing my friend," I said as I wept quietly.

The house was quiet and dark when I walked upstairs. I stood in the doorway and watched Marcus and the kids sleep. He had one in each arm.

Huh, the perfect family, I thought.

Marcus had his daughter and the son he would never have snuggled close to him, and with the number of junk lying around, it looks like they had a great time.

I moved close to him and kissed him on the forehead. He looked up at me through sleep-filled eyes and smiled.

"Baby, what time is it?" Marcus asked.

"It's twelve thirty and way past their bedtime."

"You go get in the shower, and I will get them settled," he said.

I let the water run down my face as I tried to hold back the tears. I cried for the son I lost and would never have. I cried for Carmen because I knew she rarely cried for herself, and I cried for River because I wanted him to remember how wonderful his mother was.

I finally got out of the shower, and I slid in bed beside Marcus and took in the scent of him. The last thing I remember was taking a deep breath, and I fell asleep.

The next morning, Marcus and I talked about Nikki's situation over coffee.

"Jennifer, you just don't understand what bad timing this is. You know last month when I told you Bruce and I were thinking of going into business together?"

"Yes, I remember."

"Well, we finalize the deal at the end of the week. This crap could jeopardize everything we're trying to put together. Being a sports agent and attorney is a very delicate operation, and we cannot be plagued with this kind of negative publicity before we even get the business off the ground. Has he tried to buy this woman off?" asked Marcus.

"Nik said he did, but she wouldn't bite."

"How's Nikki holding up?" asked Marcus.

"Well, she didn't torch his Benz, so I guess she's hanging in there," I said, laughing. "I have to admit, since she had her affair with Frank, she seems different. Her whole demeanor is different. Don't get me wrong, she is still tacky as hell, but she seems changed somehow."

"Jennifer, I need to try to contact Bruce to see what we need to do for damage control. I can't see this venture go down the drain because of some gold digger. Bruce and I really want to get this business going, Jennifer. You hear all the time about these agents and attorneys taking advantage of young kids and their parents who don't know the business. They invest their money poorly, and the next thing you know, they have an injury and can't play anymore, and one day they wake up, and they're broke. That could have happened to Bruce if he had not been smart enough to go to school and get a real education, instead of just taking a bunch of meaningless classes just so he could play ball. Jennifer, we wanted to be different, we wanted to make a difference, and now we may not get that opportunity because of this bullshit. We have got to find a way to get past this."

"Don't worry, baby, you will."

"Jennifer, I'm going to run to the office before you and Carmen leave, so give me about an hour, okay?"

"That's fine Marcus, but I hope you don't mind being stuck with the kids all day. Carmen is feeling a little low, so I thought I would take her to brunch." I kissed Marcus as he was walking out the door and picked up the phone to call Carmen.

The phone rang and rang, but no answer. I tried her cell, but still no answer. I slipped on some pants and went next door, but she didn't answer the door. Now I was getting worried. I ran back to the house to get my spare key.

"Mom, what's wrong?" asked Dylen.

"Nothing. You guys can eat some cereal, and then Daddy's going to take you to the park when he gets home. River, I'm going over to your mom's house to make sure she's getting dressed because we're going out to lunch."

My heart was beating fast as I ran across the yard and entered the house. "Carmen, it's Jennifer," I said, knocking on the bedroom door as I entered.

The bathroom door was open, but I didn't hear any water running, so I knew she wasn't in the shower. As I walked around the room, I saw Carmen's body lying on the floor.

I rushed to her side and grabbed her arm, looking for a pulse. As I shook her trying to arouse her, I noticed her breathing was shallow and how cold and clammy her skin was. I picked up the phone and called 911. I called Marcus and asked him to pick up the kids and meet us at the hospital. I stayed with Carmen until the ambulance arrived. The kids heard the commotion and ran to the house.

I was trying to hold River back as the paramedics tried to resuscitate Carmen.

I grabbed River and Dylen and held them tight as River fought to get away.

"Jennifer, I'm here to pick up the kids," said Marcus, looking on in shock. "Have they said what's wrong?"

"No, I left them upstairs, and I have been trying to keep the kids out of the way. Take them home and get them dressed and then meet us at the hospital. I'm going to ride in the ambulance."

I was fighting hard to hold back the tears and be strong, but it didn't look good, and all I could do was say a prayer for my best friend. On the way to the hospital, I called in cavalry and told them to meet me at the hospital. We arrived at the hospital, and they took Carmen away. It seemed like hours before the doctor came out and told us Carmen was suffering from respiratory failure.

"We will need to see the next of kin immediately," said the doctor.

"Dr. Weiner, there is no next of kin. Carmen's husband is deceased, and her son is only twelve. I have power of attorney to handle her affairs if she ever became incapacitated. I just don't have it with me. There was no time for me to bring it with me," I said.

"Okay, look, your friend is very sick. We're still running tests at this point, but it appears she has pneumocystis pneumonia or Kaposi's sarcoma. It's a rare type of cancer of the vascular tissue or internal organs. The problem is, we don't know how long she has been unconscious. The truth is, Mrs. Covington, we've put Carmen on life support. Her vital signs are very weak. We have her stabilized, but it does not look good. I'll try to keep you updated, but I must get back to her."

"Thank you, Dr. Weiner. River, come here. Now I need you to be real strong for your mom, okay? She is not feeling well right now, and the doctors are doing everything to make her better. Once they take her to a room, we might be able to see her, but until then, I need you to be really strong and say your prayers, okay? So you and Dylen go to the cafeteria and grab some lunch, and Aunt Virginia is going to come and get you in a little while, okay?" I kissed them both, and they walked away.

"Okay, Jen, give it to us straight."

"It's not good, girls. They have her on life support, and she has pneumocystis pneumonia. It's a lung infection caused by a fungus. The fungus can block the lungs from delivering sufficient oxygen to the blood. Virginia, if you don't mind, could you take the kids to your house? They don't need to be here, because we don't know how long it's going to be before we can see her."

"Sure, Jennifer, no problem," said Virginia. "Jorden is at the house with Sybil. Just keep me posted with any updates. Once I get to the house and get them settled, I'll try to come back. I know Jorden won't mind watching them."

Marcus and Bruce went to the cafeteria to get coffee as Beth, Nik, and I sat there and held one another's hands.

"Jennifer, I don't want to see that look on your face. That bitch is strong," said Nikki. "She's the glue that holds us together. After we lost Gloria, she kept girls' night going. She made us suck it up and move on, so we are not counting her out. So you and Beth wipe those tears from your eyes. Our girl is going to get past this," said Nikki.

The doctor came out again and advised us that Carmen had been moved to a private room and she could only have one visitor at a time. Dr. Weiner told us that Carmen had developed meningitis and a fungus called *Histoplasma capsulatum*. The doctor explained that the meningitis was causing the membranes around the brain to become inflamed, and the *Histoplasma capsulatum* was causing respiratory complications.

"The Kaposi's sarcoma is what causes the purple lesions you see on Carmen's skin, and it had spread to her internal organs. The bottom line is, your friend is in for the fight of her life," said Dr. Weiner.

"Doctor, I only have one request. Please, can you let us all go up to see her? We won't stay long, I promise, but we are all the family she has, and we want her to know we are here for her. Please, Doctor!" I begged.

"Okay, but remember, only five minutes," said the doctor.

We walked into the room and were not prepared for what we saw. Carmen had tubes in every part of her body. She was so pale and lifeless. A nurse was into the room with a hazmat uniform on. We had been given gloves and masks to wear, but none of us really wanted to wear them. The hospital insisted for everyone's protection that we wear the hazmat uniforms. Beth couldn't take it; she broke down, and a nurse took her outside the room to get some air.

The machine pumped air into her lungs, and a morphine drip kept her sedated. The nurse explained there was a feeding tube, a tube for antibiotics and her other medications, and a tube for this and a tube for that. I was getting dizzy trying to follow all the lines that were going into my best friend. I picked up her hand as I felt her lifeless body. She didn't make a sound. No eye movements; no, nothing. And I couldn't take it anymore, and I broke down. The nurse came back in to change the padding they had on her back, and it was totally bloody from the lesions.

"Jennifer, why didn't she tell us she was this bad off?" said Nikki. "I knew she was extra quiet last night, but I never thought she was going through all this. I really thought the medication was helping her."

"Some people suffer more misery from the treatment of the drug than they actually do from the disease itself," said the nurse.

"What do you mean?" I asked.

"The triple-therapy cocktail they had your friend on has some huge drawbacks. The multidrug therapy can be complicated. It requires the patient to take anywhere from five to twenty pills a day, and you have to do it on schedule. Some have to be taken with food, some without, and some cannot be taken with others. Just one or two missed treatments may cause the virus to develop a resistance to the regimen. Like your friend, a lot of patients find it difficult to deal with the side effects that the antiretroviral drugs cause."

"Nurse, what are some of those effects?" I asked.

"Well, nausea, diarrhea, headaches, fatigue, abdominal pain, kidney stones, anemia, to name just a few. Some drugs produce an increase in blood fat levels, putting a patient at risk for heart attack or stroke."

"Do they think Carmen had a heart attack or a stroke?" I asked.

"I can't answer that question. The doctor will be able to tell you more when her tests come back."

After the nurse finished, Nikki moved over to be closer to Carmen. "Look, Carmen, you can't leave me here to deal with these crazy heifers by myself. Plus, you're the only one that can keep me in line," said Nikki.

The nurse came in and told us it was time to leave.

Beth was sitting outside the door crying. I put my arm around her, and we walked away, not knowing what tomorrow might bring. We met Marcus and Bruce in the lobby. Marcus walked up to me and gave me a much-needed hug, and at that point, I knew he had bad news.

"Jennifer, the doctor came back out while you were in with Carmen."

"Just say it, Marcus."

"Baby, the news is not good," he said. "Carmen had a stroke, and with all her other complications, the prognosis is not good."

"Do they think she is going to die?" I asked.

"Sweetie, you need to prepare yourself for the worst."

Nikki burst into tears, and Bruce held her in his arms.

"Marcus, what are we going to tell River?"

"We're going to tell him the truth. He's a smart boy, and whether we tell him now or later, he's going to be hurt. So we have to be honest with him. I'm going to go over to Virginia's and talk to him and Dylen. The next couple of hours are going to be critical, and I know you want to be here at the hospital, so I will deal with the kids," said Marcus.

The hours turned into days and then weeks. After being in the hospital for two weeks, Carmen regained consciousness briefly. We had hope for the first time in weeks that she might come out of this episode. I went home for the first time in days to be with my family, but I promised Carmen I would be back in the morning.

I kissed Marcus goodbye as he left for his meeting with Bruce, and I left to drop the kids off at school. Nikki, Beth, and Virginia had planned to come to the hospital later that evening, so I decided to go that morning and sit and read to Carmen. That had been my daily routine for the last two weeks, because I didn't want her to think she was alone.

I was reading E. Lynn Harris's latest book; he was one of our favorites. Carmen had been off life support for a couple of days, and even though she was still on oxygen, she continued to slip in and out of consciousness. I was so engrossed in the book that I never saw her move.

"Bitch, can you please get to the good part? What is Basil Henderson up to right now?" she said in a low, gruff voice.

I smiled at her, trying to hold back the tears, but it was too late because I was bawling like a baby.

"Jen, I am so tired of this place," said Carmen.

"I know, sweetie. It's not exactly the Hilton. I've had about all the cafeteria food I can stand," I said, laughing.

"Where's everyone at?" asked Carmen.

"School and work. Girl, you know the routine. Christmas break is over, so it was time to get back to the real world, and I am so glad you decided to rejoin it."

"Jennifer, I know you don't want to hear this, but I don't have much time left, and there are some things I need to tell you. After my death, you will be contacted by an attorney with all the arrangements I've made. I want you and Marcus to adopt River. I have completed all the paperwork, and the only thing you need to do is sign if you're in agreement to become his parents. I know you love him, and it will be like giving you the son Jeff took away from you."

"Carmen, please, I'm not ready to talk about this. You are getting excellent care, and you can have rehab for the stroke, and you'll be as good as new."

"Jennifer, I'm just so tired. I'm tired in my spirit, and I'm tired in my heart. It's just time for me to say goodbye. So please let me finish. I love you so much. You're the sister I never had, and I have enjoyed our friendship much more than you will ever know. So I have to be honest with you of all people. I know you have hated Jeff for killing your baby and for what he did to me, but you're wrong. Jeff didn't infect me."

"Carmen, you don't know what you're saying. It's the morphine and other drugs they're giving you that's making you say these things."

"I know exactly what I'm saying, Jennifer."

"I read a text message from one of Jeff's partners he was having an affair with. I never told him that I knew he was sleeping with men. I just kept it to myself. Then one day while I was grocery shopping, I met this handsome young man, and we carried on an affair for six months before I decided to break it off. A month after I broke off the affair, Jeff's firm had a blood drive, and I donated blood. That's how I found out I was HIV positive. I was contacted by the blood bank and was told I needed to see my doctor immediately. That night, I told Jeff about the affair and that I knew that he had been sleeping with men. Jeff tested negative for several years, and the day before the accident, he found out that he was HIV positive. Since my affair, Jeff and I have lived separate lives complete with separate bedrooms. Jennifer, Jeff committed suicide because his lover threatened to go public with their relationship if he didn't leave me."

I sat there in shock as I listened to Carmen's deathbed confession.

"Jen, I'm sorry that I've let you and everyone believe Jeff infected me. I was angry with him about this new relationship and how it had threatened our livelihood. I just didn't want you and the others viewing me differently. I need to ask you a favor, Jennifer. Please don't tell the others. I mean, what good would come from it anyway? Just promise me that we will keep this just between friends?"

"Yes, I promise, Carmen. No one will ever know."

"Jennifer, I'm tired of hurting. My head hurts, my heart hurts, and I just want to sleep and not be in pain."

"I know, Carmen, but you will get better, and we will go out dancing again, and the pain will go away just like it has in the past when you were sick."

"Not this time, Jennifer. Just hold my hand tightly, and remember to tell River that I love him. I do not want this to be his last memory of me. When you gather up my things, you will find all the journals I've been keeping for him. All my thoughts and all my love have been written down for him to read and never forget me," said Carmen.

"Marcus and I won't let that happen, I promise."

Carmen closed her eyes, and I kissed her lightly on the forehead. I heard the machine flatline as my best friend passed away. Her pain and suffering were over now, and she was at peace. Carmen passed away on February 22, 2002, at 1:30 p.m., of respiratory failure; she was thirty-six years old.

The nurse came in and disconnected the machines as I sat there. "Mrs. Covington, would you like for me to call someone?"

"No, I'll take care of everything," I said.

"Marcus, this is Jennifer. When you get this message, please call me. Carmen has passed away.

"Hello, Nikki, it's Jen. Please call me as soon as you receive this message. Carmen just passed away, and I need you to please call the others and let them know."

"Hello, hello, Jen, I'm here. Wait, don't hang up."

"Hi, Nikki, can you just call everyone? I'm headed home so we can get together and make the arrangements."

"Jennifer, stay there. I will pick you up. You don't need to drive right now."

"Nikki, I'm fine. If you could just have everyone at the house around eight, okay?"

"Jen, I love you."

I told Nikki I loved her also before disconnecting the call.

The nurse continued to disconnect the machines.

"Nurse, can I have a few minutes alone to say goodbye?" I asked.

"Yes, ma'am, you can. They will be in to get her in about thirty minutes, so take your time."

"Carmen, I know you would not want us to dwell on this too long. You were always the one who used to say 'Just get on with it already.' Girl, who is going to keep Nikki in line now? You were always the voice of reason when it came to all of us. You were always so shy and unassuming, and I always loved and admired that about you. You were strong but demure, and yet you had the purest spirit of anyone I have ever known. My life will never be the same without you. Goodbye, my sister."

I don't remember leaving the hospital or the drive home. I went to Lake Minnetonka and sat for hours. When I finally arrived home that night at nine thirty, Marcus was a nervous wreck.

"Jennifer, are you okay?" asked Marcus.

"No, Marcus, I'm not okay, but I know eventually I will be. Where are the kids?"

"They're upstairs. I haven't told them anything yet. I wanted to wait for you, but they know something is wrong. Let's just let them get a good night sleep, and we'll tell them in the morning. Nikki, thanks for coming by. I appreciate you being here."

"Beth and Virginia were here, but it got so late they had to leave. They will be back in the morning," said Nikki.

I sat next to Nikki and held her hand. "Nikki, I don't know how much more I can take of this. First, Gloria, then Frank, and now Carmen. I know they say it comes in threes, but I can't catch a break."

"Jen, you are not in this by yourself. You can count on us. We have to be strong for one another, so don't do this to yourself. You have got to be strong for the kids, for yourself, and for the rest of us. We need you. I need you," said Nikki.

I think that was the first time I had heard Nikki admit she needed anybody. I kissed her good night and dragged my tired body upstairs to take a hot bath, but as usual, Marcus had beaten me to the punch. The tub was filled with water and his signature rose petals. I soaked in the tub and tried to imagine the effect of losing Carmen would have on River. He would need counseling to help him get through all this, I'm sure.

Sleep did not come easy for me that night, and I knew it would be a while before it would again. Marcus was supportive and tried everything he could to comfort me. He sat up with me until I fell asleep around 4:00 a.m. I don't remember what time it was when Dylen woke us up; I just remember her running into the room with tears in her eyes.

"Sweetheart, what's wrong?" asked Marcus.

"I had a dream about Grandpa Frank again," she said. "He told me to take really good care of River, because he is going to need me now that his mom is in heaven with him," she said, crying. "Mommy, did Aunt Carmen die?"

"Yes, sweetheart, she did," I said, tearing up. "We wanted to wait and tell you and River in the morning."

"Mom, it is morning, and River already knows. He told me two days ago when he was asleep, his mom kissed him and hugged him tight."

"Baby, that probably was just a dream."

"No, it wasn't, Mommy. He came into my room and let me smell his pajamas, and it smelled just like Aunt Carmen's perfume. Mommy, is River going to be my brother now?"

"Yes, baby, he is. Would you like that?"

"He's already like my brother, and I'm glad he is going to be living with us all the time."

"Okay, it's time to go back to bed, and we will talk in the morning."

"Mommy, it is morning, remember?"

"I know, sweetheart, but try to get just a little bit more sleep, because River is going to need us to be strong for him."

"You get some rest too, Mommy. You look really, really tired."

"Baby, Mom is really tired.

Marcus and I were dreading our talk with the children. When they finally came down the stairs for breakfast, they were holding hands.

"Uncle Marcus, I know what you're going to say, and it's okay," River said sadly. "I knew my mom was dying. We talked about it all the time. I know she is not in pain anymore, so I am okay with her being dead. Don't worry, I'm okay. She also told me you and Aunt Jennifer were going to be my new parents. I mean, if that's okay with you," he said in a little voice.

"Yes, River, it's okay with us. We would love to have you as our son."

The days following the funeral, we met with Carmen's attorney to sign the papers to make River's adoption final. We packed up the house and gave Carmen's clothes to Goodwill as per her wishes.

The house was paid for when Jeff died, so Carmen willed it to River. We talked to him about it, and he said he didn't want the house, so we decided to put it on the market. It was difficult for me to think of selling Carmen's house because I really couldn't see someone else living there.

We decided to take the kids to Hawaii for a couple of weeks before letting them resume their schoolwork. They went on with their day-to-day lives as though nothing had happened. I was worried about River, though. Whenever I tried to talk with him about his mother, he acted so indifferent. It was like Carmen never existed to him, but at night, I would hear him crying in his sleep. During the day, he went on with his life as normal, and that worried me, so Marcus and I had talked about getting him therapy once we returned home.

I also tried to be brave during the day, but most nights, I cried myself to sleep as well. Marcus would hold me until I fell asleep, but sleep never lasted longer than a couple of hours. I knew Carmen's dying was inevitable, but I wasn't ready. I guess, in all honesty, I would have never been ready. The days went by quickly, but the nights seemed to drag on forever.

The day came for us to return home, and the kids were exhausted. They slept the entire plane ride home. When the plane landed in Minneapolis, they looked surprised that the trip was over. We arrived home, and the kids ran upstairs to get ready for bed.

I called Beth to check on her. I knew she had been dealing with some bouts of depression since Carmen's death, and I was afraid she would fall back into her old habits of binging and purging. Just as I was about to hang up, Richard answered the phone.

"Hi, Richard, this is Jennifer. Is Beth available? We just got in from our trip, and I wanted to check on her."

"Jennifer, she is asleep right now, but she's okay," he said. "Carmen's death has been hard on her, but how are you doing?"

"Richard, I'm taking it one day at a time. That's all I can do right now, but thank you for asking. Tell Beth I called and I will try her tomorrow, okay? Take care, Richard," I said as I hung up the phone, and I went to the next call.

"Hey, V. This is Jen. I was just calling to let you know I was back from my trip."

"So did you guys have a good time?" she asked.

"It was good for the kids even though I didn't get much rest."

"Seriously though, Jennifer, how are you doing?"

"I'm good, V. Marcus hasn't left my side, but I can't continue to sit around here drowning myself in pity. Look, I don't want to hold you, girl. Just give Sybil a kiss for me and tell Jorden I said hello. I will call you tomorrow, okay?"

"Okay, Jennifer, just remember, I love you, and you are not alone in this. She was our friend too."

I didn't bother to call Nikki because she wasn't back from her trip to the Bahamas. I stretched out on the bed, waiting for Marcus to get out of the shower.

"Hey, you, are you asleep?" he said.

"No, honey, I'm just resting my eyes, waiting for you. Why don't you go get in the shower? And I will go get us a bottle of wine so we can sit and relax a bit. We can talk or watch a movie, whatever you are feeling up to."

"Marcus, I love you for what you're trying to do. But, sweetheart, I'm okay. Really, I am. It's just going to take some time," I said.

"Sweetheart, I'm just worried about you. You've lost so much in the last two years, and I'm concerned," he said.

"Marcus, I love you for loving me so much, but it will take some time, and I will be myself again. I promise."

I took a quick shower and lay down to rest. Marcus brought up some wine, fruit, and cheese. I didn't have much of an appetite, but I knew I needed to eat something. As I lay there enjoying my wine, Marcus decided to go and check on the kids. He had a strange look on his face when he returned.

"Baby, what's wrong?" I asked.

"Jennifer, I know those two are like brother and sister, but I think they are a little old to be still sleeping together."

"Marcus, I know, but they feel safe together, but if it really bothers you that much, I will talk with them tomorrow."

"Okay, baby, I will let you handle it," said Marcus. "Speaking of tomorrow, Jen, I need your signature on some papers that I had drawn up for River's trust fund. Also, when the house sells, we'll deposit the money in his trust, and if he manages his money correctly, he won't have to worry about money for his education or anything else.

"I was also thinking, Jennifer, that maybe we need to enroll them in a real school so they can start to be around other children and develop other relationships. I know River is going through a difficult time, but I think it's unhealthy for him to spend all his time with Dylen. They are getting older, and they should start getting into other activities, don't you think? Or am I overreacting?"

"No, baby, I don't think you're overreacting. I also think it's time for Dylen to get more involved in little-girl activities. As a matter of fact, I signed her up for Little League cheerleader tryouts. I just don't want her to be upset if she doesn't make it."

"Please, Jennifer, that girl has been in ballet and gymnastics since she could walk. There's no reason she can't make it."

"I know, but I don't want her to have to deal with the disappointment if she doesn't."

"I know, Jen, but it's a part of life. I didn't want to mention it, but when we were on vacation, River told me he wanted to sign up for baseball and then, in the fall, he wanted to play football."

"Marcus, that's wonderful. You will make a good father to our new son."

"Jennifer, this is a moment I've wanted for so long, and I can't wait to start enjoying it."

"Some of the girls who are trying out for cheerleading are meeting here this weekend, and I'm going to contact the parents and arrange a sleepover. I was going to suggest that you and River go away for the weekend. You guys could use some male bonding time, and maybe you can get him to open up a little."

"Honey, that is a great idea," said Marcus as he kissed me lightly on the face.

"I was just thinking, if you're not too tired, Marcus, I could dress up in my old cheerleader outfit and show you a couple of routines," I said, smiling.

"Are you trying to jump my goal pole?" asked Marcus.

"If you're not too tired," I said.

"No, I'm not tired."

"Well, come to Mama, Big Papa."

"Oh, you know I like it when you call me Big Papa."

The phone rang around ten o'clock when I was making breakfast for the kids.

"Hi, Nikki," I said.

"I hate fucking caller ID," said Nikki. "I was just calling to let you know we got back about one this morning."

"You're up already," I said.

"Hell yeah, I needed to holla at my girls. I was thinking, if you don't have plans with the kids today, all of us can get together for lunch. We really haven't spent any time together since Carmen's death, and I miss my girls terribly. Plus, I need to hear about your trip, and you can hear about mine and all of Bruce's baby mama drama."

"Okay, what time and where, Nikki?"

"Let's do P. F. Chang's, about two o'clock," said Nikki.

"That's fine. I will see if Marcus can hang out with the kids, and I will give you a call in an hour."

"So how are Nikki and Bruce doing?" asked Marcus.

"They're great, according to Nikki. We're meeting for lunch if you can hang with the kids this afternoon."

"Of course, that's not a problem. I really hope they worked everything out on vacation, because I don't need this million-dollar deal with Bruce to fall apart."

"Honey, I will give you a full report when I get back from lunch, so don't worry. What are you going to do with the kids?"

"We are going to the country club to play golf," said Marcus.

"Oh, Marcus, I hate that club. When Dylen and I go there for brunch, they treat us like crap when we're not with you."

"Who?" asked Marcus.

"Marcus, it's nothing or no one specific, exactly, and it's not everyone. It's hard to explain, really, so just forget it."

"Do you want to join another club?" he asked.

"No, honey, that won't be necessary. I don't go enough to complain, one way or the other. Just take the kids and have a good time, and I will see you when I get back," I said.

When I arrived at the restaurant, everyone was already there. My eyes started to well up as I hugged everyone. I missed Carmen so much, and all of us being together just heightened that emotion.

"How are my divas doing?" asked Nikki.

Everyone exchanged pleasantries, and Nikki ordered a bottle of champagne.

"So, Nikki, what are we celebrating?" asked Virginia.

"I am going to be a mother," said Nikki.

"You're pregnant?" asked Beth.

"No! Of course not. I'm going to adopt."

"Okay, Nikki, start from the beginning, because I am totally confused," said Virginia.

"Well, Bruce and I decided to fight for custody if it turns out that this child is his."

"What does the mother have to say about this, and is she still trying to sell you guys the baby?" said Virginia.

"Virginia, that is a horrible thing to say," I said.

"That's what it boils down to, Jennifer, when someone tells you that you can have their child in exchange for money," said Virginia.

"Virginia, calm down. We are not going to buy the baby from that tramp. We are going to take her to court and sue for custody."

"On what grounds?" I asked.

"Jennifer, the bitch is unfit, and she's trying to use her baby to make a profit, so we are going to use that against her," said Nikki. "Jennifer, what are you frowning for?"

"I don't know, Nikki, I don't like this. I understand what you're trying to do, and I know she's in it for the money, but that doesn't necessarily make her an unfit mother, just an opportunist," I said.

"Bitches, don't rain on my parade. I brought you here to celebrate."

"I'm not, Nikki. It's just that I'm a mother and I don't know what I'd do if someone tried to take Dylen from me or River, for that matter, but you're not a mother, so you couldn't possibly understand what I'm talking about."

"Thanks a lot, Jennifer," said Nikki.

"Nikki, you know I didn't mean it that way. All I'm saying is, it's hard to prove a mother unfit. There are crackheads who have retained custody of their children after clear evidence of neglect."

"Jennifer, I need you to believe in my cause," said Nikki.

"Why do you care so much what I think, Nikki?"

"I want you to represent me."

"Represent you? Nikki, do you know how long it's been since I've practiced law?"

"Well, better dust off your briefcase, girlfriend, because the reality of the situation is, you have just as much to lose as Bruce and I do. Because if this trick drags Bruce through the mud and ruins his reputation, Marcus stands to lose a whole lot of money. So get your game face on, girl, and let's eat."

"Nikki, girl, you need help because you have some issues you need to deal with," said Virginia.

"So, Beth, how much longer until the big day?" asked Nikki.

"Only six more weeks," said Beth.

"Do you know what you're having yet?" I asked.

"We're having a girl, and Richard and I are delighted," said Beth.

"Have you picked out any names yet?" I asked.

"Well, I suggested Carmen Aniyah," said Beth.

"Carmen would love that, Beth," said Virginia.

"Carmen Aniyah Ross has a nice ring to it," I said.

"I would have thought Richard would have wanted a boy," said Nikki.

"Not really, Nikki, but he did want the baby to be named after his mother."

"I can understand that," said Virginia.

"What is his mother's name?" asked Nik.

"Her name is Tallulah Mae."

"Tallulah?" we all said at once.

"Girl, who in the hell would name a baby Tallulah in this day and age?" asked Nikki.

"Nikki, Tallulah is not a bad name," said Virginia. "As a matter of fact, I think Bruce Willis and Demi Moore has a daughter named Tallulah."

"That old-timey-ass name? Virginia, please, that child is not going to like it when she is older," said Nikki.

"Beth, don't pay any attention to Nikki," I said.

"Was Richard disappointed that you wanted to name the baby after Carmen?" asked Virginia.

"No, not really, V. He knows how much Carmen meant to me, to all of us. He just wants the baby to be healthy," said Beth. "But enough about me. Jennifer, how is your new addition to the family doing?"

"Beth, he is wonderful, and Marcus is enjoying having another male in the house," I said. "I do worry about him, though. He gets so depressed at times, and I know he is thinking about his mother, and it is those moments that break my heart because there is nothing I can do to ease his pain. We arranged for counseling, and Marcus is keeping him busy with baseball practice. We're trying to get him to broaden his horizons and not spend so much time with Dylen. We agree that they both need to start cultivating other friendships."

"Jennifer, if you and Marcus ever need a break, Jorden and I would be more than happy to take them off your hands for a couple of hours or whatever," said Virginia. "Sybil loves having them around even though they are older."

"Thanks, V. We might have to take you up on your offer."

Nikki got this mischievous look on her face. "So, Virginia, tell us, how is that relationship going?" asked Nikki.

"What do you mean, Nikki?"

"I mean, Virginia," she said sternly, "do you ever miss men?"

"I don't think about it, really," said Virginia. "I have a very fulfilled relationship with Jorden. She loves my daughter, handles business, and is more committed to a relationship than Brian ever was. And just for the record, Nikki, I did Brian a disservice by marrying him, to begin with. My heart was never into that relationship. I married him because that's what my family wanted me to do. Now it's time for me to be happy, and if I'm happy and content, then Sybil will be happier. I don't think neither Brian nor I were ever totally vested in that relationship. We both wanted something different, and hopefully, he is happy, because I sure am."

"Virginia, do you ever miss him?" asked Beth.

"Not in the way you probably mean, Beth. I just wish he was willing to have a relationship with his daughter, but I can't make him want that."

"Virginia, I am glad you've found happiness," said Beth.

"Thank you so much, Beth, but I don't want your approval, just your acceptance. Now let's talk about your baby shower."

"You guys don't have to do anything. We already have almost everything we need, thanks to Richard's parents. My mother sends boxes full of stuff every other day, so we are pretty much set."

"Beth, we have to do something. This is such a wonderful occasion," I said.

"Jennifer, if you guys feel you must, then just buy some clothes. A girl can never have too many clothes," said Beth.

"Beth, when is your mother arriving?" asked Nikki. "Are you excited about her visit?"

"Kinda, sorta. My mother can be very overdemanding and overbearing, but to answer your question, she will be here in about three weeks."

"So why aren't you excited about her visit?" I asked.

"My mother was a pageant mom. She was always pushing me to be in this pageant or that pageant, never having time for what I really wanted to do. You know the type," said Beth. "So I'm a little nervous about seeing her, to be honest."

"Come on, Beth, you're a grown woman. Let's get serious for a moment. She can't make you do anything anymore, so why are you so nervous?" asked Nikki.

"Nikki, you don't know her."

"Beth, the truth is, most mothers who are like that are trying to live vicariously through their children, and the only power she has over you is what you give her," said Virginia.

"You need to let her know you want her support but that she is not going to run your life," said Nikki.

"I know you guys are right as usual, but wait until you meet her. My mother is the most overbearing, self-absorbed, selfish person you will ever meet in your life," said Beth.

"Beth, maybe things will be different now that you're going to be a mom," I said.

"Jennifer, please, this woman tried to pick out the color scheme for the nursery until Richard put his foot down."

"Beth, you're joking."

"No, Jennifer, I'm not. Don't get me wrong, I love my mother. She's always made sure I had the best of everything. Her family was very poor, and when she went to Spellman, she made a promise to herself that she was going to land herself a lawyer or a doctor. She made sure we only socialized with the best people, as she called them. I attended private school, and she made sure I was the perfect little debutante. I was Mother's little princess.

"My therapist says she is the source of my eating disorder. I didn't realize until I started therapy that perfection came with such a high price. My mother always expected me to be the perfect size 4, and anytime it looked like I was gaining weight, my mother put me on a diet. My mother made my childhood a living hell. I was miserable because she expected so much all the time."

"Beth, that's awful, but don't worry, we will be by your side the entire time, and if Cruella gets too far out of line, we will sic Nikki on her," said Virginia.

We all laughed hysterically, and momentarily, my mind drifted off, and I thought of Carmen. I missed her laughter, her corky sense of humor, and most of all, I missed her friendship. We kissed one another goodbye, and we waved to one another as we drove away.

That night, Dylen and I got things ready for Saturday's slumber party, while River and Marcus played video games. I was happy to see them bonding, and for the first time in a long time, our family felt complete. I had my daughter and my son. I wondered how River was really coping with the death of his mother. I was an adult, and I still missed my father terribly. I guess if you lose a parent, it doesn't matter if you're nine or ninety; the hurt is still the same. I wanted River to feel loved, but I didn't want him to think I was trying to replace his mother.

I had been sitting there staring off into space and hadn't realized River was standing next to me. He looked at me as though he had been reading my mind.

"Aunt Jennifer, I miss my mom too, but you're my mom now, and I love you and Uncle Marcus, so don't be sad," he said.

"I know you miss your mother, River, and I am happy she chose me to be your new mom. Now tell your sister it's time for you guys to get ready for bed."

The phone rang at 3:00 a.m., and it was Nikki.

"Jennifer, it's time. The baby's coming."

"The baby's not due for another six weeks, Nikki," I said.

"I know, but Richard just called me and said he was taking Beth to the hospital. I've already called Virginia, and she's on her way," said Nikki.

"Give me ten minutes, and I will meet you there," I said.

"Jennifer, what's going on?" asked Marcus.

"Richard just rushed Beth to the hospital. The baby's coming early."

"Do you want me to come with?" asked Marcus.

"No, sweetie, I'll call you later and let you know how they're doing."

"Honey, I know you're excited about the baby, but take your time, no speeding."

We sat in the waiting room; it seemed like hours before Richard came out and told us they were going to have to do an emergency C-section. Virginia called Beth's mom, and she said she would be on the next flight from California.

Two hours later, the nurse came out and showed us the most perfect little girl since Dylen, I thought. Richard came out next and told us Beth was doing fine and she was being taken to recovery. I called Marcus to give him the good news, and then we went to the gift shop to buy teddy bears and flowers. When they allowed us to see Beth, she was in tears from happiness.

"You guys must have bought every bear and flower they had in the gift shop," she said as she was being wheeled into the room. "It looks like a florist in here." She smiled.

"Beth, she is beautiful. What did you and Richard decide about the name?" I asked.

"We decided on Carmen Aniyah Ross," said Beth.

"That's wonderful, Beth. Carmen would be so pleased and so very proud to have her as a little namesake," I said.

"Beth, I called your mother, and she is on the way. Her plane should arrive at one thirty this afternoon," said Virginia.

"Thank you so much," said Beth. "But can I trouble one of you to pick her up at the airport?"

"Jennifer and I will do that," said Virginia. "I figure it would be good for her to see a familiar face. Richard gave me the key, so we are going to drop her things off by the house and then come straight here."

"Where's Nikki?" asked Beth.

"She went downstairs to get coffee. Girl, we have been here since three a.m., and you know how she can be without caffeine," I said, laughing.

"Honey, look, who came to see you," said Richard. "Beth, she is beautiful. I think she has your eyes and your lips."

"You're right, but I think she has your nose, Richard," said Virginia.

"Can we see the damn baby, or are you two going to sit there discussing body parts?" said Nikki.

"I'm sorry, you guys," said Beth as she handed the baby to me.

"I actually think she looks like both of you, and I just love her cocoa-brown skin," I said.

"Well, we know where she gets that from," said Richard, smiling. "Beth, we're going to give you guys some space, and Virginia and I are going to go pick up your mother from the airport, but Nikki is going to stay here with you until we get back, if that's okay."

"That's fine, Jennifer. I'll see you in a bit."

"Virginia, do you remember what Beth's mom looks like?"

"Yes, I met her when Beth and I were in college."

"So what's she like, and why is Beth so afraid of her, really?" I asked.

"Jennifer, the picture Beth painted for y'all about this woman made her seem like a nun compared to the way she really is. Well, first of all, her government name is Ruby Jean, but she changed it," said Virginia.

"Her government name? Virginia, what the hell does that mean?" I asked.

"The name she was born with, Jen."

"Oh, okay," I said.

"Anyway, when she went to Spellman, she went by Je'nae, and after marrying Beth's father, she had it legally changed. She made Beth's life a living hell. You know how the nouveau riche can be. Beth's father, on the other hand, is so down-to-earth. You are going to love him," said Virginia. "But Mrs. Winston 'Je'nae,' on the other hand, can test the patience of a saint."

We arrived at the baggage claim and saw a light-skinned lady with big hair, way too much makeup, and a fur coat on raising hell about her luggage.

"Is there anyone in this godforsaken airport that can help a lady with her luggage?"

"Ms. Winston, we'll help you," Virginia said.

"Oh, hi, Virginia, dear," she said with an uppity attitude. "Who's your friend?"

"I'm sorry, Ms. Winston, this is Jennifer Covington. She's one of our dearest friends. Sweetheart, that's Ms. Winston."

"One of my greatest accomplishments was marrying Lawrence Winston, and I don't need you diminishing that by calling me miss," she said.

"I apologize, Mrs. Winston. I meant no disrespect," said Virginia.

"Jennifer, is it?"

"Yes, ma'am," I said.

"Well, honey, if you don't have any visible disabilities, can you grab a couple of those bags? And let's get the hell out of here."

"Mrs. Winston, I thought you were only staying a week," asked Virginia.

"That's right. Why?" she asked.

"Well, because you have seven bags."

"Well, a lady has to have choices, doesn't she?"

Virginia opened her mouth to speak, but before she could say a word, Mrs. Winston said, "Don't speak, dear. That was a rhetorical question."

"Oh, I guess you're right," said Virginia.

"Who knows? I may decide to stay longer," said Mrs. Winston. "After all, Lawrence won't arrive for a couple of days. Jennifer, sweetheart, where's the driver?"

"What driver?" I asked.

"Didn't Richard hire a driver?" she asked again.

"No, ma'am, I drove," said Virginia. "Look, it may not have a driver, but it is a Mercedes," said Virginia, smiling. "I hope you don't mind?"

"I guess it will have to do. I do so appreciate your efforts, dear," she said with her nose in the air. "By the way, Virginia, how is your family, dear? And, Jennifer, I was saddened to hear about your father, dear. I know I didn't know him, but Beth does keep me up on her friends and their lives. I was also devastated to hear about your friend Carmen. That was truly tragic. Beth sent me a picture of your trip to New Mexico, so I feel like I know each and every one of you. Just remember, Jennifer, it's a healing process, and you will get through it in time, and your father's death will be a distant memory as well."

I looked at Virginia and gave a polite smile. "Mrs. Winston, I do appreciate your words of comfort," I said.

"And, Mrs. Winston, my family is doing fine. Thank you for asking," said Virginia sarcastically.

"Now, ladies, let's get going. My grandbaby is waiting."

We arrived at the hospital and not a second too soon. I was about ready to strangle Mrs. Winston, and if Virginia rolled her eyes one more time, I think they would have fallen out of her head. Virginia and I let Mrs. Winston out in front of the hospital and went to park the car in the garage.

Mrs. Winston stopped by the gift shop to get flowers, and we caught up to her just as she was getting on the elevator.

We walked into the room, and I heard Virginia announce behind my head, "Let the games begin." And I started to laugh.

"Darling, how is Mommy's baby doing?"

"I'm fine, Mother," said Beth.

"Well, don't worry about a thing. Mummy is here."

Oh my god, this woman overpronounces everything, I thought.

"Darling, where is Richard?" she asked.

"Mom, he went to the nursery to get the baby."

"Baby, I've asked you repeatedly to call me Mother," said Je'nae.

"Mother, sit down. Tell me how your trip was."

"Hello, Mrs. Winston, my name is Nikki."

"I've heard quite a lot about you, Ms. Nikki. You're the one who is always giving Beth a hard time, aren't you?" she asked with venom in her voice, but still sounding sweet.

"I beg your pardon," said Nikki.

"Beth tells me about all her friends."

"Mother, don't start, please."

"I'm joking with you, Nikki. I know Beth thinks the world of you, all of you, and please call me Je'nae."

"Je'nae? I thought your name was Ruby Jean?" said Nikki with this shit-eating grin on her face.

"No, dear, you are misinformed. My legal name is Je'nae."

"Okay, whatever, I meant no disrespect, Je'nae," said Nikki, and she looked at Virginia and frowned.

"Well, the flight was long, and first class was crowded, but I'm glad to have my feet back on the ground."

"Why don't we give you and Beth a moment? We'll just step out and get a cup of coffee or something," I said. "Mrs. Winston, would you like something."

"No, dear, I had champagne on the plane, but thank you just the same."

"Beth, if you need anything, we'll be right outside."

As we were leaving, Richard came in with the baby.

"Beth, she's awfully dark," said Je'nae. "I was so hoping she would have your beautiful light complexion and not Richard's."

"Mother, please don't start," we heard Beth saying as we made a quick exit.

"That bitch is a trip. I don't think I'll be able to stand her for the next week or so," said Nikki. "And please, who the hell wears fur in April? Nobody, that's who, unless you're a goddamn cat. I know this is Minnesota, but please, it's not that damn cold."

"Nikki, try to be nice," I said.

"I mean it, Jennifer. She has gotten on my last nerve already, and she hasn't been here thirty minutes yet."

"Well, you better get used to the idea of her being around for at least a week anyway."

"I can see why Beth's father wanted to come by himself, and I don't like the way she intimidates Beth," said Nikki.

"Imagine that, Nikki, you don't like Beth being intimidated, but you push her around all the time," said Virginia.

"Beth knows I love her, Virginia."

"Nikki, don't you think her mother loves her too?"

"Whatever, Virginia, but did you see the look on Beth's face when she mentioned the baby's complexion? That was so hurtful for her to say that shit to Beth. If that were my mother, I would have told her to shut her fake ass up," said Nikki.

After getting the coffee, we returned to the room to find Beth in tears and Richard arguing with Je'nae.

"Beth, are you okay?"

"Yes, Jennifer, I'm okay."

"If you're okay, why are you in tears?" asked Nikki.

"Beth's just being a baby," said Mrs. Winston. "I just said that I wished the baby had been a boy since it was born with Richard's complexion and nappy hair texture. Beth, you have gorgeous brown skin and nice long hair, and I just don't see that in your daughter."

"It doesn't matter, Mother. I'm going to love my baby regardless of what she looks like."

"Beth, I'm taking the baby back to the nursery so you can get some rest, and I'll be back a little later," said Richard.

"Are you taking Mother with you?" asked Beth.

"I hadn't planned on it. She can stay with you."

"I can't stay here, Beth. I need to freshen up and take a nap."

"Beth, I'll take her to my house, and she can stay in our guest room until you get home from the hospital. I know you and Richard need to spend time bonding with the baby. I will bring her back a little later if she wants to come."

"Thank you, Jennifer. I love you guys so much," said Beth.

"Jennifer, that is a splendid idea, dear. I would love to be a guest at your home," said Je'nae. "Beth, you get some rest, and I will see you either a little later or first thing in the morning, dear."

"Okay, Mother, get some rest. I will speak with you later," said Beth.

Je'nae walked away without even kissing her daughter goodbye.

"Virginia, can I get a ride home?" said Nikki as she kissed Beth goodbye. "Jennifer, sweetheart, you have my condolences, because I couldn't put up with the Wicked Witch of the West."

We all rode down in the elevator together, and I invited everyone over for dinner. "We can have an early dinner and plan the welcome-home party for Beth and Carmen."

"Who?"

"Your granddaughter, Mrs. Winston."

"Is that what they're really going to name the baby?" she asked.

"Yes," I said sternly.

"Mrs. Winston, is there a problem with the baby being named Carmen?" asked Nikki.

"No, I'm sure she did it for sentimental reasons, but I was hoping she would name the baby after me."

"Who names a baby Ruby Jean these days?" said Nikki.

Mrs. Winston snapped her head around and looked at Nikki. "Young lady, I have informed you my name is Je'nae. I had it changed before you or Beth was ever born, and I resent the fact that Beth told you my name was Ruby Jean. She had no right to even tell you that was my name," she said.

"Mrs. Winston, I meant no disrespect, but I think you need to know that you are hurting Beth's feelings with your comments about the baby," said Nikki.

"Well, I appreciate your concern, but Beth is my daughter, and you're just a friend, and I think you need to know your place when it comes to my relationship with my daughter."

"Nikki, let me handle this, please," I said. "Mrs. Winston, you have to realize that we are so much more than just friends. That's why Beth named the baby Carmen. We share a very special bond. We were all born an only child, and we couldn't have been closer even if we had been born sisters," I explained.

"Jennifer, I can appreciate your position, but Beth is still my daughter, and I must do what's in her best interest."

"Yes, ma'am, I understand."

"Jennifer, don't waste your breath," Nikki said as she stormed off the elevator.

"Remember, dinner is at eight, and I am expecting everyone to be in attendance."

"Okay, Jennifer, Jorden and I will be there. And, Mrs. Winston, it was good seeing you again," said Virginia.

"Virginia, dear, don't be so formal. I will see you for dinner tonight, and I'm going to be around for at least a week, so we will have time to catch up. I can't wait to meet your new gentleman friend. Beth tells me that Jorden is really nice and is an attorney too. What a nice catch for you."

"Mrs. Winston, Jorden is…Oh, never mind, you'll meet Jorden tonight."

"This is going to be a hoot!" Nikki laughed as she walked away.

"That is a strange girl," said Mrs. Winston as she was getting into the car. "Jennifer, dear, I don't mean to pry, but are things okay with you and Marcus financially?"

"Yes, why do you ask?" I asked with amazement.

"Well, Beth told me that he came from money and that you're both attorneys, so I was just wondering why you're driving your own car."

"Mrs. Winston, my husband and I don't view our social status that way. We raise our children to earn the things they get, and we try to provide them with a first-rate education so they will be able to be successful in life and choose their own path. We don't want them to be spoiled trust-fund babies."

"Dear, you could at least hire a driver, that's all I'm saying. That's a small amenity that most people with money deserve."

"Mrs. Winston, I'm just a regular mom. I drive an SUV most of the time that I use to haul the kids around in, and then I have this Mercedes that Marcus bought for my last birthday, and that's enough for me."

"Well, it's not enough for me. I have money, and I enjoy spending it."

"Mrs. Winston, don't get me wrong, I enjoy our life, but the love Marcus and I share and the values we teach our kids are more important than the money we have. I enjoy my Chanel sandals, my Prada and Gucci handbags, but I also shop for bargains just like the next soccer mom."

"If Beth had been smart, she would have married herself a rich white man."

"I don't mean any harm, Mrs. Winston, but why didn't you marry one?"

"Well, it was forbidden in my day, but I married a man who was light, bright, and damn near white. I wanted my children to have a chance in life and not be held back because they were dark skinned with nappy hair."

"Mrs. Winston, light-skinned and mixed kids have problems just like dark-skinned blacks. It's just a different set of problems. There is no sense of real belonging to one group or another. The blacks have a problem with you not being black enough, so you're always trying to prove your blackness, and the whites have a problem with you—period! So, Mrs. Winston, don't be complicit in giving your grandchild a complex about her skin color. I went through that my entire life. You just need to accept her for just being your blood regardless of how light or how dark she may be."

"Jennifer, that is easy for you to say because you have it all: that rich white husband and that beautiful daughter of yours with her curly blond hair. Honey, you have it made and just don't know how to take advantage of what you have."

"Mrs. Winston, I have love, and that's the most important thing to me," I said as I pulled into the driveway. I couldn't wait to get out of that car, where I was no longer subjected to this woman's poison.

Marcus greeted us at the door, and I couldn't wait to get rid of Mrs. Je'nae Raquel Winston.

"Honey, I would like for you to meet Beth's mother, Mrs. Je'nae Winston. She's going to be staying with us for a couple of days until Beth gets out of the hospital."

"Welcome to our home, Mrs. Winston," said Marcus.

"I wish all of you would call me Je'nae, just plain Je'nae," she said.

"Okay, Je'nae, if you will give me your bags, I will take them to the guest room."

"Thank you, honey. I'm not used to dragging bags around myself. We have servants for that. I understand. I grew up with servants also, but we try to maintain a certain level of normality for the kids."

"I know. Jennifer explained your theory of child-rearing during our drive home, but I am of the opinion that if you have it, flaunt it." Je'nae laughed.

"Mrs. Winston, I don't understand because Beth is not a materialistic person," I said.

"I know, sweetheart. She gets it from her father. He made the money, and I spent the money. I call it an equal division of labor," she said, smiling. Listen, kids, I just believe that if you have money, you might as well enjoy it, because you certainly can't take it with you."

"You're right, Je'nae. You can't take it with you, but you can invest it for future generations," said Marcus.

"I understand, but maybe we can finish discussing this over dinner. It's been a long day, and I need a good, hot bath and a nap," said Je'nae.

Marcus took all the bags upstairs, and I proceeded to help Mrs. Winston unpack and show her around the house.

"Je'nae, the guest suite is all-inclusive. You have your own bathrooms, complete with sunken tub and Jacuzzi. You have a full-length, walk-in closet, your own wet bar and mini fridge. You have everything but room service, so make yourself at home, and dinner is at eight."

I walked into the kitchen to find Marcus pouring a glass of wine and a scotch for himself.

"Wow, that woman is a barracuda. I feel so sorry for Beth and Richard, and you said she's going to be staying with us until Friday?" he asked.

"Unfortunately, yes."

"So, honey, what's for dinner?" asked Marcus.

"I was thinking of cooking chicken marsala, with spaghetti carbonara, garlic bread, and salad."

"That sounds great, honey. You need any help?"

"No, but I would like some company in the kitchen."

"Jennifer, what was on your mind inviting that ratchet woman to stay with us?"

"Marcus, you should have seen her at the hospital going after Richard and Beth. I thought Nikki was going to kick her ass. She was being mean to Beth, and Nikki stepped in to protect her."

"How is Beth holding up?" asked Marcus.

"She is a wreck. Her mother criticized the baby because she has Richard's complexion. Baby, it was horrible the way she behaved. Richard just got fed up and took the baby back to the nursery, and Beth just cried. That's when Nik jumped in and went after Mrs. Winston. It was funny as hell."

"Jennifer, I have to be honest, sweetheart, I don't know if I will be able to put up with her for an entire week," said Marcus.

"Honey, let's just take one day at a time. You're talking about the week, and I'm thinking about getting through dinner," I said, laughing.

"Nikki, Virginia, and Jorden will be joining us. This should be very interesting," said Marcus. "I'm going to make sure I have a ringside seat for this show," he said, laughing.

"You devil you," I said. "Have the kids eaten yet?"

"They had lunch earlier, but I promised them McDonald's for dinner."

"Well, if you take them for burgers, I will get started on dinner," I said, kissing my smiling husband.

I sat at the table at seven thirty, and the guests started to arrive.

"So where is that old bitch?"

"Probably still asleep in her coffin, I bet," said Nikki.

"Nikki, please be nice."

"I can't stand her treating Beth that way. I know Beth and I have had our differences, but she is still one of us, and I am not going to let anyone mistreat her. I don't care if Vamprilla is her mother."

Mrs. Winston came downstairs making a grand entrance, and Nikki rolled her eyes.

"Mrs. Winston, would you like a glass of wine? We are still waiting on Virginia and Jorden."

"I would like a martini dirty, if you know how to make one," said Je'nae.

"Well, I'm playing bartender tonight, and I make a fabulous martini," said Marcus.

"Mrs. Winston, how was your nap?" asked Nikki.

"It was okay, Nikki. Thank you for asking, dear."

"What was wrong?" I asked.

"Dear, don't get me wrong, I really appreciate your hospitality, but your bed is just a little too firm for my taste, but it will do for right now," she said.

"Excuse me," said Nikki, "but if I'm not mistaken, Jen and Marcus paid ten grand for that plush mattress."

"Nikki, why must you be so combative, dear?" said Je'nae. "I think you may have an anger management problem."

"Why are you such a bitch?" Nikki mumbled under her breath.

"Nikki, you seem to find fault in everything I do. Why is that?"

"Mrs. Winston, I don't mean any disrespect, but I find you very abrasive, and you seem to go out of your way to make everyone around you feel inadequate, especially Beth."

"Well, Ms. Nikki, thank you very much for that analysis, but unless you have children, you could not possibly understand the heartache of a mother when her child makes the wrong decision, and I really don't care to discuss my family with you. I happen to find you to be ill-bred, childish, and dumb," said Je'nae.

"Excuse me, lady, you don't know shit about me, but I will tell you this: I keep it real, and you're a big-haired country wannabe."

"Ladies, I think we really need to change the subject. I am going to get the door. And, Nikki, you can finish setting the table, unless you plan on burning Mrs. Winston at the stake," I said.

"Hello, ladies, did the party get started without us?" said Virginia. "I heard the yelling coming up the walk."

"Virginia, we weren't yelling. We were just having a difference of opinion," said Je'nae.

"In my opinion, you should mind your own business, Je'nae," said Nikki.

"I am done with this childish conversation, Nikki, if you don't have anything else to say, because I want to talk to Virginia and her friend. So, Virginia, is Jorden running late, or is he not joining us for dinner?" she asked.

"Mrs. Winton, I beg your pardon, but this is Jorden Parrish," Virginia said, introducing Je'nae to Jorden.

"I beg your pardon. But, Virginia, this is a woman. Does this mean you're a dike, Virginia?"

"No, Mrs. Winston, it means I am a lesbian."

"I do not understand," said Je'nae. "Virginia, you were married to a very handsome man, and you have a beautiful little girl."

"Mrs. Winston, I know it may be difficult for you to understand. It certainly was for my parents," said Virginia. "But this is my life, and people who love me are going to have to understand. If people can't be tolerant of my choices for my life, as well as my daughters, then they cannot be a part of our lives."

"Virginia, you could be a beautiful girl if you just lose a little weight. I think men would find you attractive again."

"Excuse me, Ms. Winston, but are your tracks too tight? Because Virginia clearly said this is her life, so why don't you let it go?" said Nikki.

"Nik, just let it go. She just doesn't get it. Anyway, dinner is ready," I said.

"Thank you, Jennifer, but I do believe I'm going to my room. I refuse to sit here and be attacked by Nikki."

"Je'nae, that is not necessary," said Virginia.

"V, let her go if that's what she wants," said Nikki. "She has done nothing but keep up hell since she arrived, and I'm tired of it. I feel so sorry for poor Beth."

"Well, Ms. Nikki, you are entitled to your opinion, young lady. After all, they are like assholes. Everybody has one," said Je'nae as she stormed upstairs.

"Okay, Nikki, I just passed Mrs. Winston in the hallway, and she almost knocked me down, so what did you do?" asked Marcus, smiling.

"Marcus, what makes you think I did something to her?" asked Nikki.

"I have been around you long enough to know your handiwork," said Marcus.

"Marcus, get out of here. She just better be glad I didn't throw some holy water on her, because that woman is dealing with some demons."

"Jennifer, if you get a tray together, I will take it up to her," said Marcus, laughing. "You women are a trip, you know that, Jennifer? The woman hasn't been here a day yet, and you guys are ready to tar and feather her. Thank God men don't have this kind of drama."

"Marcus, please, you guys have just as much drama as women," said Nikki. "Look at Bruce. If he had kept his drama in his pants, we wouldn't be in the middle of a paternity suit right now."

"I guess you got a point, so how is he holding up?" asked Marcus.

"How is he holding up? The question should be 'How am I holding up?'" Nikki said playfully. "But the answer to that question is, I'm holding up one martini at a time."

"Don't worry, Nikki, you guys will get through this. I have every confidence," said Marcus.

"I'm glad someone is confident, because sometimes I just don't know, Marcus. Is dinner ready yet? Because I am starving," said Nikki.

"Yes, it's ready. Now that I have fed Cruella de Vil, we can eat."

We sat down to eat, and dinner was a blast. It seemed like forever since we had sat down and enjoyed one another's company without any drama. Marcus stuck his head in the room and announced that Mrs. Winston had retired for the evening. He said his good nights to everyone, and then he went to bed. Nikki was, of course, the last one to leave as usual. We sat and talked about our lives and how much we missed Carmen. After about an hour, we said good night and agreed to meet at the hospital tomorrow at noon. Although Nikki was the queen of bullshit, I was glad to have her back in my life.

The afternoon of April 25 was warm and sunny with a slight Minnesota chill in the spring air; the flowers were starting to blossom, and the grass was turning green. Virginia and I decided to meet at the hospital at noon to check on Beth. Mrs. Winston had decided to sleep in and would take a taxi to the hospital if Marcus was unavailable to drive her.

When we walked into the room, Beth was already in tears from a conversation she had had with her mother.

"Beth, sweetie, what is wrong?" I asked. "Why are you so upset?"

"It's Mother. I just don't know how I'm going to get through these next couple of weeks with her. Everything I do is wrong, and she hates Richard and the baby," Beth said, sobbing.

"Beth, your mother is different," I said, searching for the right words. I didn't want to aggravate the situation. "Beth, I do believe your mother loves you and the baby, but she just has a different way of showing it," I said.

"Jennifer, I know she loves me, but she hates Richard, and how can I choose among my mother, my husband, and my child? She's always resented him, even though he is a wonderful husband and an excellent provider. I can't help it that I didn't fall in love with a light-skinned man."

"Why is his skin color such an issue with her?" asked Virginia. "All I can say is that this color thing is her issue, not yours, Beth, and you need to sit her down and let her know how you really feel. Let her know you would love for her to be in the baby's life and to be a part of your life, but it is not a prerequisite for your happiness, because you have your own family now."

"Enough about my problems," Beth said, wiping her eyes. "Tell me, Jennifer, how was dinner last night?" Beth asked.

"It was a fucking nightmare," Nikki said, walking through the door. "Your mother—and I mean no disrespect, Beth—but that woman gives new meaning to the word 'bitch.'"

"Jennifer, I am so sorry you have to put up with Mother. I know she can be a handful," said Beth.

"Beth, I feel so sorry for you. No one deserves a mother like that," said Nikki. "Je'nae is self-centered, egotistic, and downright cruel to people. She called Virginia a dike to her face last night at dinner, for God's sake."

"Well, ain't that the pot calling the kettle black?" said Virginia. "Can you believe it? We finally found someone even more uncouth than Nikki!" said Virginia, laughing.

"That's all fine and good. Go ahead, have a laugh at my expense, but we still have a serious problem: Mrs. Je'nae Winston," said Nikki.

"Nikki, stop talking about my mother like you're looking for the answer to germ warfare," said Beth.

We all started to laugh; it felt really good seeing Beth smile.

"So what's so funny?" said the voice everyone dreaded.

"Hello, Je'nae, how are you today?" I said as we exchanged pleasantries.

"I'm good, Jennifer. Thank you for asking, dear. I had your lovely husband take me to the Four Seasons so I could arrange accommodations before my husband arrives tomorrow. Lawrence has decided to fly in on Friday before Beth is released from the hospital, and that way, we won't impose on your hospitality any further, Jennifer."

"Oh, Mrs. Winston, it's no trouble at all, but I do understand that you miss your room service," I said, smiling.

Beth sat there watching her mother's theatrics and rolled her eyes. I could tell she was upset by the way her nostrils flared when she tried to smile.

Suddenly, we heard footsteps at the door, and we all turned around just in time to see Richard enter with the baby. Je'nae looked around the room as if she was looking for something. Everyone knew she was trying to ignore Richard and the baby. I could see the perspiration starting to form on Beth's forehead. I could tell she was holding her breath, waiting on her mother to say something hurtful.

"Well, Richard, is this little…What's her name?" said Je'nae.

"It's Carmen, Mother," said Beth with anger in her voice. "You know what the hell her name is," said Nikki sternly.

Richard just stood there with the baby, looking frustrated with Je'nae.

"Beth, you will not speak to me in that tone, and I do apologize for forgetting the baby's name. I will eventually get used to it," said Je'nae.

We all gathered around the baby to admire her beauty, and Je'nae just stood back watching.

"Mrs. Winston, would you like to hold her?" I said, extending the baby toward her.

"No, not right now," said Je'nae. "She's just so tiny, and it's been so long since I've held a baby, and frankly, I wouldn't remember how. After all, Beth had a nanny, and I rarely had to handle her at all."

"That's a shocker there," said Nikki, laughing.

"Well, maybe I will just go get a cup of coffee. The room is getting a little crowded," said Je'nae.

"There goes my mother, the most self-absorbed bitch on the planet," said Beth.

I could see the tears starting to form in her eyes, so I put my arms around her and tried to comfort her. I felt so sorry for Beth and what she was going through. This should have been one of the happiest moments in her life, and her mother was ruining it.

Friday finally came, and it was time for Beth to go home. Richard told Beth he had an important meeting he couldn't miss and that Virginia and I would pick her up from the hospital. When we arrived, Beth was sitting there with baby Carmen in her arms, and for the first time in over a week, she looked extremely happy.

"Hey, girls, thank you for picking me up. I wish Richard could have been here, but I'm just happy to be taking Carmen home," said Beth.

"Don't worry, Beth, he will be home as soon as his meeting is over, and just think, since your father won't get in until tonight, you won't have to put up with Je'nae alone," I said, laughing.

"Yeah, that is the upside, Jennifer. I didn't think about that," said Beth.

We arrived at the house just as Nikki was pulling into the driveway.

"Hi, Nikki, I didn't know you were going to be here," said Beth.

"Baby girl, I wouldn't miss your and baby Carmen's homecoming for the world, regardless of how I feel about your wretched mother," said Nikki.

"Be nice, Nik," said Virginia. "This is a happy occasion," she said, opening the door.

Once inside, everyone jumped out and yelled "Surprise!"

Carmen was so happy and startled that she started to cry.

"The biggest surprise is yet to come," said Richard, hugging his wife.

"What surprise?" asked Beth.

Out of the shadow walked Lawrence Winston, Beth's father.

"Oh my god, Daddy!" said Beth, unable to hold back the tears, bawling like a baby.

Beth's father held her in his arms and wiped away her tears.

Je'nae walked up to hug Beth and whispered in her ear, "Beth, pull yourself together. You have guest."

It was apparent that Beth's father adored her and that Je'nae was jealous of their relationship. Lawrence continued to hug Beth and then asked to see his granddaughter.

"Beth, she's beautiful," he said. "She reminds me of you when you were born."

"No, she doesn't," said Je'nae. "Beth was the most beautiful baby I'd ever seen. Even nurses said they had never seen such a beautiful little girl. She was flawless, perfect skin and a head full of the prettiest hair you have ever seen. My baby girl won 'beautiful baby' contest. She was so gorgeous."

"Je'nae, please," said Lawrence, "this is not the time or the place for one of your little tirades."

"Daddy, don't worry about it. I'm going to take the baby upstairs and lay her down for a bit," said Beth.

We followed her up the stairs, and when she opened the door, Nikki, Virginia, and I yelled "Surprise!" We had the nursery decorated with clowns and balloons in bright primary colors. Beth was so happy she started to cry again. We waited with her as she changed the baby's diaper and was preparing to go back downstairs when we heard Richard announce it was time for Beth and the baby to get some rest and say he appreciated everyone for welcoming his family home.

"Are you throwing us out of your house?" said Je'nae.

"In a manner speaking," we heard Richard say. "Look, lady, I have allowed you to disrespect my wife, our child, and our home, and I am here to tell you that if you can't respect our life together, then you can get your shit and get the hell out of my house. You're not going to treat my wife like this anymore, and if I ever hear you say another negative word about my daughter, I will kick your uppity ass from here to California."

We sat in the room giggling, listening to Richard tell off Je'nae.

"Where is your father?" asked Nikki.

"I don't know, but he is sick of Mother also and has been for years."

"Lawrence, are you going to let this fool speak to me this way?" asked Je'nae.

"Je'nae, just get your coat. We're leaving, and don't say another word until we're back at the hotel. Is that clear?" said Lawrence.

"Lawrence, I'm getting real tired of being talked to in this way."

"Well, Ruby Jean, I'm real tired too. I'm tired of the way I have allowed you to control me and drive our daughter away. You want to do this? So let's do it. I stayed behind because I needed some time to think. I needed to search my heart to see if I'd really had enough, if I could walk away from a thirty-year marriage and the mother of my child. Je'nae, your actions here today have proved I made the right decision. Consider yourself served," Lawrence said, pulling a white envelope from his breast pocket.

I turned and looked at Beth as a tear rolled down her face.

"I'm so sorry, Beth."

"It's okay, Jennifer. I'm just happy my father finally had the nerve to do it, that he is finally going to find some happiness."

"You mean, you're not upset?" said Virginia.

"Hell no, that bitch has had this coming for years, and I am so happy."

Beth slowly walked down the stairs toward her parents.

"Baby, I am so sorry this had to happen on your homecoming. This is not the way I wanted to do this," said Lawrence, half apologizing.

"Daddy, it's okay. I'm glad you finally had enough," said Beth.

"Beth, what are you saying?" said Je'nae.

"Mother, you have made Daddy unhappy as long as I can remember. You have made me unhappy my entire life, and I'm not going to allow you to disrupt my life and disrespect my husband anymore. I am sorry, Je'nae, that I wasn't the daughter you wanted me to be. I am sorry that I have been such a disappointment to you, but you can't hurt me anymore, and I will never, never allow you to hurt Carmen. Daddy, you're welcome to stay here. In fact, we would love to have you here with us," said Beth.

"We certainly would," said Richard.

"You ungrateful bitch! After all that I've sacrificed for you to have a good life, and this is how you repay me!" shouted Je'nae.

"I'm sorry, Mother, I didn't know I was required to repay you for giving me life. That was your decision, not mine."

"Actually, it was your father's, because I wanted an abortion, but he wouldn't allow it, so you see, you do owe me."

"Ruby Jean, that is enough," said Lawrence. "Now I have left you the main house, considerable funds, and the Jaguar if you don't contest the divorce. If, for some reason, you get it in your head to contest the divorce or the assets I have provided you, then I will make sure that you walk away with only the clothes on your back."

"What the hell do you mean?" said Je'nae.

"How fucking stupid do you think I am, Ruby? I have known about your liaisons for years. I think, as of the last count, you have had eight little boy toys in our thirty-year marriage, and I've had enough," said Lawrence.

"Daddy, are you serious? I am so sorry, Daddy, that you've had to go through this," said Beth.

We all stood there in shock as this little soap opera played out in front of us.

"This is better than *All My Children*," said Nikki.

Virginia just looked at Nikki and shook her head.

Je'nae stormed out of the house, and Beth gave her father a hug.

"Look, you guys, you need some time alone, so we're going to let you have your privacy," I said. "Beth, give us a call if you need anything, even if it's just to talk, okay?"

"Okay, Jennifer, I will. Thank you guys for being such wonderful friends," said Beth.

After leaving Beth's, we all went our separate ways. I went home to be with my family. Marcus had already started dinner, and the kids were in the kitchen being little helpers. Marcus and I sat there listening to the kids and how excited they were about attending a real school.

"It's about time," said Dylen. "We're practically teenagers. I thought I was going to have to leave for college to get away from Mom and Dad."

"Come on, sweet pea, we are not that bad," said Marcus.

"Dad, I hate it when you call me that. After all, I am twelve years old, for God's sake, and in a couple of months, I will be a pre-teen."

"Yes, Dylen, I am well aware of how old you are. I was there before and after you were born," said Marcus, laughing.

"Dad, we're just saying, we would like to be treated a little more like regular kids. We have been playing with the same spoiled, rich little kids since I was little, and we would like to start being friends with some other kids too. That's all we are saying, Dad," said Dylen.

"River, do you feel like this also?" said Marcus.

"Yeah, Dad, I do. Dylen and I have been talking about it, and we would like some other friends now that she is my sister."

I sat there giggling to myself.

"Why are you laughing, Mom?" asked Dylen.

"Baby, I'm not laughing at you. I'm laughing at the situation because your father and I just had this discussion a couple of days ago, and now you guys bring it up. I just think our babies are growing up."

"Mom, don't get all weird," said Dylen.

"Well, we have discussed it, and we will be enrolling you at Jefferson Prep next year," said Marcus.

"Dad, a prep school? Oh my god. You mean to tell me we're going to be stuck in a school with a bunch of prep school label jockeys?" said Dylen.

"Dylen, what does that even mean?" I asked, annoyed.

"You know, Mom, kids that are more concerned about the labels on their clothes than world affairs."

"Oh," I said, smiling. "Why don't we just get through dinner and pick this up again tomorrow? After all, we do not have to make a decision right away. You have one more month left in school and then three months of vacation before school starts."

"Speaking of vacation," said River, "where are we going this year for vacation?"

"Do you have somewhere in mind?" asked Marcus.

"I was thinking maybe Africa," said River.

"Africa? Are you serious?" asked Dylen.

"Yeah, I think it would be a great educational experience," said Marcus.

"I agree. I think it would be a wonderful idea," I said.

"Are you guys for real?" asked Dylen.

"Why? What's the problem, Dylen?" I asked.

"It's hot there, Mom. Do you know what that humidity will do to my hair?"

"And you have the nerve to talk about the label jockeys. Come on, little sister, you sound just like them."

"Brat," said Dylen, putting up her middle finger.

"Mom, did you see Dylen give me the finger?" said River.

"Okay, guys, cut it out," I said walking into the living room.

Marcus followed me out of the room, but not before I heard Dylen say "Mama's boy" and River respond "Daddy's whore."

"Guys, I can still hear you. Cut it out right now," I said. "Marcus, did you hear them?"

"Yes, Jennifer, baby. Don't get so upset. Brothers and sisters taunt each other. It's no big deal."

"I don't think I like the idea of my daughter being called a whore. I don't care if it is by her brother."

"Okay, honey, I will have a talk with River after dinner, okay?"

"Thank you, Marcus. I know he doesn't mean anything negative. I don't want our son growing up thinking it's okay to objectify women with degrading words like 'bitch' and 'whore.'"

"I know, Jen, and I am sure he will understand why he has such a prude for a mother," Marcus said, laughing.

"Can we just eat dinner already? Who knows what they will come up with next? First school, then summer vacation. I don't know if I can handle any more inquiries tonight," I said, setting the dinner table.

"Fine with me," said Marcus. "I have my mind on other things," he said, hugging me from behind.

"You always have that on the brain," I said.

"Don't even act like you don't like the soul pole," he said, smiling.

"Oh, I like it. I like it a lot."

"Would you guys please take it upstairs? It is so disgusting to see your parents making out. Plus, you're wilting the salad," said Dylen.

We decided to stay in Minnesota for the summer after all. Marcus was about to make partner at the conclusion of a very important case he had been working on. Dylen signed up for a summer gymnastic class so she would be ready for cheerleader tryouts in the fall. River had decided on a football camp and would be spending the summer in Florida. David and Helen were excited about having him there. They took him to dinner on the weekends and promised to take him school shopping before he returned to Minnesota. Dylen was jealous, but I decided to take her to New York shopping before school started.

Our lives had pretty much returned to normal, and Marcus found out he made partner just before the summer ended. We decided to have a party at the country club when we learned David and Helen would be attending. The kids had looked at several schools during the summer but had eventually decided on Jefferson Prep. River had made the football team, and Dylen was going to be a cheerleader, and they were both excited about starting their new school.

Nikki, Beth, Virginia, and I met at the country club for the final arrangements on the party. It had been a couple of months since we had spent any real quality time together, and I was excited about seeing them.

"Why in the hell would anybody want to have a party at this snooty-ass place?" said Nikki.

"It was just a matter of time before trouble walked in," said Virginia.

"Nikki, do you always have to be late?" I said.

"Yeah, Nikki, why are you always the one never on time?" said Beth.

"Actually, I'm late on purpose," said Nikki.

"Why?" I asked.

"Because that way, I miss all that chitty-chatty, pleasant bullshit y'all always do."

"What?" I asked.

"You know, that catch-up shit y'all always do before we get to the good stuff. Okay, prime example, tell me you haven't been sitting here for the last forty-five minutes looking at baby pictures of Carmen," asked Nikki.

"So what if we were, Nikki?" said Beth. "You trying to say you don't want to see pictures of my baby?"

"No, that's not what I'm saying, but did you forget, Beth, that you e-mail me every time Carmen poops? I have more pictures of her on my e-mail than I have of River, Dylen, and Syble combined."

"Nikki, baby, that's what proud parents do—we share the accomplishments of our children with anyone who will listen," I said.

"Okay, that's cool. I don't have a problem with that. That's why I give y'all your mommy time. No harm done. Now can we start ordering some drinks and tasting some food for this uppity-ass party you're having next week?"

"So let the games begin," I said.

Saturday came too quickly, and I was not prepared. I needed at least another week.

"Jennifer, baby, slow down. Everything is going to be fine."

"Marcus, this is one of the most important nights of your life. How can you be so calm?"

"Easy, baby. 'Never let 'em see you sweat' is my motto," said Marcus. "I just came upstairs to let you know I'm going to pick up Dad and Helen at the airport and the kids are going to ride with me."

"That's great. Now I'm stuck here doing everything myself."

"Jennifer, what else is left to do? The party is at the club there handling everything. You don't have to worry about entertaining Dad. He's only going to be here for the weekend. So, baby, go soak in the tub and just relax."

You would think I had never thrown a dinner party before tonight; I was so nervous.

"My god, you're as beautiful as the day I met you," said Marcus. "Jennifer, I want you to know I would have never been able to do all this without you by my side and believing in me." Marcus handed me a black box and said, "I want you to wear this tonight knowing I love you more today than I ever did yesterday."

I opened the box and saw the most beautiful Harry Winston wreath necklace that I had ever seen in my life. "Marcus, what have you done, baby? This is way too extravagant," I said.

"Jennifer, you deserve this and everything I could ever possibly give you and so much more." Marcus took the necklace and placed it around my neck. It matched the earrings he had bought me for my last birthday.

I wanted to cry, but I didn't want my makeup to run; I wanted to look perfect for Marcus.

"Mom, can you help me with my dress?" said Dylen, walking into my room. "Mom, you're gorgeous. Who knew you were such a knockout? Oh my god."

"Thank you, sweetheart. You look like a little princess yourself."

"I know, right? Dad bought me these earrings when he picked out your necklace today. They are real diamonds," said Dylen, all excited.

"You better take really good care of them, Dylen."

"I will, Mom. I promise."

Just as I was walking downstairs, I saw Marcus in River's room helping him with his tie. *Carmen would be so proud of her little boy*, I thought. "Aren't you two the most handsome men in Minnesota?"

"Just in Minnesota?" said River. "Okay, today Minnesota, tomorrow the world," said River laughing.

The night was magical, and everything was perfect. Marcus thanked the children and me in his speech, and he talked about things to come. As I stood there holding a glass of champagne, toasting his honor, I realized how lucky I was to have him in my life. I sat there looking at my handsome husband and thought that our life would only get better from here. We would be able to put all the bad things behind us and enjoy our life and our children, and that was something I so wanted in my life…real happiness.

The months seemed to fly by, but it normally does when you're happy, and we were happy. The children were enjoying being in a real school, and Marcus and I enjoyed watching them play sports. I watched River playing football as Dylen cheered him on, and I thought, *Life is as it should be*.

The time started to fly by as our lives returned to normal. All our lives had changed so drastically. It barely seemed possible that in a couple of months, baby Carmen would be six years old, and Sybil was turning eight. Jorden and Virginia had decided to have a civil ceremony to consummate their relationship, and Richard and Beth were trying to have another baby. Nikki and Bruce were even talking about adopting. Life was good, and I was enjoying every moment of it. I was even looking forward to the winter.

Winters in Minnesota can be brutal and beautiful all in one breath. The softness and the fresh smell of the newly fallen snow are always so breathtaking. The harshness of the cold winter wind against your skin could be brutal as well, but I loved it here. I couldn't imagine living anywhere else.

It was days like this that I would sit by the window and think of my life, my husband, and my children. How resilient kids could be. They experience tragedy, and they keep moving forward. It's adults who just can't seem to let go of loss, of heartache, and of pain. The last couple of years, we have all lost so much, weathered so many storms, but we have always remained friends. My friendship with Carmen was a friendship I counted on, one that got me through the bad times and helped me look ahead to the good times, and I missed her every day, but I didn't know how to help Marcus get past losing his father. David had turned into a wonderful father after Shelia died. His heart attack was so unexpected and left a great void in Marcus's life. I was so happy that he had the chance to see Marcus make partner. It was truly a proud moment for him.

"My god, where does it end?" And if you ask that question, you have to be able to look at your own immortality and accept the fact that you too will one day die. Regardless of the death of loved ones, life must and will always go on.

"You see, Carmen, this is why I need my best friend. After six years, I still sit here by the window and talk to you about the good in my life and the sadness and the shit that really try a bitch's patience," I said, smiling to myself.

The phone rang, snapping me back to reality.

"Hello. May I speak to Marcus Covington?" I heard a little voice say.

"I'm sorry, Marcus isn't available. May I help you with something?" I asked.

"My name is Marco, and my mother said she would let me call my dad since my grandfather died last month."

"Sweetheart, what is your father's name?" I asked.

"It's Marcus Covington, and David Covington was my grandfather."

"Is your mom around so I can speak with her?"

"No, ma'am, she's at work. I got your number from her address book."

"Sweetheart, what is your mother's name?" I asked.

"I'm sorry, but my mother said I should never give out personal information over the phone."

I couldn't help but laugh even though I had a knot in the pit of my stomach. "Is Pam your mother?" I asked.

"Yes, ma'am, my mother and father worked together a long time ago."

I tried desperately to hold back the tears and be polite. After all, my feelings had nothing to do with the child. "Marco, have you ever talked to your dad?" I asked.

"No, just my grandfather. He said I could meet my dad when I got older. I really miss my grandpa, and I just want to talk to my dad."

"Okay, Marco. Is this your phone number?" I asked.

"Yes, ma'am, you must have caller ID," he said.

"Yes, we do, sweetheart, and my name is Jennifer, okay? And I promise you I will have your father call you tonight, okay?"

"Thank you…Jennifer," he said.

I hung up the phone and called Helen.

"Helen, this is Jennifer, and I need to speak with you."

"Sure, baby, what's the problem?" she asked.

"Everyone's fine. I just needed to ask you something."

"Sweetheart, Marcus, isn't here. He's probably out tying up loose ends for his father."

"No, Helen, it's not about Marcus. It's about Marco."

"Marco? Baby, who is Marco?"

"I assume his name is Marco Covington," I said, but I'm not sure.

"Oh my god," she said.

"Helen, it's okay, really. I spoke to him when he called the house for Marcus."

"Jennifer, baby, don't be upset. David just thought he was doing the right thing. He found out about Marco four years ago. He had his DNA tested against his, and it proved he was a Covington. He sent money every month to make sure he has been well taken care of. He set up a trust for Marco so college will be paid for. He just didn't want this to affect your marriage and your life together once you had put the affair behind you. Jennifer, David loved you like a daughter, and once you found out you couldn't have any more kids, he thought you would be devastated to learn Marcus had a son."

"Helen, how could you and David keep this secret? Marcus had the right to know he had fathered a child."

"We didn't want some other woman to give him the one thing that you wouldn't be able to: a son," said Helen.

"I know you meant well, but it was not your and David's decision to make."

"I know, Jennifer, but we thought we were doing the right thing," she said right before I gave her dial tone.

Marcus finished his last-minute business and flew back to Minnesota. I was afraid Helen would warn him, but to my surprise, she didn't say a word.

"Hi, hun, I'm home," said Marcus.

The glass of red wine I was drinking had gotten hot a long time ago, but I still sat there in the dark holding it in my hand.

"Baby, what's wrong?" asked Marcus, kissing me softly on the lips.

"Congratulations," I said.

"On what, baby?"

"You have a son," I said.

"Jen, what the hell are you talking about?" asked Marcus.

"Your liaisons with Pam produced a son. His name is Marco, and David and Helen have been supporting him and his mother for the last four years. Marco called the house today to speak with you. He sounds…he sounds delightful," I said, trying to hold back the tears. "Here's his number where he can be reached," I said, handing Marcus the slip of paper.

"Jennifer, maybe this was Pam's way of extorting money from my family."

"David had his DNA tested four years ago. It would appear he is a Covington heir. Go figure, you sleep with that bitch once, and she produces a son."

"Jennifer…"

"Marcus, don't. I'm fine. I don't need your pity. I'm a strong woman, and I will get through this, just like I got through the affair."

Marcus took the number and sat down on the bed.

"Hello, may I speak with Pam?"

"This is she. May I ask who is calling?"

"You know who this is, Pam. Cut the shit," said Marcus.

"Why, Marcus Covington, isn't this a surprise. What brought on this phone call? You barely spoke to me at your father's funeral."

"Look, Pam, this is not a social call. I need to ask you a question. Do I have a son named Marco?" asked Marcus.

"Where did you hear that?" she asked.

"Pam, he called my house today and spoke to Jennifer."

"Marco, get in here!" we heard Pam yelling in the background.

"Jennifer, do you want me to keep her on speaker?" asked Marcus.

"That's fine, Marcus. I'm okay. I want to hear everything."

"Marco, did you speak to a lady named Jennifer today?" she asked.

"Yes, Mom, I wanted to talk to my father, so I got his phone number out of your address book."

"Marcus, I am so sorry you had to find out this way."

"Pam, why didn't you tell me?" asked Marcus.

"Okay, Marco, go watch TV. I will talk to you later," she said. "Marcus, look, after you left Florida, I had no way to reach you, so I contacted your father. I told him I needed to speak with you, but he would not give me any information. Then four years ago, I lost my job and could not afford to take care of Marco, so I contacted him again. We had the DN test done, and he has been supporting Marco ever since. He made me sign a confidentiality agreement that I would never tell you, and he would make sure we were well taken care of."

"So basically, what you're saying is, you let my father buy you?" asked Marcus. "You kept me away from my son for a fucking trust fund. How could you do that? If you were that hungry for money, I would have paid you and provided for my son."

"How would that little wifey have felt about you spending time with your baby mama? I'm sure she would not have appreciated you spending time with the other woman regardless of whether she had your son."

"Pam, you were never the other woman. You were a very regrettable mistake," said Marcus.

"So I guess that makes your son a mistake also," said Pam.

"You bitch, don't make me call you what you really are," said Marcus.

"What kind of way is that for you to talk about the mother of your child?" Pam said, laughing.

"Look, Pam, this is not about you, and it's not about Marcus," I said. "This is about Marco. It's about your son, because obviously, he wants to get to know his father, or he wouldn't have called."

"So the question is, where do we go from here?" Pam asked Marcus.

"What do you mean?"

"I mean, how do you want to handle this?"

"Do you want to fly here, or do we come there?" asked Marcus.

"Look, Marcus, I'm not sure. I will talk with Marco and then get back to you, if that's okay," said Pam.

"Pam, don't make this about money, please. I want to get to know my son," said Marcus.

"Marcus, what makes you think this is about money?"

"I just think that since my father is dead, you're going to need a new cash cow, because you know you can't touch Marco's trust until he turns twenty-five, if I know my father."

"Wow, it's always about money with you Covingtons," said Pam.

"Again, Pam, just speak with Marco and get back with us as soon as possible."

"Yeah," said Pam, and she disconnected the call.

Marcus turned and looked at me. "Jennifer, are you okay?" he asked.

"Yes, Marcus, I'm fine, but please, Marcus, don't make this about me. This is about a little boy who obviously needs his father, because his mother is a gold-digging whore who's going to use her son for every dollar she can get."

"I know, Jennifer, but I just want to make sure we're okay."

"Yes, Marcus, we're okay."

"Well, babe, you go get ready for bed because your man needs some attention. I really missed you and the kids."

"You need to go and say good night to the kids. They waited up for you. The kids…Marcus, what are we going to tell the kids?" asked Jennifer.

"The truth! Always the truth, Jennifer," Marcus said with conviction. "Don't worry, they can handle it," Marcus said with a smile.

"I hope you're right, Marcus. I really hope you're right."

The next morning, I felt tired and mentally drained. I was sitting at the table staring out the window, having my first cup of coffee, when Marcus came downstairs.

"Were you able to get any sleep last night?" he asked.

"A little, but like I said, don't worry about me, Marcus. I would like to know what the next step is, though, other than telling the kids, I mean."

"Unfortunately, Jen, I don't know. I mean, it's really not our call. The ball is in Pam's court, whether we like it or not. The only thing we can do is hope she does the right thing for our son."

Hearing Marcus say "our son" cut like a knife, but I tried not to show the hurt on my face the way I felt it in my heart.

"Jennifer, baby, I owe you such an apology. I can't tell you how sorry I am for all this and for any heartache this may be causing you."

"Marcus, like I said before, this is not about me. You just need to make sure things are okay for your son, for Marco," I said softly.

"Jennifer, would you mind the new addition to our family?" asked Marcus. "I was thinking last night that if it is okay with you and the kids, maybe Marco could live with us—I mean, if that's what he wants, of course."

"Marcus! Are you talking permanently? Do you really think Pam would just let him live with us?" I asked.

"I think for enough money, Pam would be willing to do just about anything," said Marcus. "I was thinking last night that if she is agreeable and if it's okay with you and the kids, maybe I would get full custody and you could adopt him."

"Marcus, that's an awful lot to ask of me at this point," I said, startled. "I mean, we don't know anything about this kid: his personality, likes, dislikes, anything. Don't you think that you're jumping the gun a bit, Marcus?"

"Jennifer, I was just thinking out loud, baby, but I would like you to give it some thought because this is what I want. I want all my children here with us."

"I knew you would, but let's not make this decision over breakfast, okay?"

"You're right, baby. We'll talk about it tonight after we tell the kids, okay?"

"Okay, Marcus, have a good day at work," I said, kissing him lightly on the lips.

I was making breakfast when the kids came downstairs.

"Ma, are you okay?" asked River.

"Yeah, Mommy, you do look tired," said Dylen, chiming in.

"Yes, you guys, I'm fine. Don't worry about me. Just get ready for school," I said sternly.

"See, now I know something's wrong because you have an attitude," said Dylen.

"Dylen, I don't have an attitude. I'm just cranky because I didn't sleep well last night."

The kids ate breakfast in silence, and I felt bad that I had snapped at Dylen. "So whose turn is it to drive today?"

"You're going to let us drive?" asked River.

"Sure, your dad and I have been discussing it, and we decided to let you guys take turns driving during the week, and if you do well, you may be able to get your cars before graduation."

"Okay, so what are we driving?"

"The Hummer, the Mercedes, the Jag, what?"

"Actually, you're driving the Denali," I said.

"The Denali? Mom, Dad normally drives the Denali. What up with dat?"

"'What up with dat?' River, we spend a hundred thousand dollars for you and Dylen to attend a private school, and that's the kind of language you're using?" I asked. "Back to your question, your father took the Hummer today, and there is no way you are driving the Mercedes or the Jaguar."

"Come on, Mom, please?" said Dylen.

"No, and that's final, and if there is a need for further debate, I will drop you off myself. Is that understood?"

"Yes, Mother, and I'm sorry. I can tell you're stressed this morning even if you won't say why."

"And, River, just for the record, you are taking English this semester, correct?"

"Yes, Mom. Why?" asked River.

"'What up with dat?' Baby, that's no way to talk. Do you really think they will let you into Harvard talking like that?"

"Mom, I think we've covered the English thing already, and can we please not get into the college thing right now?"

"Okay," I said graciously.

After the kids left for school, I decided to call Nikki.

"Hey, girl, what's up?" asked Nikki. "And what's wrong?"

"What makes you think there is something wrong?" I asked.

"Come on, Jennifer, after all this time, I know you, girl, so spill it."

"I do need to talk, if you have a minute?"

"Do you need me to come over? Because you know I will be there in a New York minute."

"No, all that is not necessary at this point, Nik. I just need a friend right now. Do you remember me telling you guys about the affair Marcus had right before we moved to Minnesota?"

"Yeah, what about it?" asked Nikki.

"Well, it has been brought to our attention that Marcus fathered a child with this woman."

"Get the fuck out," said Nikki. "Did he know about it and not tell you? Is that why you're so upset?"

"No, he didn't know, but I'm upset that he didn't use a condom. I mean, I knew back then he didn't. That's why I made him get tested every six months, but the thought of a child never entered my mind, Nikki. I'm not trying to put all the blame on her, even though it is her blame, because how do you sleep around with everybody in the office and not use some type of protection or birth control?"

"Because she was trying to trap the first unsuspecting man that came along," said Nikki. "So, Jennifer, how did you find out? Wait, she wanted money, so she called to blackmail Marcus?"

"No, Nikki, that's not how it happened at all, and can we please keep the dramatics to a minimum? Actually, she wasn't the one who called. It was his son, Marco."

"It's a boy? Damn, girl, so now he has a real heir."

"Nikki, people don't care about heirs and shit like that anymore."

"The hell they don't. Rich people do care about that, and Marcus's family was wealthy. You know, Jennifer, now that I think about it, bastards are not considered legitimate heirs."

"Nikki, don't call him a bastard. He is just a child. Besides, this is not about money. Marcus's father has been providing for him for four years and has already set up a trust for him."

"So why in the hell is his mother contacting you now after all this time?" asked Nikki.

"She's not the one who called, he is," I said again. "He misses his grandfather and would like to get to know his father."

"So what is the mother saying about all this?" asked Nikki.

"Not much of anything at this point, but I do know she has not worked since David found out about his grandson and started picking up the tab for her expenses. I talked to him, and he sounds really smart and quiet, charming actually."

"So what are you and Marcus going to do?" asked Nikki.

"We haven't discussed it in any great detail at this point, but we plan on telling the children tonight. If I know Marcus, he's going to want him to come and live here."

"If his mother is agreeable," said Nikki.

"Knowing her, I don't think she will object as long as there is something in it for her," I said.

"How do you feel about that, Jennifer?" asked Nikki.

"I don't honestly know, but I don't want Marco to be without his father any longer, and you know how much I love children."

"I know you do, Jennifer, but this is different. You would be raising your husband's bastard child from his tawdry little affair," said Nikki.

"Tawdry? Nikki, come on, it was never all that. It was more like a one-night stand," I said. "And for the last time, stop referring to him as a bastard."

"Can I help it if his mother is a slut and his father is an adulterer?" asked Nikki. "You are right about one thing: it's not the child's fault. But you know I always tell it like it is. Jennifer, really, though, are you prepared to raise another woman's child?"

"I don't know, Nikki. That's why I wanted to talk to you. You were almost in the same situation, so I wanted to know how you would have handled it."

"I don't know, Jennifer. That's why I'm so glad that the paternity test proved the baby wasn't Bruce's child. Child, you know that I am not gracious under pressure, so God knew not to try my patience with that situation," said Nikki.

"Nik, I can always count on you to keep it real and make me smile." I laughed.

"Hun, the best advice I can give you is to be honest with Marcus about how you really feel, and stop trying to be Superwoman."

"I'm not, Nikki. I'm trying to do what is best for this child, who did not ask to be born into this situation, and I'm trying to do what's best for my family."

"Jennifer! Girl, 'please take control over this situation before it gets out of hand' is all I'm saying," said Nikki. "And trust me, you do not want this little bitch coming back into your life and destroying your family. Please, one-night stands are not supposed to be this complicated. Believe me, I know."

"Let's not go there, Nikki," I said.

"What?" said Nikki.

"Remember Frank, Nikki?" I said.

"Oh yeah, sorry, girl," said Nikki.

"It's okay, Nikki. Girl, you know I don't trip on that anymore. You know you got your girls, Jennifer, and I don't think the kids are going to have a problem with having a new little brother. They're friendly and loving, and they will accept him with open arms, because they are not the typical, privileged, spoiled little brats, and you have yourself to thank for that."

"I've told myself that over and over again, and I really hope you're right, Nikki."

"Don't worry, Jen, it will be fine. Girl, I hate to cut you off, but I have a dentist's appointment, but I will call you when I get back."

"Thanks for listening, girl. I have a lot to think about," I said.

Marcus came home early for dinner, and the kids could tell something was wrong. The air was so thick you could cut it with a knife, but we tried to keep a smile on our faces.

"Okay, I'm not sure what's going on, but if you two are getting a divorce, I want to be emancipated, because I cannot choose between you guys."

"I second that," said River.

"No one's getting a divorce, little girl," I said.

"Okay, Mom, then what's going on?"

"Your father has something he wants to talk to you guys about."

"Okay, Daddy, let's hear it," said Dylen. "I mean, tell us something. What? Are we broke? We're going to have to go to a public school, sell the house? What?"

"Dylen, it's nothing like that, and if you pipe down and put a lid on it for two seconds, I will tell you," said Marcus. "This is difficult for me to admit to my children, but thirteen years ago, I cheated on your mother. We learned last night that you have a thirteen-year-old brother from this indiscretion."

"Get out of here, Daddy. You're one of the most honest people I know," said Dylen.

"I made a mistake, Dylen, and I'm just thankful your mother forgave me, but now we're all going to have to deal with the consequences of my actions."

"Mom, are you okay?" asked River.

"Yes, baby, I'm fine. Your father and I dealt with this a long time ago."

"So why are you just now finding out about this kid?" asked Dylen.

"Sweetheart, it's complicated. The only thing that's relevant to you and River is the fact that you have a brother."

"So is this kid going to come and live with us? Is that what this is all about?" asked River.

"I don't know, maybe, at least for a visit anyway," said Marcus.

"Dad, are you sure this is even your kid?" asked Dylen.

"Yes, Dylen, your grandfather had a DNA test done," said Marcus.

"River, you're awfully quiet," I said.

"It's okay, Mom. I mean, you guys took me in and adopted me, so I'm cool with it. It's the brat you're gonna have to worry about," said River.

"If you are talking about me, I resent being called a brat, and second, if it's okay with Mom to take care of Dad's love child, then I guess I'm okay with it."

"Dylen, watch your mouth and be more respectful of your mother's feelings," said Marcus.

"Mom, I'm sorry, I wasn't trying to be, you know, a bitch or anything," said Dylen.

"Yeah, Dylen, I know. It's okay your father and I put this behind us a long time ago, so that's not the discussion here. The discussion is your little brother."

"Oh, okay, so when do we get to meet the brat?" said Dylen.

"Dylen, I mean it. Enough with the sass," said Marcus.

"Okay, Dad, so what's the family discussion about? You want to know if River and I will have a problem if he comes here? Well, my answer is 'I don't care,'" said Dylen.

"It's cool, Dad," said River.

"Oh, Dad, one more question. Is he mixed?" asked Dylen.

"Does it really matter?" said Marcus.

"Not really. I was just curious. Dad, I didn't think you did white women," said Dylen.

I shot Dylen a look that could peel paint off the wall.

"Okay, Mom, okay, I'm sorry for asking that question."

The rest of dinner was full of whimsical remarks by Dylen, and I just couldn't take it anymore and went to bed.

The next morning, Dylen once again apologized for her remarks at dinner. "Mom, are you mad at me?" she asked.

"Dylen, I'm not upset. I just figured that was your way of dealing with the situation, so no, I'm not upset."

"Mom, are you really okay with all this?" asked Dylen.

"Yes, I told you last night that the affair is not important anymore, but the fact that it produced a son upsets me a little. Your and River's feelings are much more important to me. Besides, Marco is just a little boy, who deserves to know his father, his sister, and his brother."

"You're right, Mom, and I can't wait to meet Marco," said Dylen. "So when will he be here?"

"We're not sure yet, but you will be the first to know," I said, kissing Dylen on the cheek.

After a week of waiting to hear from Pam, she finally called and said Marco could come for Christmas break.

"Okay, Pam, whatever," I heard Marcus say. "If that's the earliest we can see him, I guess I will have to wait. Can I at least speak to him?"

"Yes, of course," she said.

"Hello, Marco, this is your dad."

Marcus seemed so excited to talk with Marco. I sat there looking at him while he talked to Marco on the phone. The conversation was short, and Marcus looked out of sorts when he hung up the phone.

"So is everything okay?" I asked Marcus as he hung up the phone.

"Yes, he's excited about coming here for the holiday and meeting his sister and brother. Jennifer, he's just so polite. It was like talking to a small version of me. He's the perfect little gentleman."

"I guess all the money your father spent on that fancy school paid off," I said sarcastically.

Marcus ignored my comment. "I wish he could come sooner, but his mother insists that he can't make it before the holiday. I did promise him I would call him once a week so he can get familiar with everyone, if that's okay with you, Jennifer," Marcus said excitedly.

"Yes, Marcus, that will be just fine. I'm sure the kids will get a kick out of that."

The week before Thanksgiving, Pam called to ask when arrangements would be made to have Marco picked up.

"Well, Pam, when is his last day of school?" I asked.

"It's Friday, the seventeenth of November, Jennifer," said Pam.

"Well, Pam, is he afraid to fly?"

"No, he's not, Jennifer. As a matter of fact, we fly quite frequently, thank you."

"Well, do you think he will be afraid to fly alone?"

"No, my son is fearless and very mature for his age. After all, he is a Covington," Pam said smugly.

"That's fine, Pam. I will let Marcus know, and I'm sure he will make all the arrangements this evening and get back with you."

"Make sure you tell Marcus that Marco is used to flying first-class."

"Yes," I said, hanging up the phone.

As soon as Marcus got home from work, I told him about my conversation with Pam. Marcus immediately called the airline made all the necessary arrangements. He called Pam with all the information and told Marco we would be at the airport to pick him up on Friday.

Marcus took off work on Friday, and we all drove to the airport to meet Marco's plane. The airline paged Marco and told him his party was waiting at baggage claim.

When we arrived at baggage claim, there stood the handsomest little boy. He looked just like Marcus.

"Hello, I'm Marco Covington," he said as he stretched out his hand.

Marcus introduced everyone, and he politely said hello. Dylen gave him a big hug and kissed him, and River tried to give him some dap.

"I'm sorry, but I'm not allowed to assimilate urban mannerisms," said Marco.

"Don't worry, dude, we'll change all that," said River.

Marco just stood there and smiled.

"So, Marco, where would you like to have lunch?" I asked.

"It doesn't matter, Mrs. Covington," said Marco.

"Sweetheart, please call me Jennifer."

"Okay," he said.

"So, little brother, how does it feel to find out you have a black brother and sister?" asked River.

"It's okay. I don't think about it, really. My mother told me my dad has jungle fever," said Marco.

Marcus smiled, but I didn't find it amusing.

"Marco, do you understand what the term 'jungle fever' means?" asked Marcus.

"It's when white and black people date each other or when someone white only likes things that are black," he said.

"Not actually," said Marcus. "But we will discuss it later."

"So are you saying you don't like blacks?" asked Dylen.

"Dylen, don't start this," I said.

"Mom, I'm not. I'm just saying that if he has a problem with us being black, he probably shouldn't have come," said Dylen.

"No, Dylen, I don't have a problem with black people. I love that you're my sister, and I'm sorry if I hurt your feelings," said Marco.

"No, it's cool, Marco. This is as strange for us as it is for you, but believe it or not, we do have the same father," said Dylen.

"Yeah, I know," said Marco, smiling.

I sat through lunch thinking what a remarkable little boy Marco was. He sat through lunch answering all of Dylen's prying questions with the style and grace of a true Covington, and a part of me was overwhelmed with his presence. Watching him made my heart melt and made me want to love him.

Dinner was better than lunch, and the kids seemed to settle down and get used to the idea of having Marco around. They even made plans to take Marco to the movies to see *Harry Potter and the Goblet of Fire*.

"Why did you choose that movie?" I asked Dylen.

"Because, Mom, I just thought Marco would like it better. Let's face it, you can't get any whiter than that," said Dylen.

I shot her a look, and she rolled her eyes.

"Actually, I would prefer to see *Are We There Yet?* when it comes out," said Marco.

"Way to go, bro," said River.

"I thought your mother didn't like you to assimilate black culture? Doesn't that include black movies?" said Dylen.

"I don't know. We never talk about black stuff," said Marco.

"Black stuff? What the hell does that mean?" said Dylen.

"Dylen, I'm not going to tell you again to watch your mouth," I said. "You're starting to come off really rude, and I'm tired of it," I said.

"That's fine, Mother. I will let the bros hang out together. I just want to go home," said Dylen.

Marcus looked at me and said, "This is going to be a problem."

Marcus decided to take the boys to the movies, and I stayed home with Dylen to have a little mother-daughter bonding time.

"Mom, I'm sorry, but how am I supposed to accept a brother who acts like he doesn't like the black culture?" asked Dylen. "As a biracial person, I've had to put up with this all my life, but now I have to put up with it from someone who is supposed to be my brother? This is bullshit."

"Dylen, watch your language, young lady."

"I'm serious, Mom, and he probably has that superior attitude because he is all white and we're not."

"Dylen, just give him a chance, please. This is our first holiday together, and I just want everyone to have a good time. So promise me you will be on your best behavior?"

"I will, Mom, dang," said Dylen with an attitude.

The holidays were fabulous. The kids seemed to be getting along, and I think they really bonded by the end of the holiday vacation. Marco had become a real part of the family, and the kids hated to see him go. As we drove him to the airport, I could see the tears well up in his eyes as I looked at him in the mirror.

"It's okay, Marco. You are welcome to come back anytime you get ready," I said.

"Thank you, Jennifer. That is really nice of you."

"Don't worry, bro, we'll talk at least once a week," said River.

"Yeah, brat, don't worry, we'll let you come back. As a matter of fact, why don't you ask your mom if you can come and live with us," said Dylen.

"Are you serious? You guys wouldn't mind if I came to live with you?" asked Marco. "I really would like to live here, if that is okay. That's funny, because I've been thinking about asking my mom if I can come back and live with you guys."

"Marco, we haven't talked about this, but why didn't you say anything to Jennifer or even to me?" said Marcus.

"I don't know, Dad, I guess I was scared. I really would like to live with you on a permanent basis. To tell the truth, Dad, I don't think my mom would even miss me. Dad, I would be willing to give her all the money in my trust fund and the entire money Grandpa left me if she would just let me stay with you," said Marco.

"Marco, I don't want you to worry about any of this, okay? Jen and I will handle this. And, son, you don't have to worry. We will work something out."

We put Marco on the plane, and we all kissed him goodbye. The drive home was quiet, and everyone was sad.

"Mom, do you think Marco could really come and live with us?" asked River. "Dude was so happy here."

"Plus, he knows his mother is a gold digger and only had him for the money," said Dylen.

"Dylen, why would you say such a thing?" I asked.

"I said it because it is true. Marco overheard his mother talking to Granddaddy about how she never wanted him anyway and if she couldn't get any financial help, she would give him up for adoption."

"My son heard his mother say that?" asked Marcus.

"Yes, Daddy, I promise. He told me and Dylen that one night when we were watching TV in the living room," said River.

"He's miserable there. He didn't want to go back," said Dylen.

"Okay, kids, your mother and I are going to talk about Marco's situation, and we're going to make the best decision for him and all of us, so don't worry, okay?"

When I entered the bedroom, I could hear Marcus talking to Pam.

"How much is it going to cost me for you to hand over my son?" said Marcus. "That much, huh? It was always about money with you, wasn't it, Pam? Why can't you do this because it's what's best for Marco? You can't be much of a mother if you would agree to sell your own son just so you don't have to work.

"I will have the papers drawn up tomorrow for the adoption. You will relinquish all your rights, and I will have two million dollars transferred to your account once I have been notified that the papers have been signed and filed with the courts. I will also instruct my attorney to pay off your mortgage and your car. After that is completed, I never want to hear from you again.

"If Marco ever wants to see you again, that's fine, but it will be his decision and on his terms. And if you're wondering what brought all this on, it was your son. He overheard you telling his grandfather that if you did not get money for him, then you would put him up for adoption. Now everyone wins. He will be adopted in a family who loves him, and you will get your money. I will have a ticket waiting on him when he gets to the airport. You make damn sure you have him there, or you will regret the day you ever messed with me. Now stay the fuck out of our lives," said Marcus as he slammed down the phone.

"Jennifer, I'm sorry I didn't discuss this with you first, but I needed to do what was best for Marco. I made the decision because somehow I knew you wouldn't mind."

"Marcus, I don't mind. I know that child is miserable with that woman, and the kids love him, so it's perfect."

Marco returned a week later, and we got him registered for school the very next day. The kids at Jefferson were a little shocked when the kids introduced Marco as their brother. They didn't mind, especially River. He thought it was cool having a little brother.

I met Virginia and Nikki for lunch, and Nikki, being her usual self, could not refrain from making wise cracks about Marco being Marcus's love child.

"So what does he think about being around so many black folks?" asked Nikki.

"I asked him once if it was going to be an issue, and he said no, he was proud to be a Covington and be a part of such a culturally diverse family."

"He is something else," said Virginia.

"I can't believe that little Ms. Priss accepted him so easily, though," said Nikki. "After all, she had the only real Covington heir for so long."

"Nikki, my children don't think about things like that."

"Please, Jennifer, get real. Kids that come from money always think about things like that," said Nikki. "And if you ladies don't mind, I am ready to order. I need some buffalo wings or something. Damn, I'm starving. By the way, how are Beth and her two little rug rats doing?"

"They're great, Nikki. I was over there yesterday, and little Richard is getting so big."

"Child, I know damn well they are not planning on calling that boy Li'l Richard," Nikki said, laughing.

"Speaking of babies, when are you and Bruce going to have a little crumb snatcher?" asked Virginia, laughing. "Oh my god, girl, I am so sorry, Nikki, for being insensitive."

"Girl, you're fine," said Nikki. "Actually, we have stopped trying. I mean, if it happens, it happens, and if not, maybe we'll try adoption. I don't know, but it is not something I spend a whole lot of time worrying about, to tell you the truth. Where the hell is that bitch with my wings?"

"Girl, will you calm down? Damn," said Virginia.

I sat there shaking my head; it was so good to be with my girls. During lunch, I realized how much.

People always say time flies when you're having fun, and the kids were having fun. Six months had gone by already, and Marco no longer felt like he was a guest. He was right at home with the other kids. He no longer asked if he could eat snacks or drink sodas. He just went into the refrigerator and got them like the other kids. I no longer thought of him as Pam and Marcus's son. He was my son, and I loved him.

As we sat there at the dinner table, I watched the kids laughing and talking, and I decided to bring up the subject of summer vacation. As usual, Dylen wanted to go to an island. River wanted to go to an amusement park, and Marco wanted to do something educational.

"Well, whatever we decide to do, you need to take into consideration football camp and cheerleading camp and all the other activities you kids have going on during the summer. Marco, is there anything special you would like to do for the summer?" asked Marcus.

"Well, Dad, I did pick up a brochure at school regarding space camp."

"Space camp? Bro, come on, how nerdy is that?" said River. "We need to do something where we can pick up girls."

"Girls? I really don't think I'm ready for all that yet, River, but thank you for thinking of me," said Marco.

"You know I gotta look out for my little brother."

"Ugh, River, you are such a man whore," said Dylen. "Is that all you think about? Come on."

"Dylen, watch your mouth," said Marcus.

"Dad, come on, River has had four girlfriends already this year. You better hope you don't have somebody knocking on the door, saying 'River's my baby daddy.'" Dylen laughed.

"It's not my fault all the ladies want the soul pole."

"Just make sure that pole is wearing a condom before you get something that doesn't require a child support payment," I said.

"Mom, come on, I'm not that stupid," said River.

"Son, we're not saying you're stupid. We just want you to be responsible for you and your potential partner," said Marcus.

"And Dad would know," said Dylen.

"Young lady, one more word out of you, and you will be grounded for a month," said Marcus.

"Can we please change the subject? This is not exactly dinner conversation, you know," said River.

"Well, you guys give it some thought, and we will discuss the summer vacation plans on Sunday, so be prepared. It's already February, and we need to start making some kind of plans and reservations," said Marcus.

"I can't believe summer vacation starts in three months," I said.

"Yeah, Mom, ain't it cool?" said Marco.

"Yes, it's real cool, sweetheart, real cool," I said, smiling.

The three months went by quickly, and the decision had been made to go to Rome. Dylen would get to shop, Marco would get the educational summer he wanted, and River was happy no matter what.

At times, I felt like Marcus and I were drifting apart and the only real connection we had was the children. I enjoy being a wife and mother, but sometimes I really felt like something in my life was missing. Sometimes I just got tired of the charity fund-raisers, the country club snobs, the brunches, and all the trivial nonsense that made up my life. Most of all, I missed Carmen. I missed our lunches together and our play dates with the children. I missed my best friend.

"Mom, you and Dad need a vacation alone. Sometimes you look so unhappy," said River, snapping me out of my pity party.

"Baby, I'm having a great time, and your father and I will have plenty of time with each other when you and Dylen graduate next year. I can't believe you two are juniors already. Where did the time go? Your mother would be so proud of you, River."

"I know she would, Mom. I miss her so much, and there is not a day that goes by that I don't think about her, but I've had a good life, and you and Dad have been the best parents I could have asked for. Just remember I love you," he said with tears in his eyes.

"Okay, enough of this. Let's finish packing. We have an early flight tomorrow. I love you, River! You have a good night," I said, kissing him on the forehead.

The kids were very excited about the 2007 school year. Over the summer, they found out they had enough credits to graduate early but decided against it because of sports and the fact that they hadn't decided on what colleges they would attend. Dylen had talked about attending an Ivy League school, but River wanted to go to a predominantly black university. Marcus and I wanted them to attend the same school but ultimately decided it was their decision.

Three months had passed since school started, and it was time to get ready for the holidays. This Thanksgiving and Christmas was going to be special. Marco had been with us an entire year and hadn't asked to see his mother once. Marcus had talked to him about it, but he said there was no need. I asked Marcus if he thought Marco needed counseling to deal with possible abandonment issue, but Marco said he didn't have any issues. He even told me, "I'm a Covington, and this is my home."

I've always been an early Christmas shopper. Marcus, however, always waited until the last minute then complained about the crowds. I decided to take the kids one by one so they could shop for their father and for their other siblings without them knowing what they were getting.

I had been rushing around all day, trying to get the grocery shopping done before picking Marco up from school to take him Christmas shopping. He was going to be the first of the kids to go since he was only in school a half day today. After picking Marco up, we headed to Mall of America. Shopping was hectic already, and we spent three hours in the mall and only went to four stores. I started for home and realized I needed to run to Saint Paul and drop off three dresses to my seamstress.

"Mom, this is going to take forever. It's already five o'clock, and we're going to hit rush-hour traffic," said Marco.

"I know, honey, but I don't know when I will be able to get back out here, but I promise I will hurry," I said, unlocking the car door. "I know you're hungry, but we will order out when we get home, whatever you want."

"Whatever I want?" asked Marco.

"Yes, honey, whatever you want." I was just about to pick up the cell phone to call Marcus when the phone rang.

"Baby, where are you? I came home early to take my favorite girl to dinner, and you're not even home."

"Marcus, I'm sorry. I picked up Marco early from school, and we decided to do some early Christmas shopping, and I lost track of time."

"So what time do you think you'll be here?" asked Marcus. "I know the traffic has got to be murder this time of day."

"Yeah, we're stuck going five miles an hour coming across the bridge."

"The bridge? Jennifer, it's six four now, and at this rate, it will be eight o'clock before you get home." Marcus laughed.

"Well, go ahead and order something for you and the kids, and Marco and I will stop and get something before heading home."

"Mom…Mom, look! That car just fell off the bridge!" screamed Marco.

"Marcus, hold on, there's some sort of accident or something."

Just as Marcus started to call my name, I heard a huge cracking sound, and the bus in front of us started to slide into the big gaping hole that was once the bridge. A semitruck was being held up by leaning against the side of the railing. As the bus started to slide sideways, the bridge started to collapse. The car started to slide forward as more cars slid into the Mississippi River.

"Jennifer? Jennifer, what is going on?" I heard Marcus screaming.

"Marcus, the bridge has collapsed, and cars are falling into the river. I don't know if I can hold on much longer." I pulled up the emergency brake, but the cars behind me were pushing me forward.

"Jennifer, where are you, exactly?"

"I'm just before the SE University exit. Marcus, this doesn't look good, baby. Marco, talk to your dad while I try to get us over by the railing."

"Dad, I love you, and I'm so scared," said Marco.

"I know, but you have to be strong for your mom. She needs you right now. So just be brave, okay? And, Marco, I love you, son."

"I love you too, Daddy."

"Marco, give the phone back to your mother."

"Marcus, there are too many cars in the way. I can't make it to railing."

"Jennifer, listen to me. Get out of the car, get to the edge of the bridge, and jump into the water. You and Marco are strong swimmers. You might be able to survive the fall," said Marcus. "It will be more difficult to try to get out of the car once it has hit the water and is sinking."

"Marcus, we can't get out. The cars around us have us pinned. Marcus, listen to me. There are two rows of cars in front of us, and I can still hear the bridge cracking and breaking."

"Jennifer, try to break a window or something. Baby, don't give up."

"Marcus, tell Dylen and River I love them and I will be with them always. I love you so much, Marcus."

Before I could finish my sentence, I felt the bridge give way, and we started to fall. As I reached for Marco, I dropped the cell phone and couldn't reach it as I felt the car hit the water. The impact knocked Marco into the windshield. I grabbed for him as water started to pour into the car. I tried to find a pulse but got nothing. As I searched for the phone, I felt the blood pouring from my nose. As I shook the cobwebs from my head, I tried to push open the door. The door wouldn't open. I quickly picked up Marco's book bag and began searching for his cell phone. As I dialed the number, I thought about Carmen and Virginia and my father.

"Hello, Marco?"

"No, Marcus, it's Jen."

"Jennifer, what is happening?"

"Marcus, the car fell into the water and is slowly sinking. I can't get the doors open, and Marco is still unconscious."

"Listen, baby, hang in there. Someone will get to you before the car sinks completely. Jennifer, are you hurt?"

"I have a head injury, and my leg is broken, but I'm okay. I'm just worried about Marco. He has been unconscious since the car hit the water. Marcus, can you put the kids on the phone?"

"Go ahead, baby, I got you on speaker."

"Dylen?"

"Yes, Mommy."

I could tell Dylen was crying, so I knew I had to suck it up and control the pain in my voice. "Dylen, you know Mommy loves you very much, and I'm going to be with you always, but I need you to be strong. I need you to be strong for me, for your father, and for your brother, okay?"

"Yes, Mom, but I'm scared I'm never gonna see you again."

"If, for some reason, you don't, baby, just remember that I love you very much and I will always love you. You were one of my greatest accomplishments, baby, and I am so proud of you," I said, trying to hold back the tears.

"Mom, you will be okay, and I will keep the house in order until you get home, okay?" said Dylen.

"Listen, all of you, I don't think I have much time. The water is really starting to come into the car, and I still can't get the door open. Marcus, I love you. I've always loved you. I know I don't have to tell you to take care of the kids, because I know you will do that. River, you have been the best son any mother could ask for, and Carmen would be so proud of you." I heard Marcus call my name, and the call went dead.

The windshield broke, and the water rushed into the car. I tried to move but still could not free my leg. I tried to hold my breath as long as I could, but there was no use, and I slowly drifted off to sleep.

* * *

"Dad what's going on? Have they gotten to Mom?" asked River.

"Maybe we need to go down to the bridge," said Dylen.

"The news said the traffic is backed up for miles and they're only letting emergency medical personnel through at this time."

"Dad, we just can't sit here and do nothing," said River.

"Baby, I know what you're feeling, but we just need to be patient and wait. That's all we can do right now."

"Daddy, try her cell number again," begged Dylen.

"I just tried it," said River. "But it went straight to voice mail."

We paced and paced, but still no word came.

"Daddy, call the police again," cried Dylen.

"Sweetheart, I just did, but they had no additional information. Kids, I know this is difficult for you, but all we can do is pray that they reach them in time."

By the time the word came that her car had been located, Nikki, Beth, and Virginia had come to the house.

"Marcus, what in the hell is the po-po doing to find our girl?" asked Nikki. "This is bullshit that they can't tell us anything, and here it is almost ten o'clock."

I answered the phone, and it was the police again.

"Shh, shh! Aunt Nikki, Daddy can't hear."

"So they haven't found any bodies yet is what you're telling me?" asked Marcus.

"That's a good sign," said Virginia. "Maybe that means she escaped with Marco somehow."

"Mom is very strong and very smart, Dad. Maybe she did get out," said Dylen.

The doorbell rang, and everyone froze.

"Don't answer it, Daddy," said Dylen. "If we answer it, then we can't take it back," Dylen said, sobbing.

Beth opened the door, and a police officer stood there with a chaplain.

"Goddamn it, this can't be happening again," said Nikki.

"Calm down, Nikki," said Bruce as he held her in his arms.

"I need to speak with Marcus Covington," said the officer.

"Did you find my mother and little brother?" shouted Dylen.

"Folks, if we can just come inside for a moment," said the officer.

Everyone stood motionless as the police officer stepped inside the house.

"Mr. Covington, there is no easy way to say this," said Officer Rice. "When we found your vehicle, there were no occupants inside. We found out that some bystanders jumped in and pulled them from the vehicle."

"Thank God," said Beth.

"Ma'am, please let me finish. The woman and child were already dead by the time the paramedics reached them. We need you to come down and make a positive identification."

"Dad, I don't want you to go," said Dylen.

"Just because Dad doesn't go won't change the fact that they're dead," said River.

"You don't know that, River. Plus, she's not your real mom, so it doesn't matter to you."

"Kids, please, this is not helping anyone, and your mother would not want you arguing like this. This is difficult for everyone, so please let's just get through this and find out if the bodies lying in the morgue belong to your mother and your brother or if they're lying in a hospital somewhere."

"Mr. Covington, with all due respect to you and your family, we believe that the bodies in the morgue belong to your wife and son. I just don't want you to get your hopes up," said the chaplain.

"Thank you, Father. We will be there first thing in the morning. I really don't think we can handle this, this evening."

"I understand," said the chaplain. "If you need me for anything, please feel free to call us day or night."

I walked the police officer and the chaplain to the door, and I held River in my arms as I wept uncontrollably.

"Officer, can I ask you a question? What is the current death toll?" I asked.

"Mr. Covington, everything is still so chaotic we still have no idea how high the death toll will reach."

"Thank you, Officer. You have a good evening," I said.

"Oh, Daddy, why did this have to happen to our family? It's not fair," said Dylen. "How could a bridge just fall down? This just doesn't make any sense to me."

"Marcus, brother, if you need anything, please don't hesitate to ask," said Bruce.

"That's right," said Nikki. "We are all here for you. You know we loved her very much."

"Don't talk about my mother like she's already dead. She's alive, and I don't care what anyone says!" screamed Dylen.

Beth and Virginia hugged me as they were about to leave.

"Keep the faith, Marcus. We are not sure if it's them. They may still be alive," said Beth.

"Thank you, Beth. I want that to be true so desperately," I said, trying to be strong for the kids.

"What are you people talking about? Mom would move heaven and earth to contact us if they were still alive," said River.

"I know, River, but just remember, regardless of what happens, you have all of us here for you, your sister, and your father," said Virginia.

"Aunt Virginia, right now I just feel as though God hates me."

"River, why would you say something like that?"

"How could he take both mothers away from me?" asked River.

"River, things don't work that way. This was just a horrible accident. It's not God's punishment for anything you or any of us have done. So please don't think like that, son," I said, trying to comfort him.

"We are all going to get through this together," said Nikki.

We kissed one another good night, wondering if what tomorrow would bring would leave us all sad and brokenhearted.

The trip to the morgue the next morning was quiet. The kids barely spoke, and you could see the terror in their eyes.

"This reminds me of when Grandpa died and we had to go to New York," said Dylen.

"You remember that?" I asked.

"Yes, Dad, of course. Mom cried the whole trip. How could I forget that?" said Dylen. "No matter how optimistic I try to be about this situation, I just can't stop crying. I have this ache in my heart, Dad, and it won't go away. I know she's gone, Daddy. I had a dream about her just like I had about Grandpa when he passed away, so I know she's gone and there's nothing we can do about it," Dylen said, sobbing.

"Dylen, don't get yourself all worked up until we find out for sure," I said, trying to be positive.

"Whatever, Daddy," said Dylen.

"River, are you okay? You're awfully quiet," I said.

"Yeah, Dad, I'm fine. I just don't have a lot to say. That's all," said River.

We were met in the lobby by the coroner.

"I'm Marcus Covington, and we're here about my wife and my son."

"Mr. Covington, it won't be an actual viewing because the bodies were submerged in water for so long, and I just don't think it's a good idea. You will be viewing them on a monitor. If you will follow me, I will show you to the viewing room," said the coroner.

The corridor seemed to go on forever. We were put in viewing room A, and moments later, the face of a boy appeared on the monitor. Dylen couldn't handle it, and she broke down in tears.

"Mr. Covington, is that your son?" asked the man in the white lab coat.

"Yes, that's Marco."

He looked so peaceful as if he were asleep. I could see tears start to run down River's face.

"What was the cause of death?" I asked.

"Severe head trauma. He had no water in his lungs, so he was dead before the car was submerged in water," said the doctor.

Before we had the chance to regroup, a picture of a woman flashed on the monitor. The face didn't look like my wife, but I knew it was her. Her face was swollen and distorted from the water. She barely looked like herself.

"Mr. Covington, is this your wife?" the man in the lab coat asked again.

"Yes, that's my wife, Jennifer Covington. And her cause of death?" I asked.

"She drowned, Mr. Covington."

Dylen left the room, and River followed to make sure she was okay.

"What happens now?" I asked.

"Well, the autopsies are complete, so you just need to sign the necessary forms, and the bodies can be released. I am truly sorry for your loss, Mr. Covington. This was a horrific accident and a dark time for Minnesota. You have my deepest condolences."

"Thank you. I appreciate all your assistance."

"Dad, have you called Marco's mom?" asked Dylen.

"Marco's mom died with him in the Mississippi River, and I'm truly thankful that they didn't have to die alone."

Just before I started the car, my cell phone rang.

"You son of a bitch, why didn't you tell me there's a possibility that my son is dead?" asked Pam. "Helen came by the house this morning and told me about the accident."

"Pam, look, Marco is no longer your concern, remember?"

"I am still his mother. Is everything okay with my son? Marcus, I worked with you for years, and I can hear it in your voice that something is wrong. Now tell me, is everything okay with my son?"

"No, Pam, it isn't. Jennifer and Marco are dead," I said. "They were killed when the bridge collapsed."

"You bastard, you couldn't call me and tell me our son was killed?"

"He's not your son. He was our son, Jennifer and mine. You sold him for a handsome profit, remember? Now leave my family alone." And I disconnected the call.

"Dad, are you okay?" asked River.

"Yes, son, I'm fine."

"Dad, I can drive if you're too upset," asked River.

"No, son, really, I'm okay. Do you guys want to stop and get something to eat?"

"No, Dad. Let's just go home. I'm tired," said Dylen.

"Okay, because I need to get home and make some phone calls and start arranging things for the funeral service."

"Dad, do we have to do this today?" asked Dylen.

"Yes, we do. There are arrangements that have to be made and people who have to be notified."

"Dad, I just want to get home as soon as possible," said River.

"I know that, son. We will be there in about ten minutes. Just hang tight."

The kids went upstairs to their rooms, and I got on the phone and started to make phone calls. I called Nikki, Virginia, and Beth and asked them to be at the house in an hour. I called Helen and let her know a positive identification had been made and that Jennifer and Marco were gone.

"I will be there tomorrow," said Helen. "And don't worry, we will get through this. I promised your father I would be there for you, and I plan to keep that promise."

Nikki and Bruce arrived first, and from the moment I answered the door, she could see it in my eyes.

"So it is really them?" asked Nikki. "You're trying to tell me that once again, one of my best friends is dead."

"Yes, Nikki, it's them. They're gone, and they are never coming back," I said, becoming overwhelmed with tears.

I had never seen Nikki so emotional as Bruce held her in his arms.

"Baby, calm down," said Bruce.

"How am I supposed to calm down, Bruce? This should not have happened. Somebody has to pay for this. This government cannot continue to ignore the infrastructure in this country. Wasn't hurricane Katrina enough? How many more lives have to be destroyed because this fucking country is falling apart while George W. Bush is on the goddamn golf course? My best friend is dead, and she didn't have to die, and somebody needs to pay."

Beth and Virginia walked in in the middle of Nikki's little tirade.

"What is going on?" asked Virginia. "Please, please don't tell me it's them."

"Yes," said Bruce.

Beth broke into tears, and Virginia held her hand.

"Marcus, what can we do?" asked Virginia.

"Well, we just got back from the morgue, and I have got to get my bearings. So I really don't know where to start. If one of you can get her address book and notify her friends, I will take care of her family in Arkansas. Even though she really didn't stay in constant contact with them, I know she sent Christmas cards every year. So I feel obligated to let them know she's gone."

"Have you contacted her father's side of the family yet?" asked Nikki.

"No, I haven't contacted anyone outside of you guys. I am not looking forward to contacting the Farillos. These people just lost their son in one of the most horrible acts in US history, and now this freak accident," I said.

"Marcus, would you like me to do it?" asked Virginia.

"No, I'll do it."

I dialed the number and secretly prayed no one would answer.

"Hello, this is Angelo. How can I help you?"

Who answers the phone that way? I thought. "Yes, I'm sorry. This is Marcus Covington."

"Jennifer's husband, yes," said Angelo.

"Yes, that's right," I said.

"We have been following the bridge thing down there," said Angelo.

"Actually, that's why I'm calling."

"Is everything okay?" asked Angelo.

"Not exactly, Angelo. Jennifer and our son Marco was on the bridge when it collapsed."

"Is she in the hospital? Go get Isabella," I heard Angelo saying. "Go get her now!" shouted Angelo. "There has been an accident, and Jennifer is hurt."

"Angelo, listen, put me on speakerphone and gather the family," I said calmly.

There was a brief pause, then I could tell I was on speakerphone.

"Hi, everyone."

"Hello, Marcus. This is Isabella. Are you okay?"

"No, Isabella, we are not okay. This is one of the most difficult things I've ever had to do," I said, choking up.

"Son, just tell us what's happened," said Angelo.

"The day the bridge collapsed, Jennifer and our son Marco were on it. We were contacted by the police on Friday evening that two bodies were found, and we went this morning to identify the remains." I could hear Isabella sobbing.

"Marcus, was it them?" asked Angelo.

"Yes, it was them. Jennifer was trapped in the car and couldn't get out and drowned. Marco died of head trauma before the car sank."

"Marcus, we will be there tomorrow. Isabella, contact the rest of the family and let them know we are coming to Minnesota," said Angelo. "How are River and Dylen holding up?" asked Angelo.

"It's difficult, and I think you and the rest of the Farillo family being here will help Dylen tremendously. Thank you so much, Angelo, and if you need me to make reservations for anyone, just let me know. The house is pretty big, so we have a lot of room, and we have tons of friends who have offered to open their homes to any family we have coming into town. So just let me know what time your plane arrives tomorrow, and I will send someone to get you. Also, as soon as you know, can you give me a head count on how many family members will be attending?"

"Okay. Yes, Marcus, and thank you very much. We love you," said Angelo.

"Marcus, I contacted the school and sent an e-mail out to everyone on Jennifer's email address book," said Virginia. "Beth is still contacting people from the address book we found in Jennifer's desk, Marcus. Is there anyone else you want us to contact or anything else you need us to do?"

"No, Virginia, I think I can take it from here. You have been wonderful, and I appreciate everything you guys have done. I know you have lives of your own, but if one or two of you could hang around and help out with the kids, I would really appreciate it."

"Marcus, that's not a problem. I would be more than happy to stay and help out," said Nikki.

"Me too, Marcus," said Virginia.

"Marcus, I can come during the day while the kids are in school," said Beth.

"That's fine. I just need someone here to keep the kids company while I'm out making arrangements. I'm concerned about Dylen, but I'm really worried about River. He's not showing any type of emotion at all, and that's scaring me."

"Marcus, would you like me to speak with River?" asked Nikki.

"You? Why you?" asked Beth.

"Why you gotta say it like that?" said Nikki.

"You're not exactly the maternal type," said Virginia.

"That may be true, but all the kids know Aunt Nikki doesn't sugarcoat the truth. They know out of all of us that I will not bullshit them and will tell it like it is. Y'all know in most situations like this, people are all about the sugarcoating to spare everyone's feelings, but maybe that's not what they need right now. So, Marcus, if it's okay with you, I would like to talk to the kids," said Nikki.

"That's fine with me, Nikki, if you think you can get through to them, because right now, I think they're feeling kind of lost, and I don't know what to do or say because I'm lost as well."

"Knock, knock, it's Aunt Nikki. River, can I come in?" asked Nikki.

"Sure, Aunt Nikki, what's up?"

"Nothing, baby, I just wanted to make sure you're okay. I know this is a lot for you to digest, but we just wanted you to know that if you need to talk, we are here for you. You know, River, most people have to live a lifetime before they experience the kind of grief you have gone through at such a young age. First, your father and mother, now your brother and Jennifer. It's a lot for anyone to handle, and I totally understand you being withdrawn."

"Aunt Nikki, it's cool really. You guys need to stop worrying so much about me. I'm just trying to be strong for Dylen. She needs me right now. I mean, she was there for me when my first mom died, and now it's my turn to be there for her."

"Sweetheart, you can be strong for your sister without shutting down your emotions."

"Aunt Nikki, I'm not shutting down, I promise, and if I start to feel all creepy and weird, I promise I will let you know, okay?" said River.

"Okay, sweetheart, I will drop it for now, but you try to get some rest."

"Aunt Nikki, I love you," said River.

"I love you too," said Nikki before walking away with tears in her eyes.

"Dylen, knock, knock, it's Aunt Nikki," she chimed out. "Can I come in?"

"Sure," said Dylen.

"I can?"

She smiled.

"I can come into your domain?"

"Whatever," said Dylen.

"So what does that mean, Dylen?" asked Nikki.

"Nothing, Aunt Nikki. How can I help you?"

"Sweetie, I didn't want anything. I was just making sure you're okay."

"No, Aunt Nikki, I'm not, and what exactly is it I'm supposed to be okay about?" asked Dylen.

"Okay, Dylen, I know you're in pain, so I'll let that smart-ass comment slide this time, but don't forget whom you're talking to, Ms. Thang," Nikki said, smiling.

"Aunt Nikki, I know you're only trying to help and you're just being concerned, but I know if I can do this, if I can get past losing Mom."

"Sweetheart, this is not something you can just get past. This is something that's going to affect you for the rest of your life," said Nikki. "We're just trying to make sure that you're coping with this situation in a healthy manner, and if you're not, your father can get you some help. You can see a grief counselor, which probably wouldn't be such a bad idea for you and River."

"Why River?" asked Dylen. "Aunt Nikki, River is fine."

"No, he's not, Dylen. He's cried, what, once since this whole thing started. That's not healthy, Dylen."

"What do you people want?" asked Dylen. "If I cry too much, it's a problem. If River doesn't cry at all, it's a problem. So what do you people want from us?" screamed Dylen.

"Baby, we just want you to be able to cope with the loss of your mother and be able to get on with your life, that's all. Do you realize how hard it is for us to stop crying ourselves to sleep at night because we didn't get the chance to say goodbye or tell her how much we loved her?" said Nikki, crying. "She was our best friend, and we never got the chance to say goodbye to her," sobbed Nikki. "We have to find a reason to get up in the morning when all we want to do is lie in bed and grieve hoping that this too shall pass."

"Aunt Nikki, it's going to be okay," Dylen said, putting her arms around her.

"I know it will eventually," said Nikki. "I just keep losing my best friends, and there's not a damn thing we can do about it. First Gloria, then Carmen, and now your mother. Believe me when I tell you that it takes everything I have to go on each day. So kill me if I'm overly concerned about the welfare of my best friend's children. I have to make sure that you guys are okay. That's the least I could do for her."

"Aunt Nikki, I am so sorry for acting like a brat," said Dylen. "I didn't stop to think about her friends and how you're feeling. All of you were like her sisters, and she loved you all very much. I should have stopped to think how much you're hurting too."

"It's okay, baby. We are going to get through this together. Everyone is here for you, River, and your dad. And no matter what, I will always be here for you," said Nikki. "So wash up and come downstairs for dinner."

"Sure, Aunt Nikki, I will be down in a couple of minutes, okay?"

"So how did the talks go?" asked Marcus.

"They're going to be fine, Marcus. River is just being strong for his sister. They are leaning on each other for support, and right now they feel as though that's all they need," said Nikki. "I just told them we are all here for them. Bruce, you can go home, sweetheart. It's been a really long day, and I know you're tired. Virginia and I are going to spend the night and help Marcus get ready for his Sicilian storm that will be blowing in tomorrow." Nikki laughed. "Beth is going to come back in the morning. So, baby, just go home and get some rest. I love you," said Nikki, hugging Bruce goodbye.

"Marcus, brotha, if you need anything, please don't hesitate to call me," said Bruce.

"Yeah, man, thanks for everything. You and Nikki have been a big help."

Nikki and Virginia spent most of the night drinking wine and reminiscing about when they first met.

"I can't believe all the friends we've lost," said Virginia sadly. "I thought we would all grow old together."

"I know. I can't believe there are only three of us left," said Nikki. "It seems like yesterday we were hanging out at the Gay 90s, kicking it, and now we're burying another friend. It just doesn't seem fair somehow."

"I know, Nikki, but we can't go down this road of self-pity, or it will eat us alive," said Virginia. "We have to be strong for Marcus and the kids. I don't know how much more this family can take. Girl, let's try to get some sleep. It's going to be a long day tomorrow."

Nikki kissed Virginia goodnight and went upstairs to take a shower. As she stood there with the water running down her face, she started to tremble and cry uncontrollably.

"I have so many regrets, so many things I'd never even said I was sorry for. I had disappointed so many people, none more than Jennifer. If I hadn't confronted Jeffrey that day, you never would have lost your baby. Then I had the nerve to sleep with your father and cause you more pain. I always had to be the big shot and shoot off my mouth. And, Jennifer, I am so, so sorry that I hurt you. I know you said that you forgave me, but I guess I never forgave myself. As God is my witness, Jen, I will always be here for River and Dylen. So you can rest peacefully, my friend, and I will love you always."

Nikki finished her shower and was about to call Bruce when her cell phone rang.

"Baby, are you okay? You sound like you've been crying," said Bruce.

"Bruce, I need you. Please come back."

"Baby, what's wrong?" asked Bruce.

"I just need you, and I don't want to be alone tonight."

"I'll be right there, sweetheart. I promise you, I will be right there."

"Dad, what time are the Farillos getting here?" asked Dylen.

"The plane arrives around one thirty, I think. I need to check the confirmation, but I'm pretty sure it's one thirty, but we will get there around one o'clock. Why do you ask?"

"I don't know, I'm just going to miss the peace and quiet. You know how loud those Italian people are," said Dylen, frowning.

"Dylen, those Italian people are your family, and they love you very much. So please don't refer to them as 'those Italian people.'" I laughed.

"Dad, I'm just saying they're loud. That's all."

"They're just as unhappy as you are. They loved your mom, and they love you too. I just need you to be tolerant. That's all I'm saying. So if you don't mind, go upstairs and get your brother because Virginia and Nikki made breakfast. And after we eat, we need to get ready for the loud Italians," I said, smiling.

We arrived at the airport at one o'clock, but the plane arrived even earlier.

Just my luck. I would keep them waiting.

We quickly went to the baggage claim and spotted half of Sicily standing there. Isabella grabbed Dylen and started crying.

"How's Grandma's *bambina*?" asked Isabella.

"Grandma, I'm okay."

"River, my little bambino. Give Grandma a kiss."

River reluctantly kissed Isabella.

"Marcus, how are you holding up?" asked Angelo.

"I'm doing fine, Mr. Farillo."

"Marco, darling, how are you doing?" asked Isabella.

"Mrs. Farillo, I'm good. I mean, I'm hanging in there." It felt weird to hear Isabella call me Marco, but I didn't have the heart to ask her not to, since she had done so on several other occasions.

"So if everyone has their bags, we can get started before they kick us out of the airport for having a family reunion." I smiled.

"Gus, you and your family can ride in the limo with Rudy Maria and Marco. Marco…" I said as my eyes filled with tears.

"Marcus, are you okay?" asked Angelo.

"Yes, I'm fine. You know, my son's name is Marco—was named Marco," I said quietly. "It's just difficult hearing you call me Marco and we got little Marco over there. Don't worry, I'm okay, Isabella. Now you and Angelo can ride with me and the kids. There should be enough room in the other limo for eight people, and the other four can ride with Nikki and her husband."

"Daddy, can we just go? I'm tired," said Dylen.

"Hold on, Dylen. We're trying to get everyone settled," I said sharply.

"Yeah, girl, chill out," said River.

"It's okay, Dylen. Grandma is tired too. It's been a long trip."

"I'm sorry, Grandma. I'm not trying to be rude. I haven't been sleeping, and I'm just tired."

"Don't apologize, child. I totally understand."

During the ride home, everyone was very chatty and was trying really hard to avoid the real topic and what brought us all together: the death of my wife.

"So, Marcus, what really happened?" asked Angelo.

"Angelo, I would really like to wait until we get to the house to discuss this. That way, I don't have to repeat the story again for the rest of the family."

"That's fine, Marcus. I totally understand, son."

I enjoyed the rest of the ride because of the peace and quiet.

Dylen held her great-grandmother's hand as she drifted off. She somehow felt comforted because she knew the same blood that ran through her veins ran through hers. River sat there with his headset on, oblivious to everything around him.

When we finally arrived at the house, she was exhausted. She couldn't stand to hear the details of her mother's and her brother's deaths again.

I mean, how many times am I gonna have to relive this fucking nightmare? thought Dylen. *Doesn't anyone read the newspaper?* "Dad, I'm going upstairs to my room," said Dylen.

"Okay, Dylen, we will call you when lunch is ready."

"Whatever!" said Dylen as she made her way up the stairs.

"Marcus, is she all right?" asked Isabella.

"She's having a hard time, just like the rest of us. It's just going to take some time. It's going to take some time for all the families that lost someone on that bridge."

"Marcus, can you please tell us what happened?" asked Angelo.

"I will tell you everything I know, Angelo. The police haven't given us a lot of information. It's been classified as a horrific accident with not many details."

"Just tell us everything you know, please."

"Jennifer had picked our son Marco up from school, and she had to drive into Saint Paul for a dress she was having altered. On the way back across the bridge, she hit rush-hour traffic. While they sat there waiting in traffic, the bridge collapsed. Jennifer called me on her cell phone, and I stayed with her until the call was disconnected. She had cars on both sides of the vehicle that blocked her in.

"From the initial impact of the first vehicle, my son hit his head on the dashboard and was knocked unconscious. Jennifer's leg was pinned, so she could not exit the vehicle, and by the time the vehicle hit the water, Marco was dead. We know this because there was no water in his lungs," I explained as tears started to run down my face. "Jennifer wasn't so lucky. She drowned when the vehicle was submerged."

Isabella said a prayer and made the sign of the cross and started talking in Italian. "My little *bambina*," she said over and over.

Angelo broke down; he couldn't take it anymore and left the room.

"So what's being done?" asked Gus. "Because someone needs to pay for this. I don't know what's worse: 9/11 or this travesty."

"Yes, Gus, I agree. Somebody needs to pay, and I don't mean monetarily. I mean, somebody needs to go to jail to pay not only for the loss of Jennifer but for everyone who lost someone that day."

"Okay, Marcus, so what happens now?" asked Angelo, reentering the room.

"We bury Jennifer and Marco. I have an appointment at the funeral home tomorrow to make arrangements. I've already spoken to the archbishop at Our Lady of Lourdes Catholic Church about holding the service there. It's kind of poetic justice, actually."

"Why is that, Marcus?" asked Angelo.

"It was built on the east bank of the Mississippi River, and the Mississippi River took Jennifer's life."

"I'm really happy, Marcus, that she will have a Catholic service. Her father would be very happy."

"Well, I'm sure everyone is tired, so I will show you to your rooms, and you can shower and rest before dinner. Anyone who's hungry is welcome to anything that's in the kitchen. Make yourselves totally at home," I said. "I'm going to go check on the kids and take a nap myself," I said, feeling totally drained. "Isabella, you don't have to worry about trying to cook. People have already brought food and will continue to bring food up until the day of the service."

"That's all fine and good, Marcus, but how many Italians cooks are there in Minnesota?" She smiled. "These people are, what, Swedish? They know nothing about fine dining. So, Marcus, you get some rest, and we will take care of everything else. Don't worry, we are here to help you and the kids get through this, I promise."

I felt like I hadn't slept in days. I got the Farillos settled and went to my room. I could smell Jennifer's perfume. I could feel her presence as though she were in the room with me.

"Jennifer, baby, I know you're always with me. I can feel you. I get a whiff of your perfume at the oddest times. Jennifer, I need to know that you and Marco are in a better place. I need you to know that you are the love of my life and every day I live, I will love you, whether in this life or the next. Baby, if you can just give me a sign, anything, Jennifer."

I turned on the radio before getting into the shower, and the radio station was playing her favorite song, "My Funny Valentine," by Chaka Khan. I remember the first time we heard that song and she fell in love with it.

"Thank you, Jennifer, thank you for loving me all these years. Baby, I will never forget you, and I will always take care of our kids and make sure they never forget what a wonder mother you are."

I slept so peacefully I couldn't believe it was eight o'clock already. I felt like a huge weight had been lifted, and I felt at peace. "Thank you, Jennifer, for allowing your spirit to touch me and for giving me such a wonder sign of your love."

Isabella had commandeered the kitchen, and food was everywhere. The house was chaotic, and I welcomed the noise. I wasn't really up for entertaining, but I knew I had to at least be social. As usual, Nikki was entertaining the masses. She was telling a funny story about girls' night out, and everyone seemed to enjoy hearing any story that involved Jennifer.

After dinner, everyone sat around talking and making suggestions about the service. I was just ready to get this over with. To lay Jennifer and Marco to rest would be a huge weight lifted from my shoulders. The doorbell rang.

"Who in the hell could that be?" I asked myself.

Nikki answered the door, and it was Helen.

"Helen, why didn't you tell me you were getting in today? I would have sent a car for you," I said.

"I know you got a lot going on, so I just rented a car at the airport, and here I am," said Helen. "Come here and give me a big hug."

"It's good to see you, Helen. How have you been?" I asked.

"I'm good, but enough about me. Where are the kids?"

"They're probably upstairs in their rooms. We just ate dinner. Come on in so I can introduce you to everyone, and I'll go get your bags out of the car."

"Sweetheart, that's not necessary. I checked into the Grand Hotel in Minneapolis. It's off Second Avenue. Do you know it?"

"Yes, it's really nice. But, Helen, we have enough room here, or you could stay with Nikki and her husband."

"Marcus, it's not necessary. I don't mind, really."

"Well, don't stand on ceremony. Come on in so you can meet everyone," said Isabella, introducing herself. "This is my husband, Angelo Farillo, and these are our children: Rudy, Lucilla, Marco, and Maria. Allesandro is Maria's son, and we call him Alex. Franco and Alisa are Lucilla's children. Sofia, Gia, and Francesca are Rudy's daughters, and Adriana is Marco's daughter."

"Isabella, you're going to be up all night making the introductions," said Gus. "I'm Gus Farillo, and this is my wife, Alma. These are our sons Anthony and Baltazar. Santino, Alexandra, and Allegra are Anthony's children. Bianca, Rina, and Sarafina are Giana's girls. She is unable to attend because of work."

"Hello, everyone," said Helen, visibly overwhelmed by the Italian invasion. "I am hungry, and the food looks fabulous."

"Alma, do you mind fixing Helen a plate?" asked Isabella.

"Helen, it is great seeing you again, but it's been a long day, so I'm about to call it a night," I said.

"So what are the living arrangements going to be, Marcus?" asked Nikki.

"Well, Helen is staying at the hotel, so that means we have fifteen other accommodations that need to be made. I have four guest rooms, so I was thinking Isabella and Angelo, Gus and Alma, Franco, Anthony, Santino, Alex, and Baltazar can all stay here. One room has a couch that lets out into bed, so three of them can sleep in one room. You guys will have plenty of room, but be aware, the wet bar will be locked. Nikki, I guess you can take some of the girls to your house, and Virginia can take the rest, I guess."

"That's fine, Marcus. We have three guest rooms, so we can accommodate six, and Virginia can take the other four," said Nikki. "Two girls to a room, if that's okay with you ladies, and I will leave it up to you to decide. So, ladies, grab your luggage, and everyone who is coming with me, let's get this party started."

"Okay, since all that is settled, we can call it a night and meet back here tomorrow in the morning around eleven o'clock for brunch, and then the meeting at the funeral home is at three, and the church after that. Isabella, I would like you to help Dylen pick something out for Jennifer to wear. Virginia and Beth are working on the obituary," I said, going down the list of things to do in my head. "It must be ready to turn in by Wednesday. The viewing of the body will be on Friday, and the service is Saturday at two."

"We got this, Marcus. Don't worry, we will not let you down," said Virginia.

"So if there's nothing else, girls, let's boogie," said Beth, patting Marcus on the shoulder.

Isabella and Alma cleaned the kitchen, while the men sat around playing cards with River and Dylen. I kissed the kids good night and turned in.

I woke up sweaty and hot. The noise downstairs startled me, so I went downstairs to see what was going on.

Isabella sat quietly at the table, drinking a glass of Chianti. "Oh! I'm sorry, sweetheart, did I wake you?" she asked.

"Not really. I've been awake for a while. I just went in and checked on Dylen and River and was coming downstairs to get something to drink, and I heard a noise. Are you okay, Isabella?" I asked.

"I was just sitting here thinking about how happy I was when Jennifer came into our lives after Francis died. She was such a comfort to Angelo and me. I always felt so close to Francis having his little *bambina* around, and it hurts me to my soul to think that she died such a horrible death. It just breaks my heart," she said, sobbing.

"I know it's difficult, Isabella. It's difficult for all of us."

"Marcus, I just want you to know that we're going to be here for you and the kids for as long as you need us to be."

"Isabella, there really isn't a need for that. The kids and I will be okay."

"Maybe the need is ours. Maybe Angelo and I need to be around you and the kids right now, if that's okay with you."

"That's fine, Isabella. I'm sure the kids will like that a lot."

"Do you want me to fix you some coffee or something to eat, perhaps?" she asked, suddenly feeling overjoyed that I had agreed to let them stay and help out.

"Isabella, I'm fine. No coffee for me. Thank you anyway."

"When is Marco's mother arriving?"

"Isabella, my son's mother died with him on that bridge on August 7."

"I know, Marcus, but doesn't the lady who gave birth to him have the right to mourn her son?"

"Not as far as I'm concerned," I said. "She gave up that right the moment she took my check."

"I understand your frustrations with his mother, but at least extend the invitation to her, and if she shows up, great, but if not, your conscience is clear. Marcus, that is the proper thing to do," she said. "I know this woman hurt you and, at one time, you both hurt Jennifer, but let that go. Allow her to say goodbye to her son."

"Isabella, I know you're right, but it's just really hard. Jennifer was my life, and I hurt her badly with that woman once."

"Yes, but she forgave you, and your lives moved forward. You just need to forgive yourself."

"I know you're right," I said, tearing up. "It's just really hard because she never loved my son. He was her meal ticket, nothing more than that."

"He was her son too," said Isabella. "Sweetheart, just call her and extend the invitation. You know Jennifer would have told you the same thing."

"You're right, Isabella. I know you're right."

I looked at the time. It's almost 4:00 a.m.

"Why don't you go upstairs and get some rest before the chaos starts?" said Isabella.

"It's going to be a really long day for all of us," I said. I kissed Isabella good night and went to my room. "Hi, Pam, this is Marcus."

"Marcus, do you know what fucking time it is?" asked Pam, sounding very annoyed.

"Yes, Pam, I am aware of the time, but I need to say this."

"What is it?"

"I want you to attend the funeral. It is Saturday at two p.m."

"Go to hell, Marcus. You can go straight to hell," she said, hanging up the phone.

I was about to apologize for not telling her sooner about the accident when I heard the dial tone. "What a stupid bitch," I said before closing my eyes and falling asleep.

The time went by quickly, and before I knew it, it was eight o'clock. I could smell the bacon and coffee in the air. I was tired, probably the most tired I had ever been in my life. I was ready for peace and quiet.

It was Monday morning, and the Minnesota sky was very gloomy. "I think winter is going to come early this year," I said to myself. I stood there dreading the afternoon ahead of me. I wasn't aware of all the noise downstairs until I heard a knock at the door.

"Hi, Daddy," said River.

"Are you okay? I was just standing here thinking about how happy your senior year should be, and now it's totally distracted by this horrible accident, and to top it off, the holidays are right around the corner."

"Dad, it's okay, really. I just want you to be okay when we leave to go to college next fall."

"Thanks, sweetheart, but I'll be okay. Now let's go downstairs and have some breakfast. I'm starving."

"Good morning, everyone," I said.

"Good morning, Marcus," said Alma. "Marcus, Nikki and Virginia called and said they would be here around ten o'clock, so just sit down, and I'll get you some coffee, and breakfast will be coming up shortly."

"So who is going to the funeral home with us?" asked Angelo.

"I know Nikki, Beth, and Virginia are going. The kids said they do not want to go, so Alma said she and Gus would stay here with them."

After Nikki and the rest of the family arrived and had breakfast, we decided to head out.

"Marcus, I'm going to drive, and Beth and Virginia are going to ride with me, so where is this funeral home?" asked Nikki.

"The funeral home is located on Lyndale Avenue, so if you guys want to just meet us there, that will be fine."

Everyone arrived at the funeral home and was greeted by Mr. Pike.

A short, stocky man who has a creepy demeanor that makes working for a funeral home the perfect job for him, I thought.

After showing us pictures of the caskets and the burial plans, we made the final decision on all the arrangements. No expense was made when it came to the services. Jennifer and Marco would be buried in style.

"Mr. Covington, you have my deepest condolences. This has been truly a tragic time for the state of Minnesota. It's been really difficult trying to help the families deal with this tragedy," said Mr. Pike.

"Difficult yet very profitable," said Nikki under her breath.

"Stop it, Nikki," said Virginia.

"V, you know there are vultures all over this state that are making a profit from this situation, so don't front."

"I know that, Nikki, but this is not the time or place to discuss it. So stop it."

As everyone stood there talking, Isabella walked away. She couldn't handle the thought of Jennifer dying at such a young age. *And her being unable to save that poor little boy must have been devastating for her*, she thought.

Virginia walked over and tried to comfort her.

"I'm okay," Isabella said. "We have all lost so much, Virginia, it makes it really hard to go on sometimes. I know that death is the natural order of things, but it still doesn't make it any easier to handle."

After dropping the obituary off, everyone headed back to the house. Everyone's mood was pretty somber, and Dylen was still in her room.

I opened the door, and the air was stale and musty, and Dylen was sitting in the dark.

"Dylen, are you okay?" I asked.

"I'm okay. The house is just so noisy, and I just want to be alone."

"I understand, but open up a window or turn on some lights. It is not healthy for you to be up here day after day in the dark, and you know your mother would not want this."

"I know, Daddy, but I'm sorry if I can't laugh and joke around like everyone else. She was my mother, and I miss her every day," Dylen said, crying. "And Marco, he might have been a brat, but he was my little brother, and I miss him too."

"Dylen, there is nothing anyone can say that is going to make you feel better, but I assure you that with time, the pain will ease, and you will be able to go on with your life, and that is what your mother would have wanted for you and River."

As I tried to comfort my daughter and shield her from her pain, I knew the words fell on deaf ears, and the only thing I could do was be there for her.

The next four days went by quickly, and it was finally Friday. Everyone was rushing around, getting ready for the four o'clock viewing. Everyone decided to meet at the house and then drive over together.

The funeral home was very quiet and had an antiseptic feel about it. I hated the music that was playing.

What is the purpose of that music anyway? I thought. It wasn't soothing or comforting. It just added to the sadness everyone already felt.

The bodies were laid out in a chapel-like setting. The room was filled with flowers from family and friends. Jennifer and Marco looked as though they were sleeping.

I held the kids' hands as they approached the caskets. Dylen couldn't take it and fainted. Nikki and Bruce took her to the waiting area and watched over her while everyone else viewed the bodies. River kissed his mom on the lips and sobbed as he touched Marco's hand.

This is the first time River has displayed any real emotion since we had learned of the deaths, I thought.

Isabella broke down as Angelo tried to comfort her. "I can't take it, Angelo. First, Frank, now his poor *bambina*," cried Isabella. "Somebody needs to pay for this, Angelo. How can this happen?" she asked over and over again.

"Isabella, this is not the place. Try to stay calm. We can get through this together," said Angelo.

After the viewing, everyone went back to the house for dinner. Dylen had to be sedated, and everyone talked about whether she should be allowed to attend the service in such a fragile state.

"I think she will regret not coming," said Nikki. "She is her mother's daughter, and she will get through this. Jennifer was one of the strongest people I'd ever met, and she would want her daughter to be there."

"I know what you're saying is true, but we have to leave it up to her. If she doesn't think she can handle it, then she should stay home, Nikki."

"Daddy, I will be fine," said Dylen, walking into the room. "It was just a shock seeing Mother today, but I will be okay for tomorrow, I promise."

The rest of the evening was quiet and somber. Everyone dreaded tomorrow, but they knew it would come, whether they wanted it to or not.

The next morning came quickly, and everyone walked around the house quietly while they dressed for the service. Dylen and River hung tightly to each other as we rode to the church. The limousines pulled up to the chapel, and everyone knew that this was it. This would be the last time we would ever see Jennifer or Marco again. That fact had not crossed my mind, and I was unable to hold back the tears. I felt Dylen squeeze my hand, and the tears began to pour down her face.

"It's going to be okay, Daddy, I promise," said Dylen as we walked into the chapel.

After laying Jennifer and Marco to rest, everyone had dinner at the house. Of all of Jennifer's friends, Nikki took the service the hardest. She was always the strong one and appeared that nothing ever bothered her, but today that couldn't be further from the truth.

I raised my glass and tapped it lightly. "Can I have everyone's attention, please?"

The room became quiet, and I began to speak.

"I would like to thank everyone for all the love and support that have been shown to me and my family. Jennifer was a devoted wife and mother and a loyal friend to everyone. She never held a grudge toward anyone and always found a way to be forgiving even when she had been wronged. I would like to ask everyone here today who is able to donate to the Jennifer and Marco Covington foundation in lieu of flowers. This foundation will help provide care to special-needs children. This is a cause that Jennifer believed in deeply. When you leave here today, please don't mourn her or my son. Rejoice in the fact that Jennifer loved life and would have given hers to save Marco.

"And to her girlfriends, please continue girls' night out. She always loved that special time you shared together, and I'm sure she will take comfort in knowing that all the secrets you guys shared together will always be just between friends."

About the Author

Cindi Gaines, born in 1963 in Pine Bluff, Arkansas, was raised by her grandmother until she graduated in 1981 and joined the United States Air Force. The mother of three children currently resides in Arkansas and is currently working on a new novel.

CPSIA information can be obtained
at www.ICGtesting.com
Printed in the USA
LVHW031056311220
675393LV00004B/531